Nephilim the Awakening

Wrath of the Fallen Book 1

Elizabeth Blackthorne

Edited by Elemental Editing and Proofreading

Cover by Avdal Designs

Graphics by Etheric Designs

CONTENTS

For my family who kept me grounded.
For my friends who keep me dreaming.
For the RH Rogues who kept me believing.

And for my husband
who supported me all the way through.

All hope abandon, ye who enter here.

DANTE ALIGHIERI

AUTHOR'S NOTE

Thank you for taking the chance on a new series!

Although several people have edited and proofread this book,

typos and mistakes still manage to slip through. If you do spot any we've

missed, please email me at elizabethblackthorne-books@gmail.com so I can correct

them. Please don't contact Amazon as it could result in them taking the book

down!

As I am a British writer, and the main character is also

British, the book is written in British English.

The Wrath of the Fallen series is based on ancient Abrahamic

mythology and religion, using sources such as the Apocrypha and the Bible.

However, creative liberties have been taken and this series is meant as a work

of fiction and is not meant to cause offence.

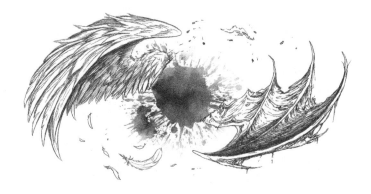

PROLOGUE

FAITH

It was the voices that tipped me over the edge. The whispering, the growling, and the cruel, terrifying laughter that filled my skull until I screamed and screamed. The sound faded away, but I kept screaming. Somewhere deep inside, a small voice whispered that this was what happened when people lost their minds and went insane, that I'd be trapped forever in this darkness and pain, but I knew it would end eventually. It always did.

My senses returned slowly, and I could feel my blood thumping in my ears, my heart hammering in my rib cage. I concentrated on my breathing, each rise and fall of my chest, until my heart rate slowed. I turned my head, pressing the side of my face against the cool stone floor. Somewhere far below, in the depths of the earth, a deep rumble resounded, so quiet I almost missed it. Then there was another, slightly louder now, and this time the building shifted with a soft rustle of dust descending as ancient stonework stubbornly resisted the slight movement of its deep foundations. Taking a deeper breath, I opened my eyes. My gaze travelled along the flagstone floor, up the massive stone column that towered above me, along the path of the carved chevrons, and up the great pillars to where they arched over the cavernous ceiling before curving back down to old dusty pews waiting for a congregation that had never arrived.

Rolling onto my side, I pushed myself onto my hands and knees, and using the stonework to steady myself, I slowly got to my feet. My head spun, so I leaned back against the pillar, feeling the cold seep through my clothes and into my skin. I'd been dreaming of this place for months now. I always awoke here after experiencing darkness and pain or hearing the voices that haunted me. There was no one else here, and it felt as though no one had been here for a very long time. Time seemed to move differently in this place, and I relaxed slightly as I stood alone in the deserted cathedral, watching the dust fall from the vaulted ceilings, glinting in the late evening sunlight as it drifted towards the floor. Intricate, stained-glass windows threw coloured light across the grey floor, the most beautiful being an immense rose window at one end of the nave. Beneath it stood the altar. A polished metal cross was the only item that stood upon it, and something about the way it shone in the golden light fascinated me. I walked slowly towards it, my eyes never leaving its glow as I moved through the pews, my outstretched hands running over the arms of each bench as I passed. The ancient wood had been smoothed to silk by the hands of hundreds, if not thousands, of people throughout the ages.

I reached the steps and hesitated. Turning, I glanced back at the cathedral. I hadn't seen or heard anyone since I arrived in this place, but I was still anticipating for someone to tell me I shouldn't be here. Religious buildings were like that. There were always places you couldn't go, things you couldn't touch, and words you shouldn't say. Much like religions themselves, really. Despite my given name, I'd never been a big believer in the Heaven and Hell thing, preferring history and science over a belief in the supernatural. Growing up with biblical archaeologists for parents, I learned to look at everything with some degree of scepticism. Hell was here, it was real life. Something a person had to survive and fight against. Heaven. Now then, Heaven was riding fast, the rumble of a powerful engine between my legs, the wind in my face, or a man in leather. Heaven was an excellent whiskey and dancing like I'd live forever or die tomorrow. I turned back and climbed the stone steps to stand in front of the altar.

The sun was setting, and the cross now reflected the rosy hue of the sky outside, shiny and perfectly smooth, except for the small engraving at its centre. Interested, I leaned closer, my green eyes reflecting back at me in the horizontal arms of the cross. The etching was a stylized depiction of a tree with a vertical trunk that branched at the top with no leaves or flowers, and roots that spread under it in a mirror image of the boughs above. As I looked at it, the branches and roots seemed to move slightly. I frowned and reached out to run my fingers over the shallow grooves, but when my skin touched the metal, the tree glowed red. I drew back, gasping as the deep crimson colour spread through the cross and spilled out of its base, pouring onto the snowy white altar cloth it stood on. In disbelief, I touched the cross again, feeling only metal, and yet the ruby colour flowing across the pedestal and streaming down the sides to pool on the dusty stone below was most definitely liquid. A sharp, metallic smell hit the back of my nose and throat, and I gagged as I realised what was happening—the cross was spilling blood. I sank to my knees, the blood covering my skin as the darkness began to descend, flooding my body with pain, and as the terror overtook me, I began to scream again.

CHAPTER ONE

FAITH

I opened my eyes slowly and stared across the room at the poster of a Harley Davidson Road King tacked to my wall. I followed every contour of the sleek metal, imagining the wind in my hair and the rumble of the engine as I slowed my breathing and calmed my heart rate. The sheets were tangled around my body, damp with sweat. It felt uncomfortably like being tied down, so I kicked them away. An annoying whine from my phone on the bedside table reminded me I had things to do and places to be. I rolled over to grab it, knocking a box of tablets onto the floor. I let them lie there. These sleeping pills had lasted even less time than the previous ones. I was already doubling up, and the dreams were breaking through again. Time for another trip to the doctor for a different prescription. Until then, whisky would have to do. A damn good fuck would hit the spot too.

Untangling myself further from the sheets, I balled them up and chucked them towards the growing pile of dirty laundry in the corner, and then I grabbed a towel and headed to the bathroom. I needed a hot shower. I sighed as I stepped under the steaming water, feeling it drench my hair and my body with heat. I washed my thick locks, and then worked conditioner through my long red tresses, watching as the dark strands flowed down, seeming to merge into my tattoo. I traced the ink with my fingertips. The intricate feathers began small on the side of my neck and drifted down across my collarbone, the side of my breast, my ribs, and waist, before curving over my hip and disappearing into the curls between my legs. I'd always loved feathers. They symbolized freedom, a notion I was always chasing, which was ironic for a woman trapped inside her own nightmares. Maybe I should see someone about them. Though I didn't think a fluffy counsellor would do me any good. With what went on in my head, I'd probably be better off with a priest who could perform an exorcism. I grinned to myself and rinsed the conditioner away. That was a thought. Maybe my dreams were warning me I was going to Hell. Fuck, even crosses and cathedrals were showing up in them now, so I must have really pissed someone off up there. Hmm... cathedrals...

I turned the shower off and wrapped my towel around my body before padding back to my bedroom. Wandering over to the window, I pulled up the blind and looked out over the city. My tiny apartment was quite high up, and I definitely paid extra for the view—not by choice, but cheap accommodation was scarce in a student city. The view was gorgeous at any time of the day. Creamy sandstone buildings were dotted between swatches of trees, the wide river winding through. Not exactly a bustling metropolis, but it was home. The skyline displayed the distinctive outline of the castle and the cathedral, golden in the evening sunlight. My eyes settled on the towers of the cathedral as I remembered my dream. I'd recognised it as soon as I saw the famous rose window. I'd visited it many times when I was younger, both on school trips and visits with my mother, who worked nearby at the university and often used the cathedral library for research—one perk of being a top lecturer at the university. I pushed any thoughts of Rose Matthews out of my head, a habit so ingrained now I didn't really need to think about it. Switching on my stereo, I blasted some rock music as I scrambled around trying to find some clean clothes, determined to block out any memory of my dreams.

At six in the evening, the cathedral was still surprisingly busy with tourists. I heard at least four different languages as I traversed the broad path between the gravestones and stuck my tongue out at the lion-headed knocker on the enormous doors. I'd done it ever since I was little. My parents had brought me to visit the cathedral one weekend, and I'd been scared to walk through the door because of the way the knocker glared at me. My dad had told me he was just being grumpy and to stick my tongue out at him. He'd done it too, and so had my mum, and we'd all gone into the cathedral laughing.

What's with all the sentimentality, Faith? Get a grip, woman, that life is long over. Dad's gone, and Mum... well, she may as well be.

A twinge of guilt threaded through me at the thought of my mum. It had been six years since we'd spoken. My fault mainly. At eighteen, when her parental authority ran out, she'd completely lost it and had me committed. At the time, I'd hated her for it. When they'd finally let me out, it had taken me precisely twelve minutes to pack my shit and announce I was leaving for good. It hadn't gone well, but now that the dust had settled and I was older and slightly wiser, I could see it from her perspective. I hadn't exactly been an easy teenager once my dad had died. I should give her a call. Maybe we could have a drink together or something, if she wasn't digging up pots in the Middle East...

I sighed and stepped under the huge archway. Once inside, I veered off to the right, heading for the main part of the cathedral. Not for the first time, I wondered what the hell I was doing here. Some sadistic part of me wanted to check the details in my dreams to see if the cross was there, but a sick, nagging feeling inside me wanted to avoid confronting the place. I came to a pause near a low stone sarcophagus just before the column I had woken up next to in my dream. I stood with one hand flat against the pillar to my right as memories of the pain and torment swept over me in a cruel reminder of what my fucked up imagination could do when I was asleep. Around me, visitors started to file out as closing time for the cathedral approached, and I was pretty much alone near the pulpit. The altar was positioned way back behind the choir stalls, but the path that had been open in my dream was roped off with a warning not to cross. I walked up to the rope, trying to see the altar, and a mixed feeling of relief and disappointment filled me as I realised the metal cross on it looked nothing like the one in my dream. *Silly girl*, I chided myself. *Why would it be the same? It was just a dream.*

"Excuse me?"

I turned to see someone's chest. A rather attractively toned chest mainly concealed by a maroon shirt open at the first two buttons. Fighting a sudden indescribable urge to run my hands over it, I looked up at the face belonging to the muscled perfection. Longish auburn hair fell into deep emerald green eyes, which were framed by thin wire glasses, and I watched as generous lips curved into a shy smile. I froze, and a tremor ran through me. For a second my breath caught, and I swear my heart stopped. I felt strange, like something had almost gone *click* in my brain. Realising I was staring, I moved back slightly and focused on his eyes again.

"We were looking for the cloisters and got turned around. Would you be able to point us in the right direction?" His voice was deep and smooth, and there was a faint accent there, but I couldn't quite place it.

"Of course, yes, um... you go down that way, and the door to the cloisters is on your left."

"Thank you so much." Another man, this one slightly shorter, stepped up behind him. "Alex is a closet Harry Potter fan. We couldn't pass up the opportunity to see the filming locations here."

I laughed. "No problem, we get a lot of those here in Durham."

The second man grinned at me, revealing a flash of white teeth, a stark contrast against his impossibly dark skin. I smiled back, my eyes travelling over a shaved head, chiselled jawline, and a body that looked like it lived in a weight room. He wore a tight black T-shirt and jeans, and intricate black tattoos wound around his arms, barely distinguishable against his skin. I licked my lips, imagining what it would be like to trace every detail with my tongue.

"Are you local then?" he asked. I looked over to see his eyes locked on mine, and this time, I couldn't avoid staring. His eyes were a stunningly bright blue, and I stood for a moment transfixed by his gaze. Another *click*. He blinked, and the spell broke.

Mentally shaking myself for looking like a total idiot, I managed to get out a reply. "Uh, yeah, well, I lived outside Durham when I was a kid and moved into the city when I was eighteen. Are you students?" They looked too old to be students.

The tall one shook his head. "We're from Newcastle, but farther over by the coast, really. Just fancied a change in scenery today, but we're heading home soon. It was nice to meet you though, and thank you for the directions." He turned, but the one with the startling eyes grabbed his hand, making him pause. Blue eyes fixed on mine, and I got another blindingly white smile.

"It was lovely to meet you, and you've been very helpful. Maybe we'll run into each other again next time we're in Durham. Go for a drink or... something."

I smiled then frowned slightly, glancing down at their joined hands. Getting hit on by a guy was not uncommon for me, but I'd never been flirted with by someone holding hands with his partner at the same time. "Um, aren't you guys... a thing?"

He grinned, and his eyes seemed to dance. He glanced back at his partner, who smiled softly then looked away. "Well, yes, I guess you would call us a... thing. But we have a very special relationship, and we're not averse to additional company, especially some as lovely as yours."

I couldn't help raising my eyebrows. This was a first for me. One man was enough to deal with, two would be hard work. My gaze drifted back over them and their gorgeous bodies. Yes, very... hard... work.

He held out his hand. "Amadi Gisemba. And this is Alexei Makarov."

"Faith Matthews." I put my hand in his, and he raised it to his lips, his warmth eliciting a tingle through my skin that was definitely not unpleasant. Alexei also took my hand but contented himself with giving it a gentle squeeze before releasing it quickly. Makarov... so the accent was Russian.

He turned to Amadi. "We really need to get going, we've not much time before the cathedral closes for the night."

Amadi nodded. "Of course. Tell you what, here. Call us, if you feel so inclined." He passed me a business card, and after a wink, he took Alex's hand before they turned and strolled back down the nave towards the main entrance.

What the hell was that? I glanced down at the crisp white business card in my hand. In sapphire blue letters, it read, "Amadi Gisemba, Personal Trainer," and listed a phone number and an email address. Well, that explained the bulging biceps. I certainly wouldn't mind him putting me through my paces. Did he really just hit on me in front of his partner? And did he mean what he said about having extra company? My imagination kicked into overdrive as I visualised Amadi's lips on mine, his hands tightening on my hips. Alexei stood behind me, his lips trailing down my neck...

What's wrong with me, thinking about a threesome in a cathedral of all places? I am definitely going to hell, I admonished myself. I made my way towards the door, shaking my head.

It was only later, as I was pulling up at work for the night, when I realised the two men had left the cathedral just after talking to me, avoiding the cloisters entirely.

"Hey, can I get a beer please?"

Looking up from the stack of shot glasses I was trying to separate, I locked eyes with a man leaning casually against the bar, his tanned, folded arms resting on the worn surface. He was definitely not a student, at least, not a fresher. His long, sun-streaked blond hair tumbled into his eyes, and by the looks of what lay under his half-open blue Hawaiian shirt, it seemed his tan extended beyond his arms. A brown beaded necklace with a bronze metal charm hung around his neck, and bead and shell bracelets completed the look. I took a breath as the room suddenly seemed to shift, and I heard, or felt, that weird *click* again. I shook my head, wondering if I was actually losing it or if I was just suffering in weird ways from sleep deprivation. Realising I must look as crazy as I felt, I glanced back at him, and for a moment, I pondered why on earth a guy like this was in a cramped nightclub in the north-east of England instead of on a tropical beach somewhere.

"I don't think you're supposed to ogle the clientele." His tone was deep and amused, and I blushed slightly as I raised my eyes from the exposed glimpse of his chest. His white teeth shone in the club's flashing lights as he grinned at me.

"Who said I was ogling? I would have called it staring in disbelief. You're at a nightclub, not a surf club." I arched my eyebrows and gave him a slight smile. He might be hot, but he still had to work for it.

He laughed. "Ah, but I own a surf club, and I do like to dress the part. Ever been surfing?"

"No, I hate deep water. What are you after?" I finally freed the remaining glasses and set them under the bar where I could grab them quickly.

"Just a beer, please, love. Why do you hate deep water?" He dropped a fiver into my hand, and I fed it into the till, passing him his change.

Turning, I pulled a green bottle from the fridge behind me, using the gadget on the wall to flip off the top. I passed it to him, noticing how warm his fingers were as he took it from me. "I went on a school trip to a beach when I was a kid, and a friend and I got caught exploring some caves. We liked to wander off. I guess we should have known better. The tide started coming in, and we didn't notice at first. I barely made it out. She didn't. I haven't been back in the water since."

"Well, shit, no wonder. I thought you might not enjoy getting your hair wet. I'm sorry about your friend." He took a drink of his beer.

"It's fine. Like I said, it was a long time ago, but I don't like deep water. And I have no problem getting my hair wet, I'm definitely not that kind of girl. I shower and everything!"

He laughed. "Well then, I guess I'll have to take a shower with you instead of inviting you to come surfing with me. It's not my idea of a date, but it has its benefits. No wetsuits, for starters." He took another drink, and his eyes drifted down my body. I could feel his gaze lock onto my hips, where my loose purple staff polo shirt was tucked into my tight black leather pants.

My breath caught, and my face grew warm, along with other parts of my anatomy which had been neglected for several months. Damn, it had been way too long. I slowly leaned forward on the bar, as if I was leaning in to kiss him. He froze, his blue eyes rising to meet mine before dropping to my cleavage, which was now deliberately visible as I leant farther forward, bringing my lips to his ear. "Now who's ogling?" I whispered, and quickly drew back, landing flat on my feet. He laughed, and I grinned. I liked this one. He felt... easy. Not in a bad way, he was just easy to talk to, to be with. Some guys, well, most of the guys I usually went for had this whole intense, brooding thing going for them. It was sexy as hell, but exhausting after a while.

"Hey, Faith, aren't you on at one?" One of the glass collectors dumped a full tray of dirty glasses on the bar, hesitating as she gave Surfer Dude a lingering look. I shot her an amused glance, and she blushed before wandering back off into the crowd with an empty tray. I shook my head. First years. Pulling my phone out from under the bar, I checked the time. It was five to one, so I'd better hurry. The boss wouldn't be happy if I was late to my spot. I glanced back at Surfer Dude.

"Nice to meet you, but I'm going to have to cut the ogling short, I'm afraid. Duty calls."

He cocked his head. "You're a dancer too?"

"Yep."

"Now that I need to see. Lots of opportunity for ogling." He grinned, and I felt a fluttering in my stomach that I hadn't felt in months.

Laughing, I moved away from the bar, letting another bartender move up to cover my space, and stood back out of the way while I pulled my polo shirt over my head to reveal the black satin corset underneath. It always amused me that the bartenders had to look respectable in this club when half of them doubled as dancers and had to dress for that part too. Reaching up, I pulled the clip out of my hair and fluffed out the flame red lengths with my fingers, shaking my head slightly so it fell down to my waist. It was way too hot behind the bar to leave my hair down, but it definitely got the guys going when I was on stage. Leaning closer to the mirrored wall on the back of the bar, I pulled red lipstick out of the clutch hidden from sight and dishonest hands and applied it quickly. When I turned back around, Surfer Dude was still watching me, and I felt a frisson of excitement that he was still there.

Hmmm, maybe he'd stick around until the end of my shift. I could ask him...

Nodding at the other three bartenders, I squeezed past them. I pretended to ignore Surfer Dude and slowly made my way towards the dance floor, manoeuvring between the heaving bodies. It was packed, and more and more people were drifting towards it as the alcohol they had been knocking back since eleven took effect. I edged my way to the DJ's box, the dark brown carpet sticking to my boot heels. It wouldn't have surprised me if the club owner had let more than the maximum capacity in again, and as the most popular nightclub in Durham, the students had taken full advantage. Bodies pressed in from all sides, and hands ended up in places they shouldn't. Freshers' week was always crazy busy. Everyone was rather drunk and *very* friendly, and most were looking to score. They also just received their student loans and had yet to spend the funds, which usually meant the tips for this week would be decent.

As I reached the cage at the side of the dance floor and placed my foot on the first step leading up to it, a couple of girls tottering on dangerously high heels staggered past, knocking me off balance. I stumbled and fell backwards, colliding with something hard. Large, muscular arms covered in tattoos came around me, one hand landing somewhere I definitely didn't approve of, and my elbow smashed back into his chest—a subconscious reflex from having worked in a nightclub as long as I had.

"Relax," a deep, musical voice murmured in my ear, his lips brushing my skin as he got close enough for me to hear him above the music. He moved forward carefully and gently pushed me up on the step, his large hands gripping my waist. "Just your knight in shining armour."

I turned around in his arms, suddenly recognising the voice, and nearly fell off the step again. My eyes closed briefly as I silently groaned. "Cas."

I hadn't seen him in five years, and he was the very last person I ever wanted to see ever again. Not that he wasn't insanely hot to look at. By all appearances, the last five years had added to his appeal. He was six foot four of pure muscle and tats, with long, dark brown dreadlocks and a scar cutting through one of his eyebrows. Cas had dark eyes that could see into your soul, a mouth that the Devil would lust after, and a scent all his own, a mixture of leather, whisky, and petrol.

My eyes locked onto his, and I couldn't tear my gaze away. His hands tightened on my waist. I could already feel myself leaning into him. My hands were spread over his chest, and I could feel his racing heart under my fingertips. His lips parted slightly, and for a moment, I thought he was going to kiss me.

"Still falling for me, Faith?" He gave me a cold smile instead. The spell broke, and I braced my hands against his pecs to push him away from me, feeling irritated at his arrogance and my own reaction to his presence after all these years.

"You wish." I tried to push away from him again, but his hands tightened on my waist and I froze. He grinned down at me.

"I don't need to wish. I've been there many times. And I can honestly say you've definitely grown up since I saw you last." He leaned back slightly and gave my body an appraising look, his eyes coming to rest on my breasts. "Filled out a bit too." I wanted to punch him in the face. Maybe even break his nose.

"You've got some fucking nerve." I felt a deep, primal hatred rise up inside me, and I twisted in his grip. All he did was wrap his massive arms around me, pinning me close to his body.

"Now, now, babe, don't be like that. Someone might think you didn't like me anymore." His smile was cold and mocking.

"Fucking tosser. Let me go."

He cocked his head, looking down at me. "Now, are you sure you mean that? I seem to remember you loving it when I held you." He leaned in to brush his lips against my ear. "And you definitely loved it when I was a bit rough..." I closed my eyes, trying to control my breathing. I needed him to back off, to leave me alone. Just being this close to him made my legs feel unsteady, made me feel as though I couldn't control my own body. I desperately wanted to lean forward and run my hands over his tight T-shirt again, feeling the hard, sculpted muscles I knew were underneath. I wanted to grab the edges of his biker jacket and pull him forward to kiss me with that sinful mouth of his. To feel him wrap his arms around me and kiss me like he used to... I squeezed my eyes shut tighter and snapped my head around, catching him straight in the face. He released me immediately, stepping back and bringing his hand to his nose.

"What the... What the hell is your fucking problem?" he roared at me.

"You're my fucking problem, Cas. What part of 'I never want to see you again' did you not understand five years ago?"

He narrowed his eyes. "I thought by now—"

"You thought what? That I'd have forgiven you for what you did? No fucking chance. You're a disgusting human being, Cas Hardy. I still can't believe you aren't behind bars." I couldn't believe this guy.

"Funnily enough, they couldn't get the charges to stick, no thanks to you."

"Yeah, well, stay away from me, or I'll report you for stalking. Now fuck off." I turned away from him and stomped up the stairs to the cage. When I reached the gate, I glanced back to see him disappearing into the crowd. I leaned against the bars for a moment, breathing hard, trying to let the adrenaline settle. As I scanned the crowd, I caught sight of a newly familiar face. Surfer Dude had left the bar and was standing at the back of the room with an unrestricted view of the cage I was next to. As I watched him, he glanced up, and his eyes locked onto mine. Smiling, he took a drink, never taking his gaze off me. I grinned. Perfect distraction. I slipped into the cage next to me, ignoring the whistles and catcalls that came from the crowd below.

The song switched to a popular dance track with a Latin vibe that I loved, so fixing my eyes on a certain tanned chest, I pushed all thoughts of Cas out of my mind as my body swayed to the beat. The dance floor filled up, with people grinding against each other, some in time to the music, others to their own rhythm. A small circle of men gathered around the bottom of the cage as they grinned and shouted up at me. I ignored them. At the bar, I had to talk to them, but up here, scantily dressed where everyone could see me, I was untouchable.

I glanced across the dance floor and saw Cas leaning against the wall, a glass of whisky in his hand, his dark gaze fixed on me. Surfer Dude stood near him, looking even hotter now that I could make out his tight, ripped jeans and trim waist. I considered briefly whether to make a move. It had been a few months, and I was definitely feeling antsy. Remembering his blue eyes undressing me at the bar, I made my choice. I held his gaze and began to dance like he was the only one in the room. My movements became more sensual, my hands sliding down my body, skimming over the laces of my corset and my hips, my black leather skinny trousers slick under my fingers. I stretched my arms slowly into the air, elongating my body, then let my hands drift down through my hair. Turning, I leaned back against the bars of the cage, writhing slowly to the rhythm of the music before dipping down low then sliding back up nice and slow. When I spun around, Surfer Dude had given up any pretence of looking anywhere but at me, and I held his attention for the next four songs, my moves getting sexier and more daring with every new tune.

Eventually, the next dancer showed up to relieve me. Abandoning my own pretence, I descended into the mass of heaving bodies and sashayed towards him. He opened his mouth to say something, but I reached up, slid my hand behind his neck, and brought his mouth down to mine. His lips moved over mine, soft and warm, and I felt his tongue flick against the swollen flesh. He pulled back and smiled down at me. I put my finger over his lips as he was about to speak, and ignoring the black looks I was getting from Cas, I grabbed Surfer Dude's hand and pulled him towards the corridors that led to the toilets and the back door of the club.

Outside in the dark shadows of the alley, I pushed him against the brick wall, grabbing the front of his shirt and pulling him down to kiss me again. A charge ran through me as his lips claimed my own, his tongue pushing into my mouth, much more demanding this time. I pressed myself up against him, feeling his hardness grow against my belly. Breaking away slightly, he trailed his lips down my neck, and I shivered in delight, sliding my hands up under his shirt to trace the outline of his muscles.

"Sam, we need to go. Now. Call from work," a familiar voice shouted from the back door.

I groaned. *What the actual fuck, Cas?*

Surfer Dude sighed and leaned his forehead against mine. "Sorry, baby girl, duty calls." He brushed his lips across mine again, and I pulled him close for another heated kiss, threading my fingers into his hair to keep him against my mouth as long as I could, hoping to convince him to stay. Eventually, I released him when I heard Cas sighing impatiently. I plastered a fake smile on my face and turned to my ex.

"Hey, Cas," I said breezily.

"Faith." He didn't look happy, and a perverse sense of enjoyment bubbled up inside me. I was finding it extremely amusing that they seemed to know each other, and that Cas obviously didn't like the idea of me making out with his friend. I turned back to Sam, who bent down and brushed his lips across mine again, distracting me. He smelled of fresh sea air and pine trees, and I breathed in his scent, forgetting about Cas for a moment.

"Do you really have to go? Right now?"

Sam looked from Cas to me, and I pressed my body gently against his. Desire flashed in his eyes, and he raised his hand to my face, running his thumb over my lips. "I'm afraid I do. But I really, really wish I didn't."

My skin tingled with my desire to feel his hands on me, and I completely ignored Cas as I slid my lips over his thumb, sucking gently, before pulling away. "Shame."

His eyes glittered as he took out his phone. "Can I get your number?"

I opened my mouth to answer, but Cas beat me to it. "She doesn't do numbers. Too much commitment, right, Faith? She just likes to fuck and get out of Dodge." I felt like he'd just punched me in the stomach, but it didn't stop me from stepping forward and slapping him across the face. He didn't react, just stood there smiling at me.

I glared at him for a moment then turned to Sam and smiled. "Ignore him." I took his phone from him and quickly tapped in my number. "Call me soon. I'd really love to continue where we left off."

Standing on my tiptoes, I kissed him one more time, pressing my body against his. The display was only partly to annoy Cas. This guy felt good, and I definitely wanted to explore him further.

"I'd better see you again," I murmured in his ear. I shot Cas a winning smile, then turned and walked away without looking back at either of them. I sashayed slightly up the steps to the back door, letting Sam get a decent look at one of my better attributes before disappearing back into the club, leaving the two of them standing in the alley.

CHAPTER TWO

CAS

It didn't take us too long to reach the address Hargreaves had sent me. I pulled round the back, with Sam following me in his VW, our tyres crunching on gravel that looked like it could have used a good weed suppressant spray. As Sam jumped down from the camper, I could see his slightly pissed off demeanour hadn't changed since we left the club. To be fair, mine hadn't either, so I seized the opportunity to wind him up further.

"What's with the scowl? You look like someone stole your chew toy."

He brought his hand up in front of his face and slowly extended his middle finger. "What do you think? It's supposed to be my night off."

I laughed as his glower dropped into a sad puppy dog expression. "Sorry, mate, you've worked for the Concordia long enough to know that the forces of Heaven and Hell don't take weekends off, therefore, neither can we."

Sam rolled his eyes as he slipped out of his jacket. "Inconsiderate bastards. At least humans have sick days and weekends." He continued to strip, chucking his clothes onto the passenger seat of the van. I stared at him, raising my eyebrows when he looked back over at me. "What? I've gone through enough clothes this month having to shift fully clothed. These shirts aren't cheap, and you know they don't pay me enough. I mean, it's not exactly the reason I was hoping to get naked tonight..." The jab hit home, and I turned around, taking off my helmet and leaving it on the saddle of my bike. The hot spike of jealousy I'd been feeling since I saw Faith in Sam's arms at the club needled me again.

"Yeah, well, good thing I caught you in time. Faith isn't exactly the type of girl you just bang in an alleyway." I pulled my gun out of the saddlebag and checked it over, more as a reason not to look at him.

"Hey, it was her who dragged me out there, and I'm never one to refuse a lady. Plus, I wasn't just planning on banging her in the alleyway. She's a cute girl. Funny too. I was hoping to bang her over an extended period of time and in many different places." My temper got the best of me, and I spun. He stood there grinning at me. "Thought so."

"What?"

"You two haven't just met before, have you?"

"No, we've met." I closed my eyes, fighting the urge to punch that grin off his cocky face.

"Met and... .?"

I turned back to face him, resisting the urge to snap. "And," I confirmed.

Sam looked surprised, and I didn't blame him. It was well known that I didn't even entertain the idea of dating humans. I mean, there had been times over the years when I'd succumbed to spending nights with them, but it was never long term. I'd seen others like me get sucked into relationships and then have to break it off because it became clear they weren't aging like their partner, while others stayed and watched their loved ones wither and die before their eyes. Thanks, but no thanks.

"That's not like you. Was this recent?" Sam watched me closely.

I shook my head, checking the safety on the gun, avoiding meeting his eyes. "No, about five years ago."

"Ah, okay then. So would it bother you if..."

I tucked the gun into the waistband of my jeans at my lower back. "No, it doesn't bother me if you date her. It wasn't... we only dated for a few months." I smiled grimly at the memory. "It was an assignment."

"An assignment? Faith was an assignment?" He stared at me.

I took a breath. "Yeah, but if you see her again, I'd rather that didn't become common knowledge. She hates me enough already." I glanced over at him.

"Why was Faith an assignment?" He wasn't smiling anymore.

"The Concordia wanted me to keep an eye on her, question her without her knowing. They thought she might have seen something she shouldn't have. And at the time, I was working undercover, trying to infiltrate that incubus gang in the city. She was a suitable cover, helped me get into the clubs. They like a pretty face."

Sam shuddered.

"They didn't get near her," I said firmly, addressing the concern I could see was running through his mind.

"But you did, didn't you? You fell for her." It wasn't a question, and I was getting annoyed. Besides, we had stuff to get on with.

"Look, it started as a cover and it developed a bit, that's all. You try dating her and not falling for her. But I warn you, she's trouble."

"Oh, I hope so." He grinned at me, but I didn't rise to it.

"Right, now that we've established where our dicks are at, maybe we could get on with what we came here to do?"

"Yeah, course. Sorry. She's just so—"

"Hargreaves messaged me to say there was a substantial drain on magical energies less than an hour ago, and it was established that it happened near here," I interrupted.

"Right. A local coven maybe? Did any humans witness it?"

I shrugged. "I have no idea. It could be a coven, but I doubt it. Anyway, that wasn't the problem."

"So what's the problem?" he asked.

"This is Rose's house."

"The theologist?" Sam looked confused, and I didn't blame him.

"That's the one," I replied.

"But she isn't exactly... I mean, she's a witch and all, but she couldn't raise that much power by herself."

I nodded. "Exactly. And as you might not have noticed while your mind was on other things, the windows are all blown out."

Sam glanced up at the house and whistled. "Whoa, yeah, major energy detonation. Okay, I guess I'll go scout. Take these for me and howl if you need anything." He threw something at me and slipped into the shadows.

I stared down at the crumpled briefs in my hand. "Tosser."

Tucking them gingerly into my pocket, I started skirting around the house, looking for anything else that seemed odd before venturing inside. It didn't take long. I rounded the corner and found myself in a small side garden. It might have been nice on a sunny day. There was a small lawn, surrounded by rose bushes, and a circular patio to one side with a fancy iron patio set for sipping gin and tonics. The glowing Circle of Solomon embedded in the lawn didn't really fit the pretty picture though. I peered into the shadows then edged around the circle, careful not to touch the glowing lines, and closely studied the elaborate symbols to work out what had been summoned and by who. The circle was fading. Taking out my phone, I quickly took a snapshot to study later. Whatever had been summoned must have been returned. Circles were usually programmed to fade when the being had been returned to Sheol. A rustle in the bushes to my left had me reaching for my gun, but I relaxed as a huge wolf slunk from the shrubs. I waited a moment for him to shift back, chucking him his underwear once he did.

"Well?"

"Hellhounds," Sam said, pulling his briefs up.

"Nearby?" I questioned sharply, going for my gun again. He shook his head.

"No, not close at the moment. I can't sense them nearby, but they were here, and not too long ago."

I gestured to the circle. "That explains this then. It's fading, so they must have been sent back already."

Sam raised one eyebrow. "You assume."

"Come on," I scoffed. "No one is going to leave their name on a circle that summoned hellhounds and then let them roam wildly about. It would be like marching up to Concordia with their wrists out in front saying, 'Arrest me, please!'"

"Did you get a name?"

I glanced back down at the circle, which had nearly disappeared, and opened my phone to look at the photo instead. "What the... The photo..."

I passed the phone to Sam, who looked at the red blur and grinned. "Guess someone needs to take a photography course. There's a great one for amateurs just up near Alnwick—"

"I don't need a photography course," I retorted. "This was perfectly sharp when I took it. I think the circle has been cursed to conceal the creator."

Sam whistled. "Now that's pretty advanced stuff."

"That's what worries me. Come on, let's check inside." We walked back around the side of the house, heading for the front door, but then I heard the crunch of tyres on the gravel in the driveway. Grabbing Sam's arm, I pulled him to a halt, though he'd likely heard it too. He inclined his head towards the corner of the house, and I nodded. Out of the two of us, he was definitely the quietest. I had a reputation for being rather clumsy on the ground, but I blamed my size. No one's perfect.

He inched forward a few metres, then crouched down and leaned slightly around the wall before snapping back quickly.

"It's Faith!"

"What do you mean, it's Faith? I swear, Sam, you're becoming obsessed after one kiss. Never thought you'd be the pussy whipped type."

Sam glared at me. "Funny bugger. See for yourself."

I peered around the corner to see Faith leaning against her bike, pulling off the bandana she usually wore under her helmet when she was riding to keep her wild hair contained.

"Why is she here?" Sam asked. "Do you reckon she followed us? Maybe she knew more than you thought." He looked disappointed, which I found rather amusing.

I chuckled quietly. "Don't you find out girls' names before taking them into dark alleys?" Sam stared at me, and I grinned. "Faith Matthews. She's Rose's daughter. But I don't know what she's doing here. They had a huge falling out six years ago, and I didn't think they were on speaking terms."

Sam frowned. "I didn't scent anything supernatural on her. I was convinced she was human. What is she?"

I shrugged. "She's definitely human. Every inch of her," I added, just to dig a little.

Sam appeared confused. "Even with her mother being a witch?"

I peered back around the corner to see Faith disappearing into the house. "She's adopted. We'd better wait a bit until she clears out. She might have just popped by to get something."

Sam eyed me wryly. "And you don't think she'll notice the blown-out windows? Ten quid says she'll call the police. We need to go in and stop her or Hargreaves will have our asses."

I put my hand out to stop him from charging in. "Faith doesn't trust the police. She won't call them immediately."

Sam leaned against the wall next to me. "She doesn't? Why not?"

"When Faith was younger, maybe eleven or twelve, her dad died. Well, actually, he was brutally tortured and murdered by a group of demon anarchists searching for an antique weapon he had in his possession, but Faith didn't know any of that. Rose was at a dig overseas, and Faith was at a sleepover the night it happened. She was told her dad interrupted a burglar who shot him. Anyway, she didn't cope well and went off the rails. Drinking, smoking, acting up at school. She was arrested several times, even spent a bit of time at a Young Offenders Institution. So yeah, not a big fan of the boys in blue."

Sam's eyebrows rose so high they nearly disappeared into his hair. "No wonder she and her mum had a falling out. Rose isn't exactly one for confrontations. Faith did all that? But she seemed so... normal."

I sighed. "She is now. But she was close to her dad, and his death just kind of tipped her off the edge, I guess. Rose had no idea what to do, and she was terrified Faith had seen something she shouldn't because she kept having horrific nightmares. She sent her to counsellor after counsellor, and eventually to a psychiatric institution when she started self-harming. Faith hated her for it, and when she was finally released, she ran away. Rose begged her to come home, but she refused. They've barely talked since." Sam stared at me in horror, and I felt bad for spilling Faith's secrets to someone she clearly liked. "Look, she's fine now. She was much better when I was dating her. She just won't take any shit from anyone."

"Do you think she heard something? Found something out? When her dad was killed, I mean? That would really fuck a kid up you, you know?"

"That's what I was tasked to find out. Look, she only told me this stuff because... well, I got her very drunk a few times. And high. I'm not sure if she even remembers telling me. I put it all together from a few different conversations." Sam glared at me, and I sighed. "Yes, I get it, I'm an arsehole. But it was either that or use magic, and I didn't want to fuck with her head any more than it had been already. I didn't think she'd seen anything, but she can't remember that night at all. It's blacked out in her memory, so who knows if she saw anything. The friend's dad swore she was at theirs all night. And she never opened up to any of the counsellors."

"So if her and Rose don't talk, why is she here tonight?" Sam hissed.

"Well, I haven't talked to her in five years. Maybe they're on friendlier terms, I don't know. Maybe Faith forgave her or something."

Sam opened his mouth to speak, then paused and sniffed the air. "I might do another lap. Something's... off."

I looked around at the surrounding shadows. Sam was right. The night still seemed quiet. Very quiet, in fact. "Okay, you go. I'll check inside. On the off chance you were right and she called the police, I'll need to be quick."

"Don't get caught." Sam winked at me as he dropped to all fours and melted into the shadows. I slunk over to the dark kitchen window and hoisted myself up onto the ledge. The broken glass in the wooden frame sliced my hands, and I cursed out loud. I froze, hoping no one had heard me. I felt a slight buzz as the wounds in my hands closed up, and then I jumped down onto the tiled floor. The entire house was silent, and I wondered if she'd left.

A slight tickle ran down my little finger, and I glanced at my hand. The wounds might have closed, but the blood was still on my skin. The last thing I needed was to have droplets of blood found by human police officers. The forensic tests would cause a proper flurry. Not wanting to make a sound that might give me away, I wiped my hands on my jeans rather than rinsing them in a sink. A sudden sound made me look up, my hand going to my gun. I moved towards the small door at the back of the kitchen. With my spare hand, I reached for the handle, but before I could touch it, the door flew open and something collided with my chest, knocking the breath out of my lungs and sending me staggering backwards. Instinctively, I wrapped my arms around my attacker and squeezed tightly. The next thing I knew, the heel of their hand connected with my nose, and I actually heard the crack as my bone shattered and pain exploded across my face.

"Fuck!"

CHAPTER THREE

FAITH

"Ugh, I don't know how you eat that stuff every night, Faith."
Dan, one of the other bartenders, shuffled farther along the
low stone wall we were all sitting on just so he could get away
from me, and I grinned at him before taking another huge bite.

"Dunno what you're talking about. Jane's doner kebab is the
best part of my night. Don't ruin it," I replied, not bothering to
finish my mouthful before I added, "Especially coming from
someone who puts beans, cheese, and garlic sauce on his
chips!"

"Cheesy chips are the best thing ever invented. You are a
total philistine." The three other club staff members grunted
in agreement.

I shook my head, took another mouthful, and switched on
my phone. I used to leave it on silent in the club, but it was
an old phone and the battery was going, so I turned it off
whenever I didn't need it.

*Hmm... weird. Twelve missed calls. Don't recognise the
number.*

My mind went back to the hot guys in the cathedral, and I felt a frisson of excitement when I considered they might have somehow gotten hold of my phone number in some weird and wonderful technological way. Not sure why they'd call me twelve times though. A notification popped up, saying I had a voicemail. I clicked on it, turning away from the guys as they continued the debate on chips toppings.

"Faith? Faith, sweetheart, it's Mum... it's... Rose. Look, I'm sorry to call, I know you don't want... anyway, I haven't got a lot of time. I'm going away tomorrow for a conference for a few days, but when I get back, can we talk? Meet somewhere? You can choose. I have... There's something you need to know, and then you can leave again. Or not. Whatever you want, sweetheart. Just... be careful. Keep an eye out for... well, anything strange or off. Don't go out on your own and don't come to the house. Not until I call you. I know I sound crazy, and you'll probably take no notice, but... please, Faith. I'll call... I need to go, sorry... Faith... Faith!"

The call ended, and the phone ran into its, "If you want to return the call..." ramble. With a sick feeling, I pressed two and listened to the message again.

"Everything okay, Faith?" Dan leaned over, concern on his face.

"I... er... yes, fine. Just, my... mother left me a message, and it was a bit weird." I stood up, wrapped up the last half of my kebab, and offered it around before sticking it in the nearest bin.

"She okay?"

"Yeah, yeah, she's fine. I might just call in on my way home though." I waved at them as I headed off to where I'd left my gorgeous Heritage Softail. I ran my fingers over the Harley emblem, still as in love with my bike as I was when I finally saved up enough to buy her two years ago. I mean, she'd been second-hand, but still. She was all mine. Reaching into the pannier, I pulled out a soft bandana and wound it around my hair before sliding the helmet on. As she roared to life between my legs, I smiled at the thought of flying along the country roads, even if it did mean going home.

Twenty minutes later, I pulled my helmet off and looked up at the house I'd spent most of my life in. It stood dark and silent, as though no one was home. To be fair, it was three o'clock in the morning and Rose was probably asleep. She'd kill me for waking her. I was surprised the noise of the bike hadn't done that already. Something just didn't feel right.

I opened my phone again, listening to the message one last time. The shadows seemed to grow around me as I heard my mum say my name at the end. It sounded desperate. Slipping my hand inside my leather jacket, I felt for the hunting knife in the concealed pocket, running my fingers over the hilt to reassure myself. I was well trained to protect myself. My mother insisted on years of martial arts classes and weapons training to keep me safe. I enjoyed them, preferring them to ballet or gymnastics, which was what most girls my age were doing, plus I didn't feel scared of walking through the deserted streets on my way home as most girls did. My mother wasn't trained to protect herself though. She was a full-on nerd who loved her books, her studies, travelling to digs in weird places, oh yes, and having her daughter locked up.

I stared up at the large Victorian house, taking in the details I could see in the moonlight. I hadn't been back here in six years, and it was rather dilapidated now and in need of some renovation. By the look of the wisteria and roses, it was clear my mother hadn't replaced the gardener since the year I left when George had retired. I took a few steps forward then paused. Normally the security light would have come on by now, but the only light source was the quarter moon that hung just above the treeline. It glinted off of something on the porch steps and on the gravel paths next to the house—broken glass. My eyes flicked up. The windows were gone. Each frame stood empty, and as I got closer, I felt shards crack and shatter under my boots. I headed up the steps to the entrance. The stained glass that had formed roses in the door had also been shattered, crunching under my feet as I put my hand on the door handle.

Weird. A burglary maybe? Surely she would have called the police, but there was no one here. I paused. No, that couldn't be it. All the broken glass was outside of the house, meaning the windows must have been broken from inside. The door opened with a catch, and a key wasn't required within the house, so they wouldn't need to break windows to get out. Plus, the breaks were so clean, there was hardly any glass left in the frames at all. Surely if they had smashed a window with a crowbar or something, at last some glass would have fallen inside...

Then a thought suddenly hit me—what if there was a gas explosion? What if she was hurt? But an explosion would have damaged the house, and it seemed fine. I opened the door slowly and sniffed the air. No gas smell. I stepped into the hallway and looked around, taking in the vast entrance hall and the mahogany stairs that rose up before me then split to curve around to each wing of the house. The huge, panelled oak doors leading off from the hall were all closed. I glanced at the windows. I'd been right. There wasn't a shard of glass inside the house. They had all been blown out by something from the inside. I walked to the bottom of the stairs.

"Rose? Rose? Rose!" My voice seemed jarringly loud in the silent structure. I swallowed down the sick feeling in my stomach. Ignoring the downstairs rooms for now, I headed up the stairs towards the west wing. The first room on the right was Rose's. To a casual observer, it might have appeared like the room had been ransacked, but I recognised the normal chaos of packing for digs and conferences. Suitcases and holdalls were all over the floor, and clothes and papers were scattered across the bed. The only thing missing was my mother's handbag. She obviously hadn't left early for the conference, but she still might have gone somewhere else.

I quickly checked the rest of the bedrooms and bathrooms, leaving my own last. Every now and again, I shouted her name, but the house still remained eerily silent. The fourth door on the left was mine. Well, it had been mine before she'd decided she'd had enough of my issues and packed me off to the loony bin. There had been many fights and horrible things said, on my part mostly, and even though I had softened towards her in the last year or so, my stupid pride had prevented me from picking up the phone. Things were nowhere near being resolved with my mother, but the idea of someone hurting her filled me with fear and a growing rage. As I pushed my bedroom door, it swung open violently and slammed into the wall behind it. I smiled sadly to myself. Ironic. I used to get yelled at for slamming my door shut.

Nothing had changed in here since I'd left. Seeing the gorgeous four-poster bed with its snowy white sheets and velvet navy quilt gave me a slight pang when I thought of the lumpy, second-hand mattress I was currently sleeping on. Not what you'd call luxurious by a long stretch. Avoiding the childish urge to throw myself down on it and cry, I wandered slowly around the room. Rose really hadn't changed anything since I'd left, even the stuff she'd hated. Band and motorbike posters were still tacked up on expensive damask wallpaper. A bookcase holding school books, crumbling volumes of ancient myths, arcane practices, and theoretical Bible studies remained, including tomes such as *De Arte Magica* and *Confessions of Aleister Crowley: the Most Evil Man in the World*. Two crossed swords were mounted above the fireplace, and on the wall next to the window hung a throwing axe and a morning star.

The weapons brought back memories of my lessons. Hours of combat skills, fitness, and strength training. Home schooling in various ancient languages, myths, and legends. I'd enjoyed the teachings when I was young, sitting around the kitchen table at dinnertime and arguing about translations of old books and the techniques of sword play. But that was before my dad had died. I didn't remember anything about that night, or several weeks surrounding it either, but things were never the same. I'd never felt safe, like there was something or someone watching me. I'd been terrified people could still break into the house. I'd refused additional lessons as my relationship with Rose broke down, but the training had continued. It had been the only thing keeping me going, something to throw my fear and rage into. When I'd been kicked out of school for fighting, Rose had cancelled my trainers and taken away my weapons, convinced the constant physical exertion was making me more angry and violent. Things had just got worse from there. Now, six years later, the details were fuzzy. I couldn't recall exactly what we fought about, only that we had constantly, relentlessly.

Moving over to the chest of drawers, I rooted around in the bottom drawer until I pulled out a small black box. Inside was a golden chain and a disc with the words "Beloved Daughter" engraved on it in Sumerian. On the other side was a strange symbol I'd never been able to find recorded anywhere—a circle with a half circle above and below it, and a straight line running up the middle. A gift from my mother. Not Rose, my real mother. Rose and David, my adoptive parents, had told me how I'd been handed in by someone at the hospital in Newcastle who'd found me in a cardboard box on the doorstep of the nearby church. A brief note had been tucked into my blanket, explaining that my name was Faith and that my mother loved me but couldn't take care of me. The necklace had been with it. It hadn't ever bothered me that much, since I'd grown up with it, but it had bothered Rose when I'd thrown it in her face the night I was committed. I snapped the box closed and slipped it into the pocket of my leather jacket. With one last glance around the bedroom, I closed the door softly and headed back downstairs.

The rest of the rooms were empty, though I was no longer hoping to find her in any of them. There was no sign of anything unusual except for the broken windows. Deciding there was nothing for it but a reluctant call to the police to report her missing, I walked into the kitchen to grab a glass of water. The windows in here were broken too, but that wasn't what caught my attention. On one side of the kitchen, a large wooden dresser had been pulled away from the wall, and the battered door it had concealed stood ajar. I'd always known the door was there, so that wasn't a surprise. It led down to the old cellar. I'd never been allowed down there as it was unsafe—problems with mould and asbestos—hence why the dresser stood there. The door had never stood open though. Why would Rose have gone down into the cellar?

My curiosity piqued, I pushed the door open wider, and noticing an electric light switch, I flicked it upwards. The lights came on with a slight buzz, flooding the stone steps in front of me with a pale glow. They led down to a concrete floor of a tight passageway. Taking a breath, I moved cautiously down the steps. The corridor beyond wasn't long, maybe eight feet, and ended at another old wooden door like the one at the top of the steps.

A stone lintel above the door bore the crudely scratched words, *"Hasad eli summsu mimma amelnakru."* I frowned. My Sumerian was somewhat rusty. *Something revealing something... against... enemy attack.* Okay then. Maybe it was some kind of bunker from World War II or something...

I put my hand on the iron handle and felt a shiver run through me, almost like static electricity. The lock clicked, and the door swung open, revealing only darkness beyond. I hesitated then stepped through the doorway, feeling for a light switch. A wave of sensation surged through me, almost like an adrenaline rush or a fantastic climax, but this left me shaking. I dropped to my knees on the stone floor, my head throbbing with pain. The agony overwhelmed me, spreading throughout every fibre of my body, like every cell was exploding. I opened my mouth to scream but heard nothing as a colossal roar filled my head and darkness engulfed me.

When I opened my eyes, the first thing I noticed was that the light had changed. The ceiling flickered with a soft warm glow. That led me to realise I was flat on the floor. I took a breath, anticipating more pain, but I felt nothing. The pain was gone, and all I could feel was a low buzz over my skin. I wondered if I'd tripped something and been electrocuted. Maybe I'd touched a loose wire or something when I was feeling for the lights. I scrambled to my feet and looked around, my mouth falling open in surprise.

The flickering light was coming from candles. Bookshelves and sideboards lined the fairly sizable room, and cream pillar candles covered a lot of the surfaces. The bookcases held a mixture of things—ancient leatherbound books, modern day textbooks, scrolls, and a myriad of glass jars filled with different substances. As I drew nearer to some, I saw they were mainly herbs and spices, which was odd, because Rose hated cooking with a passion. The centre of the room was empty, though I could see some kind of design etched into the wooden floor. It had obviously been there a while and was nearly worn away, but it was circular and intricate. At the far end of the space stood a high table draped with a black cloth. Two tall solid silver candlesticks bearing white candles were perched on either side of the table, and a low, wide-brimmed bowl was placed between them. The candles on the tabletop were the only ones not lit.

Glancing back at the door, I looked for a light switch, but there wasn't one. No wires either. Nothing to explain why fifty odd candles had suddenly lit by themselves. It must have been some kind of trick, like a pressure plate that was triggered when I stepped on it or a mechanism that was activated when I opened the door. Pretty cool, but creepy as fuck. I wondered if Rose even knew this was here. Drawing closer to the nearest bookshelf, I decided she definitely had. Half the textbooks were from the ancient Middle East, her speciality. A few had even been written by her.

I moved towards the table, looking down at the bowl. It was full of water. Well, I assumed it was water. I wasn't planning on touching it to find out. A memory of a passage in a book flared in my mind of a wide shallow bowl, painted black, that was filled with water—a scrying bowl for divining the future, although some said they could be used for communicating between the worlds as well. As I looked at the golden liquid reflecting the candlelight, the colour receded, and the water's surface seemed to disappear. I frowned and leaned over as I saw movement in the background. Dark shapes stirred, focusing into vague human figures. One seemed to move towards me, his features, though still shadowed, becoming clearer. The black smudges of his eye sockets softened, and then I gasped as they opened and glowing red irises gazed back at me, locking me in place and holding me transfixed as the figures grew clearer. One began to stretch his hand out towards me. I stepped back and blinked, breaking eye contact with the water. I looked again. The water was still and glowing with candlelight, reflecting my own green eyes back at me. My hands were shaking, so I slipped them into my jacket pockets. It was chilly down here. I doubt it was heated.

I turned and headed back to the door. This place was fucking creepy, and I wasn't spending any more time down here. I should probably blow out the candles to be safe, but there was no fucking way I was leaving myself down here in the dark in a confined space. It already felt like the ceiling was pressing down on me. I walked up the stairs as fast as I could without actually running, my mind focused on getting back to where there was a mobile signal and calling the police.

I pushed open the door into the kitchen and practically ran through, colliding almost immediately with a solid wall of muscle. Thick arms came around me, and I reacted instantly. My hands grabbed onto his hips and shoved them away as I pushed myself back into a stronger position. I slipped one hand up through the space between us and struck, smashing it into my assailant's face. I felt a crack as it connected with cartilage, and he released me, staggering back with a yell, his hand to his face. I took another swing at him, but it only took him a second to regain his composure. He dropped to a crouch, swinging his leg around and sweeping my legs out from under me. I flung my arm out and wrapped it around his neck, bringing us both crashing to the ground, but he managed to dislodge it, and before I knew it, he was straddling me and had my hands pinned to the floor. I looked up into dark eyes and groaned.

"Seriously, Cas? What the fuck are you doing here?"

Chapter Four

FAITH

He stared at me as I lay pinned beneath him, and my memory flashed back to a time where we'd been in a similar position. He'd been between my legs, rather than astride them, and I'd wrapped them around him, pulling him closer. His eyes had been full of lust rather than anger though. I watched his face start to soften slightly, and his gaze dropped to my mouth. Heat flashed through me and started to pool in my lower belly. He began to lean closer, and I felt my breathing quicken. I saw the tip of his tongue dart out and run across his lips. My underwear dampened as his breath tickled my neck. I was clearly having the same effect on him. A hardness pressed into my belly, sending a lightning bolt of desire to my pussy, but then another memory flashed through my mind and I froze. My hands were pinned behind my back as I was pressed down onto the floor, and the hardness of another man pressed against my ass as another forced my mouth open...

I braced my heels against the floor and slammed my pelvis up against Cas, the heavy metal belt buckle I wore hitting him square between his legs.

"Fuck..." He released my wrists and rolled onto the floor. I quickly got to my feet, righting my clothing. I turned, quite inclined to kick him wherever I could reach, but he was already struggling to his knees. "Fucking bitch."

"You deserve worse. Now what the fuck are you doing in my house?" He narrowed his eyes and backed away, using the heavy wooden kitchen table to pull himself to his feet. I noticed with grim satisfaction that he kept his distance. "Cas? I'm waiting for an explanation."

"I don't owe you a fucking thing, you crazy hell fiend."

I crossed my arms and glared at him. "You're in my house, and you attacked me hours after we ran into each other at the club."

"Your house? That's a joke, you haven't lived here in years," he retorted.

I took a breath, seriously considering pulling my knife out of my pocket and stabbing him. "Fine. My mother's house. Are you following me?"

He released a sharp laugh. "And why would I want to follow you?"

"Maybe you've had a personality transplant and decided to apologise?"

His eyes sparked with anger. "Faith, I swear to Satan, if you don't shut the hell up right now—"

"Cas! We need to... Err... Hey, Faith! Fancy seeing you... Cas? You okay, mate?" Sam leaned against the doorframe, looking amused.

Cas turned around. "Fine," he answered through gritted teeth as he readjusted his leathers. "Your girlfriend thought I was attacking her."

"And she took you out?" Sam burst out laughing, and I saw Cas send him a death glare.

"You're here too? What the fuck is going on?" Well, this was getting better and better.

"We're just... checking..." Sam hedged.

I raised my eyebrows. I was surprised that someone this friendly with Cas couldn't lie better than that. "Really, Sam? Just checking? Lame. Very lame." His gaze dropped as a guilty expression spread across his gorgeous face. I blinked. "Why the hell are you only wearing your underwear? You two aren't... together?" Jeez, I would never have pegged Cas for swinging both ways. Shame, Sam seemed like a half decent guy... and hot. My eyes travelled over the lean, sculpted muscles of his bare chest.

Cas's sarcastic timbre interrupted what were becoming quite interesting thoughts. "Together? Oh, you mean like... no, we most definitely aren't. Why, were you hoping for both of us? My goodness, you're a hungry girl. Is my poor Sam not enough for you?" I fought off the urge to throw a chair at him and settled for plastering a fake smile on my face.

"I've never been with a man who could fully satisfy me, Cas." This hit right where it was supposed to, and he stood there for a moment looking dumbfounded as Sam chuckled behind him. *Enough with the banter, Faith.* "Did you have anything to do with this?"

Cas stares at me blankly. "With what?"

"Don't act dumb," I snapped. "My mother is missing, there is broken glass everywhere, and she left a phone message that really worried me. Do you have anything to do with this? Cause if you do, Cas, I swear to God I'll—"

Cas rolled his eyes. "I wouldn't bother. You'll just embarrass yourself."

I stepped forward to hit him, but Sam caught my elbow, stopping me. I shook him off angrily, and he moved to my side.

"Faith, listen. We had nothing to do with this. We came to see if your mother was alright. We work at the same organisation, and when she couldn't be contacted, we were sent to check things out."

I frowned at him, confused. "You work at the university?"

He glanced at Cas, then back at me and nodded. "Um, yes. I mean, not... closely. We're in different departments."

I stared at him. "So you guys are like campus police or something?"

Sam nodded. He opened his mouth to say something else, then stopped.

"What?" I prompted.

He turned his head towards the door, staring straight out of the window as though he was trying to see something. I had no idea what, all I could see was darkness. "Cas? We need to leave. Now." Cas's head snapped up, and he stared hard out of the window before swinging around to face me.

I held my hands up. "Hey, don't let me stop you. What—" Sam darted past me and hit the light switching, plunging the kitchen back into darkness. "What the—"

"Be quiet!" Cas hissed.

Um no, I don't think so. "Cas, I want you and your friend out of my house right now before the police get here." I added the last bit as an afterthought.

"You called the police?" Sam's voice came from my right, but I could see Cas's outline as he moved close to the window.

"I... er... yes, just before I ran into you." I was lying, of course, but they didn't know that. I started to move back towards the door. Both guys were acting really odd, and it struck me that while Sam had seemed lovely, I didn't really know the guy, but I did know Cas, and I didn't trust him one jot. As though he read my mind, Cas's hand shot out and latched onto my arm.

"Hey—" My voice cut off as he clapped his other hand over my mouth and pulled me closer to the window.

"Somehow I'm not that bothered about the police right now, Faith," he whispered. I froze as I looked out of the window. Outside on the lawn was the biggest dog I'd ever seen. With *three fucking heads.* It was sniffing around the flowerbeds. Cas lifted his hand from my mouth, and it fell open as I gaped at the creature not six metres away from me. From where I stood, I could see that its heads would easily reach my shoulder, and the body was long and powerful, with bulging muscles and leathery skin. I couldn't tear my eyes away, yet I knew if it caught our scent, there was no way we could fight that thing off.

Sam silently stepped up to Cas and murmured something in his ear. Cas looked at me briefly then nodded. I watched as Sam slowly backed out of the room. Cas tugged on my jacket and lowered his head to mine.

"Sam is going to distract it. When I tell you, make for your bike. Mine's at the back. Wait for me to come around the front then follow me."

I wondered briefly whether I should trust him. I mean, there was no way I trusted him, but if it came down to him or facing the hulking beast on my mother's lawn, I guessed he was the slightly better option. I nodded, and he sighed—probably with relief. Even in our current situation, a small sense of satisfaction that I wasn't predictable made me smile.

A streak of movement outside caught my eye as something large and grey blurred past the window. I held my breath as the giant dog came leaping out of the bushes towards the window, then turned and bounded after the blur and into the woods at the back of the house.

"Come on." Cas grabbed my arm and pulled me to the door. I wrenched it out of his grip. He glared at me. "Fine. I'll see you at the front." He swung himself over the window ledge, landing with a crunch on the gravelled path below before looking back up at me. I held my middle finger up at him.

"Bite me." I moved quickly to the front door, opened it slightly, and checked the driveway to see if that thing was somewhere about. It seemed quiet, so I hurried over to my bike. I was just about to grip the handlebars and start her up when Cas pulled up with a roar.

He lifted his visor and looked over at me. "Are you armed?"

I nodded, pulling my jacket open to show the hilt of my knife. Cas stared at me, raised his eyebrows, and then glanced back down at the knife with silent sarcasm. I only considered stabbing him with it for a second, I swear. He grinned as if reading my thoughts and pushed something into my hand.

Looking down, my eyes widened. What the fuck was Cas doing with a gun?

"Fuck, Cas, what the hell?"

He pushed it into my hand. "In case they catch up. Send the sorry fuckers back to Hell. Safety is—" Cas was cut off as the brush around us exploded with movement. Large black shapes burst out of the shadows from which they'd been stalking us, armed with very sharp teeth and claws.

"Faith!"

I was already swinging my leg over the bike and starting her up with a roar of her own. He swung his bike around, and we took off down the driveway. I looked back to see more shapes pouring out of the trees as the first wave came level with my back tyre. They were horrific creatures. Their eyes gleamed red in the darkness, and I saw glints of white teeth as they snarled and snapped at my legs. I felt a sense of dread and fear creep over me, nausea rose in my throat, and I had a desire to freeze in place. Fuck that shit. Gripping the bike tightly with my legs, I pulled my arm back and clicked off the safety.

"Faith, hold on!" At Cas's shout, I looked up and past him. We were nearing the end of the driveway where it joined with the main road. He showed no intention of slowing down. I tightened my hold on the bike and leaned into the sharp turn, pulling out onto the road and praying to the universe that there were no late-night taxis hurtling towards us. Thankfully there wasn't, and as I came side on with my attackers, I heard another gun go off. I opened fire too, taking out the hounds closest to me. I was a little rusty though, having not fired a gun in over six years, and one got close enough that it managed to leap forward and rake its claws over my leg.

"Fucking bastard!" I yelled, feeling a sharp jolt of pain across my thigh and hearing the rip of my rather expensive leather trousers. As I straightened the bike, I planted a bullet between the eyes of the middle head, and the thing dropped back, whining.

"Clear!" I heard Cas yell from his position in front, his voice tinny on the wind that whistled past me. With an expanse of open road, he opened the throttle, and after glancing behind me to check that none of the bastards were closing in, I flicked the safety back on and stuffed the gun into the top of my zipped-up jacket. I took a deep breath, looking behind me again to watch the dark shapes fade into the distance. It took a mile or so for my breathing to return to normal and the sick fear inside to ease slightly. Trying not to think about what had just happened, I ignored the warnings in my head and followed Cas as he pulled onto the motorway and headed north.

CHAPTER FIVE

FAITH

As we flew along the deserted motorway, I tried to get what was going on straight in my head. I felt sick and shaky, and my mind was spinning. Rose had gone missing. Possibly kidnapped by someone. She had worked with Sam and Cas. They knew her. She'd met Cas... Oh God, did she know about him and me? That would be... icky. I'd dated him right after leaving home, during the period where my only contact with my mother ended in me screaming at her for trying to control me my entire life. We hadn't exactly grabbed a cuppa and chatted about boys, and she probably wouldn't have approved of Cas as boyfriend material either. But now, it was starting to look more and more as if she'd been taken against her will, and in one night, I regretted every moment I had spent hating her. I just wanted her back.

What are you mixed up in, Rose?

I shifted my grip slightly, squeezing my thighs together over the bike in an attempt to stop the shaking. I felt the hard metal of the gun down the front of my jacket and closed my eyes, picturing those creatures that had pursued us. They'd looked like Dobermans, but maybe crossed with something. Something huge. Had it really had three heads, or was I just fucking losing it? They were stockier than Dobermans too, massive and muscular. Someone really went for the freaky, fucked up guard dog angle. I loved dogs, and shooting them had really upset me. I had tried aiming over their heads, but they hadn't been fazed by the gunshots at all, and I was convinced they would have ripped us apart if I hadn't started shooting for real.

As I squeezed my thighs again, I felt a flash of pain across one of my legs. Glancing down, I saw that the dog had clearly torn through the leathers to my skin beneath. The leathers were ripped, and I could see the slickness of blood underneath, though it didn't hurt too much, so I doubted the wound was deep. To be honest, I was more pissed because these were my favourite leathers. Any guilt I harboured for shooting the fucker disappeared.

Looking up, I noticed Cas was signalling to leave the motorway, so I followed suit. We pulled up at some lights, but as they changed, we veered to the left. The famous green bridge was ahead of me, and the River Tyne was below us, and within a few minutes we'd passed into Newcastle. The roads were practically empty at this time of night, except for the occasional taxi, and it wasn't long before we were pulling into a small side road somewhere in a rather well-to-do suburb. Cas rode his bike up in front of a beautiful stone townhouse, and I did the same. As I pulled off my helmet and bandana and fluffed out my hair, I noticed the polished brass sign next to the door.

Church of the Concordia, Northeast Regional Office.

"A church? Really?" I looked back at Cas, one eyebrow arched.

"Don't make assumptions. And don't... talk too much." He turned to put his helmet on top of his bike and unzipped his jacket.

My mouth fell open. "Excuse me?"

"These are important people, Faith, and your mouth has a habit of getting you into trouble."

I didn't know whether it was the make out session with Sam in the alley or having my crotch pressed against a vibrating bike for the last twenty minutes, but instead of slapping him for being such a patronising tosser, I licked my lips and stared pointedly below his belt. "That never seemed to bother you before."

He stared at me for a moment, dropping his gaze to my mouth briefly before looking away.

"Just fucking keep it shut," he growled. I unzipped my jacket and passed him the gun he'd lent me earlier.

"Fine." I glared at him, but he ignored me, pushing past me to the entrance. Sliding a key into the lock, he tapped in a numerical code on a small box next to the door, and I heard a soft *whoosh*. The door swung open, and Cas gestured for me to enter, bowing mockingly as I did. The urge to grab his hair and slam my knee into his face was overwhelming, but I managed to resist. Just.

My grin faded as I stepped into the entrance hall. A polished black and white marble floor stretched deep into the house. High ceilings and grey walls surrounded me, with several closed doors leading off the hallway. A white, marble-topped console table to the right held a vase of red roses. I immediately felt out of place. Cas started up the stairs and beckoned for me to follow. I had a strange urge to take my boots off in case I muddied the soft cream carpet, but I saw nowhere to leave them, and Cas seemed impatient. At the top of the staircase, he ushered me along another hallway.

"Cas, where the hell are you taking me? What is this place?"

"Miss Matthews, I presume?" The door ahead of Cas opened, and a man stepped out into the hallway. Despite the fact that it was a little past four o'clock in the morning, he was immaculately dressed in a grey suit and tie, complete with waistcoat. He was clean-shaven, and his white hair was on the long side but combed back neatly. He held out his hand in greeting.

I glanced at Cas, who opened his mouth as if to say something but then shut it again. Turning back to the older man, I placed my hand in his. "Who are you? And how do you know my name?"

He grasped my hand firmly. "My name is Sir Phillip Hargreaves. I am the Head of the Northeast Division of the Church of the Concordia. As for your name, one of my officers called ahead to say Cassiel would be returning shortly with a young lady by the name of Faith Matthews. Daughter of Rose Matthews."

I nodded. "An officer... you mean—"

"Samuel Hedworth. I believe you made his acquaintance tonight?"

"She did. How's he doing, sir? There were several hellhounds pursuing us when we left, and I think he was under the impression there was only one." Cas tried to sound nonchalant, but I noted that there was genuine concern in his voice. Clearly, he and Sam were close.

Hargreaves cracked a smile. "He called asking for backup and was waiting for the team to arrive before he headed over here. The team leader checked in a little while ago, so I don't think he'll be long."

"A team? What kind of team?" I asked.

Sir Phillip looked at me. "Oh, I'm sorry. The creatures that pursued you, they were hellhounds. Creatures summoned by a magical practitioner from Sheol to Earth for a purpose. Usually the practitioner dispatches them back to Sheol after they perform their purpose, but this does not seem to have happened, so we've sent a team along to do it instead. Can't have them roaming the Earth unchecked, now can we? Shall we go in and sit down? I imagine you'll have some questions, Miss Matthews."

He stood back and gestured for me to enter. Feeling a bit out of place, I didn't say anything as I moved past him and into the room beyond. The cream carpet continued into this area, and tall mahogany bookshelves covered two of the walls with another taken up by floor-to-ceiling windows. A mahogany desk stood in front of one of the bookcases, and a small two-seater sofa and two velvet covered chairs took up the rest of the space. He gestured for me to sit, and I took the sofa, secretly amused as I watched Cas perch on one of the chairs. He was a big guy, and it looked like a child's seat under him. Sir Phillip took the other chair.

"Now, Miss Matthews, we need to have a little chat about your mother. I need you to tell me what you know about her disappearance." He leaned back, tapping his fingertips together, clearly waiting for me to speak.

Oh, hell no. I leaned forward, my elbows propped on my knees. "You know what? You might be a sir, and Cas here might bow and scrape around you, but I don't know or care who you are, so maybe this conversation should go more like... who the hell are you people? Does my mother work for you? If so, for how long, and why doesn't she work for the university anymore? What's with the weird room under my house, and, oh yeah... where the hell is she?" To my right, I saw Cas roll his eyes dramatically, and I vaguely remembered something he'd said about these being important people and my mouth getting me into trouble. What the fuck? Since when did Cas give a shit about how he acted around anybody? Bugger that, I wanted to know what had happened to my mother, and this Sir Whatsit knew something. I leaned back, pressing my fingertips together as he had, clearly taking the piss. Sir Phillip stared at me for a moment, then smiled. It wasn't a warm smile, but there was no way he was intimidating me.

"Of course, my dear. I do apologise. Naturally you are shaken and confused and worried about your mother. Let me see if I can illuminate you. Your mother does work for me, and she still works for the university. She is a consultant. I contact her when I need help acquiring artefacts or documents, and also for validating them. She is the top of her field in this country, and it is a rather specialised field."

I frowned. "I thought she specialised in biblical archaeology and theology. Surely there are loads of people who do that?"

Sir Phillip nodded. "There are, but your mother has a distinct advantage in that she has unique sources to work from, like various documents and artefacts that belong to the Church of the Concordia. We have an extensive archive that the wider world knows nothing about."

"What, even the Catholics? Or are you Catholics? I don't really know how this stuff works, not really a churchy person." And what the hell did this have to do with her disappearance? Last I checked, biblical archaeologists weren't in high demand. She wasn't exactly Indiana Jones.

Sir Phillip laughed. "No, we're not Catholics, dear. We are an organisation that exists to maintain a balance on Earth between Heaven and Hell. You might see it as policing a no-man's-land between two sides at war."

"Heaven and Hell? Really?" I didn't try hard to keep the scepticism out of my voice, but I let him get away with calling me dear. For now.

Sir Phillip opened his mouth to answer, but there was a knock at the door, and he glanced over as it swung open. "Ah, Samuel, come in."

Sam walked in and dropped onto the sofa next to me. He grinned. "Hello again, come here often?" I let out a small amount of the frustration I was feeling by punching him hard in the arm. He recoiled, rubbing the spot with his other hand. "Not the time for flirting, got it."

"Mr Hedworth, if you could possibly restrain yourself..." Sir Philip shot him a firm look, and Sam immediately went quiet. I looked at him, raising my eyebrows.

What was it about this guy that had everyone on their best behaviour? He was like a posh headteacher. Mind, I never was very popular at school, so this could be interesting. I looked back at Sir Phillip to find him watching me appraisingly. He glanced over at Sam, then back to me as if considering something.

As I opened my mouth to ask about my mother again, he held his hand up to silence me. I bristled at the patronising gesture, and it was shock that kept me quiet rather than me doing as I was told. He seemed to sense my mood, because he hastily tried to explain himself.

"I realise you have questions, but this will go faster if I finish what I was trying to explain before. Our organisation exists to maintain a buffer zone on Earth between Heaven and Hell, both of which are real and exist. I am not going to insult your intelligence by telling you everything in the Bible is true. As a daughter of a biblical archaeologist and theologian, you will know that is not the case. However, Heaven and Hell do exist. Heaven is populated by angels, and Hell by demons and fallen angels and other creatures. On Earth, there exists several other supernatural species created in various ways, but mainly by angels and demons interbreeding with humans. With me so far?"

"Um, no, not really. You're insane, and I'm leaving."

I went to stand up, but Sam caught my hand. "Stay, Faith, this is important. Please."

I sat back down, though I pulled my hand away from Sam, ignoring the hurt expression on his face. I was still pissed about the whole showing up at my house thing, and he wasn't getting away with it that easily.

Sir Phillip continued, "I realise this is a lot to take in, and I won't bore you with the details, just so far as to say Heaven and Hell have been at war since time began. A cold war as such, with a ceasefire that has lasted millennia. Entities from both also live on Earth, and the Church of the Concordia is tasked with keeping the peace and ensuring that humans do not find out about any of this."

"Why not? If they already know all the stuff in the Bible, why shouldn't they know it's real?" I was still finding it hard to link all this with a quiet, middle-aged woman who liked to dress in dungarees and binge watch documentaries in her spare time.

Cas leaned forward, resting his elbows on his knees. "Are you dumb? Or just incredibly naïve and stupid? Can you imagine the effect it would have on humanity?" I opened my mouth to argue, but he spoke over me. "It would be devastating. Societies would collapse, there would be mass suicides, murders, and wars. Especially since not one Earth religion ever got it all right. The truth, well, what we know is represented in so many ways in so many religions. There would be chaos. Humanity needs to be protected from that." His dark eyes bore uncomfortably into mine.

I tried to hold his gaze, but I had to look back at Sir Phillip, who nodded. "It is as Cassiel explained. We are comprised of members from all planes of existence, both human and supernatural, sworn to secrecy and the protection of humanity, even from itself, to a certain extent. Everyone who works for us knows the truth. And now, so do you. It goes without saying, you cannot repeat any of this outside of these walls."

I raised my eyebrows at him. "Oh yeah, cause I'm dying to go and shout all this out on a street corner. Maybe if I'm quick, I'll get committed in time for lunch."

Sir Phillip gave me a smile that didn't quite reach his eyes. "It is a lot to take in, and I realise it's hard to understand that everything you've been told about Heaven and Hell is a lie. That's why I'm glad Samuel is here."

I heard Sam groan quietly next to me.

"Sam? Why?"

Sir Phillip glanced over at him. "As I said, the majority of people who work for the church are supernatural beings themselves. Samuel, would you mind demonstrating for Miss Matthews, please?"

It wasn't really a request. Sam squeezed my hand before letting go and standing up. He moved behind the sofa to a space on the carpet and began to strip. As much as I'd wanted to see him naked tonight, I hadn't planned on doing it in some old, creepy guy's office with my ex looking on. Well, maybe Cas being there could have been quite fun, especially with how he reacted to me kissing Sam earlier. I could quite enjoy making the bastard jealous again, but definitely not the creepy old guy. When Sam got down to his underwear, he paused and glanced over at Sir Phillip, who nodded at him. Sam locked his blue eyes with mine, and then his body began to change. I jumped to my feet and stared in horror as fur began to grow, first on his chest then spreading down his legs and along his arms. His face was covered last, and by then, that was already changing shape, his mouth and nose pushing forward to form a muzzle as his teeth lengthened. He dropped to his knees, his legs and arms contorting to form four powerful legs. A tail rose behind him, and a growl came from his mouth as the transformation completed. I gaped, not realising I was backing away until I collided with a pair of knees and nearly landed in Cas's lap.

He sighed with exasperation. "For pity's sake, Faith. It's just Sam."

I jerked away from him and looked back at the very large, very real wolf that stood in front of us. With a movement that made me jump, he suddenly sat down and raised his hind leg to scratch behind his ear. I smiled slightly at the very domestic gesture and walked slowly, very slowly, around the chair. The wolf stropped scratching and sat very still. I edged forward, reaching out tentatively. His white fur was thick and warm, and he had grey over his face and legs, which deepened to black along his spine. I met his eyes, and familiar blue pupils gazed back at me.

"That's... insane... amazing..." I glanced up at Sir Phillip. "So what are you? A demon?"

He laughed, though there was no warmth in it. "I am not, though I am amused that was your first assumption. I am a witch. A human descended from a bloodline that runs back to the beginning of the human race, when a group of angels came to Earth and damned themselves by mating with human women. Many of the stronger, more deformed offspring were slaughtered, but those that were more or less human remained and were permitted to survive. As a result of our angelic blood, we can manipulate the energies of the Earth, giving us abilities you humans would call magical."

"Okay, now we have witches too. Are there... a lot of you?" I kept running my hands through Sam's fur. It was lovely and thick, and I had a sudden urge to curl up with him and fall asleep. It was easier to pretend he was just a cuddly dog, and it had been a long night.

"Yes. All humanity has the ability to manipulate the energies of the Earth, but most don't believe in it. Those who do are more powerful than others. We invite the ones that excel to join the Concordia, and also to keep an eye on their less skilled or experienced brothers and sisters to make sure they aren't endangering themselves or anyone else."

"Okay... so, my mother?" I wasn't sure I was liking where this was all going, and to be honest, I wasn't entirely sure I believed a word of it. He reminded me too much of the shrinks I'd seen in the past.

"Your mother is a witch, yes. She is fairly powerful, but not exactly in the top ranks. She specialises in ancient religious relics, which are often imbued with enchantments, spells, curses, and so on. She works to ensure they don't fall into the hands of humans. Same for ancient documents that might attract too much attention. She is very good at her job. In the past, things have made it into museums and collections that should never have come to light. Thankfully, the Catholic Church doesn't like anything that contradicts its monopoly, so they are also a handy accomplice, even if they aren't actually aware that they are."

"So, if all she was doing was archaeology, why would some-one have taken her?" That was the part I just couldn't work out.

Sir Phillip shrugged, an oddly casual gesture for him. "To be honest with you, Miss Matthews, I have no idea. Rose had her own projects running alongside those I gave her. There is the possibility she discovered something others wanted to acquire. Knowledge, or an artifact maybe. But without knowing more, I can't give you any answers. May I ask what she has told you? When did you last speak to her?"

I sighed and came back to the sofa. Sam followed me, resting his head on my knee.

"I haven't spoken to her in a while, bar a few text messages. She rang me earlier, I mean, last night, and left a message saying she had to go away tomorrow... today. She sounded strange, I don't know."

Sir Phillip gazed at me, his steely grey eyes hard under his bushy white eyebrows. "Anything else to go on? It doesn't seem like much. You're her daughter, surely you know more than this? Even about her current work projects."

He didn't seem happy with me, and his tone was really starting to annoy me.

"You know what? No, she doesn't tell me about her current work projects. To be honest, we barely speak at all, really. Now she's missing, and apart from all this churchy mumbo jumbo bollocks, you don't seem to know shit! So don't come across all preachy to me!"

He didn't respond, just looked at me. I wondered whether he was trying to decide what to say, attempting not to lose his temper, or just shocked. By the way Sam and Cas acted around him, I bet he didn't get spoken to this way very often. I took a deep breath, trying to tamp down my anger. Plus, he might, like, turn me into a frog or something.

"Look, sorry. It's been a long night and I'm worried about her. On the phone message, she told me not to come to the house. I thought that was weird, but that's all I know."

He nodded. "Of course, Miss Matthews. I apologise if you felt I was in any way blaming you, that was not my intention. And you are correct, it has been a long night. Samuel, perhaps you could shift back now please."

Sam made a quiet *ruff* noise and headed behind the sofa. I avoided looking at him as he got dressed again, as his underpants lay on the floor in shreds.

Sir Phillip sat quietly for a moment, tapping his fingers together and looking at each of us in turn. Finally, he turned to Cas. "Cassiel, I'm assigning your team as a security detail to Miss Matthews until this matter is resolved."

I jumped to my feet with a loud, "What?" just as I heard Cas say, "Sir, no, we can't..."

Sir Phillip glared at both of us. "I believe Miss Matthews may need looking after. We don't know the circumstances of her mother's disappearance yet, so I think it would be safer for her at your house with you watching over her. I will dispatch a team to her apartment in the morning to make sure it has not been tampered with, and to pack some clothing for her for the foreseeable future." Cas sat down heavily, his lips pressed in a thin line. He looked pissed, but nowhere nearly as much as I was.

"With all due respect, *Sir* Phillip. There is not the slightest fucking chance of me staying in a house with Cas, or with Sam either, seeing as we've only just met, and to be honest, I don't trust any of you as far as I can throw you. I'll be staying at my own place, and you can call me there to update me on what's going on with Rose." I stared down at him, watching as his face tightened. Clearly, he wasn't used to being spoken to that way. He stood too, and while he wasn't much taller than me, his presence seemed overbearing, and I felt my indignation crumble under his iron gaze.

"My dear, perhaps you do not understand the gravity of the situation. If your mother has been taken, it will be for something of major importance. Therefore, I would hazard a guess that if she does not have or cannot tell them the information they require, the people that have taken her may use you as leverage to force her to talk. I do not think you are obtuse enough to not comprehend what I mean. Besides caring for your general well-being, I also do not want to add to my agent's vulnerability nor to the chance that she may then give away information that could compromise our mission here. Therefore, you will stay with Cassiel and his team, and they will protect you until this situation is resolved. If you do not agree, please remember that we do not fall under mortal jurisdiction. We can and will restrain you by force."

I opened my mouth to argue, but then I felt Cas grip my upper arm tightly. "Oh, please give me a reason to restrain you." He grinned darkly, and I glared up at him.

"If you drag me anywhere, it'll be with me kicking and screaming," I snapped. His grin widened, and he stepped closer to me. I jerked backwards. "Fine. I'll go."

He smiled pleasantly, as if I'd just agreed to meet him for lunch. Wanker. Sir Phillip also smiled in an annoyingly patronising way. "Good. Cassiel, I will keep you informed of the progress of the investigation." Cas nodded and began to usher me out of the door, Sam following close behind us.

I paused for a moment and looked back into the room. "Sir Phillip? The magical abilities you spoke of... how did Rose get them? Did she learn them?"

Sir Phillip was just sitting down at his desk. "Magical abilities pass down through sacred bloodlines. Your mother is also descended from angels, though abilities do take a lot of study and practice to master. In short, no. Only faint magical remnants can be picked up by humans, even with decades to study. As you were adopted, it's highly unlikely that you possess any significant magical ability. If you were by some small chance a descendant, then we have powerful charms set upon the front door which would have alerted me to it. They were not activated."

I took a disappointed breath. It had been a long shot, after all. "Thanks, I just wanted to know for sure." *That I wasn't anyone special,* I silently added. Not that I was surprised. Why would I be?

Chapter Six

FAITH

I stayed quiet all the way downstairs and out to the bikes. Sam's VW camper was pulled up next to my bike, but I ignored him as I climbed on and fastened my helmet. He sighed and got into the van.

"See you at home," he called over to Cas, then he pulled out of the driveway and disappeared. Starting the bike, I swung it around slowly, waiting for Cas. He was looking at me with a weird expression.

"What?" I asked.

He shook his head. "Nothing, doesn't matter." Sliding his helmet on, he gestured towards the road. "We live closer to the coast, so we'll cut onto the bypass near the bridge. It's a bit of a drive."

"Well, especially if you ride like an old lady," I muttered.

"Oh really?" Cas laughed. "Well then, I can't let that slide. Come on, Peaches. Make sure you keep up." He revved the engine and took off in a shower of gravel. I followed him, keeping pace as we tipped and turned around corners, drove down smaller streets, and sped along larger ones. He glanced back at me as we approached the bypass, and I lifted a hand to wave at him. He answered by revving his bike again, and I did too, though I dropped back a little to create some distance between us. Not too much though. He turned off down the slip road to the long bypass that would lead us to the coastal road, and I indicated to do the same as he looked back to check I was following. He faced forward, and at the last moment, I swung back across the lanes, away from the slip road, and across the bridge. I opened the throttle, and my Softail zoomed away from the city, leaving Cas heading in the opposite direction.

He didn't catch up with me on my way home, but I took a roundabout way to get there just in case. He'd never seen my current apartment, but I wouldn't put it past him to be able to find out somehow. That organisation he worked for seemed pretty well funded, and I bet they had a lot of fingers in a lot of pies. It would be a cold day in hell when I went home willingly with Cas Hardy again.

The sky was growing light as I pulled up outside my apartment, and there was already traffic on the streets as people started their daily commutes. Stashing my bike securely in the lockup across the road from my building, I climbed the stairs slowly, still processing everything that had happened, trying to decide what to do next.

If I called the police, what would I tell them? That I'd waited this long because my ex-boyfriend showed up with a mate who could turn into a wolf and then told me that my mother was a witch? They would have me committed before I could say straitjacket. I sighed, pushing open the fire door to the corridor where my front door was. Maybe I should just do some research on this Concordia thing. Rose might not even be missing. She might have been attacked or something and just left. Maybe she went to the conference in a hurry and didn't go back for her stuff first.

What the...?

I stopped a few metres from my front door. It stood slightly ajar, like someone had pulled it closed but not hard enough for it to latch. The lock was slightly dodgy, so I had developed the habit of always checking that it was properly closed before I left. I reached into my pocket and took out my knife, pushing the door open slowly. It swung inwards, and I stepped into my apartment, listening for any sound of an intruder. It was silent. Stepping carefully, I checked every room thoroughly. It didn't take long, since it only consisted of a small hallway, bedroom, bathroom, and a slightly larger room that had a small kitchenette and a rather worn sofa. My TV and media box were still in place. In fact, everything was as I'd left it, though had I called the police, they might have believed someone had ransacked the place—I wasn't the tidiest person in the world. To my eye, though, there were small details that were wrong. The battered old trunk I used as a coffee table was straight on to the sofa. I usually had it at an odd angle, otherwise I always walked into it when I went to sit down. The empty cans of Diet Coke were still on top, but the pizza box from the night before was on the floor.

Someone had definitely been here, and they had been searching for something. I shivered at the thought of someone going through my stuff. Quickly rechecking the rest of the apartment, I shut and locked the door. After a moment of staring at the back of the locked door, which someone had already got through today, I went to my bedroom and started pushing at the heavy wardrobe. Luckily, it slid fairly easily along the laminate floor. The chest of drawers followed, then the chest, which I filled with books. As a last-ditch effort, I grabbed my weight set from the living room and hoisted the whole lot on top of the chest.

The sun was finally up when I checked every window and pulled all the curtains closed. I stripped off my leathers, donning an oversized Nirvana T-shirt, and plugged in my phone. Grabbing my first aid kit from under the kitchen sink, I cleaned the wound on my leg, wincing as the disinfectant stung like a bastard. The wound wasn't deep, so I pressed a pad on top, before tying a bandage firmly to hold it in place. I could barely keep my eyes open, and I knew I needed sleep before I did anything else, so I climbed into bed and lay staring at the ceiling for a few minutes before admitting defeat and rolling over to grab a couple of the sleeping pills from my bedside table. They might not keep the nightmares away, but they'd knock me out pretty damn quickly, and right now, that was what I needed.

The sun was high in the sky when I woke to the sound of banging and yelling on my front door. I sat up and squinted at the brightness that invaded my otherwise dark room from the edges of the curtains. I squeezed my eyes shut again, but the banging continued. Rolling over and grabbing my phone, I saw I'd managed about three hours of sleep. I stretched and hauled myself off the bed. As I got near the door, I recognised Sam's voice.

"What do you want?" I yelled, pausing in the hallway.

"Faith, is that you?"

I rolled my eyes. "No, it's my landlord kicking me out cause of the nutter who's banging on my door and disturbing my neighbours," I called, moving closer to the door. There was a short pause.

"Sorry. Would you open up and let me in then?" He sounded somewhat contrite.

I cocked my head and thought for a moment. "Is Cas with you?"

"No. He thought it would be better if I came on my own."

"Fine, hang on." I sighed with relief and began shifting the furniture away from the door.

"Are you okay? What's all that noise?" Sam shouted. I managed to move everything over enough to unlock the door and let him squeeze in. He stood in the hallway, surveying the furniture towers, and grinned at me. "Expecting a siege?"

I gave him a shove in response, then stepped past and locked the door behind him. He followed me into the kitchen, and I switched on my coffee machine, needing a serious caffeine boost.

"I'm impressed," he remarked.

I looked at him. "With my coffee machine?"

He laughed. "No, ours is better, but you'd be finding that out right about now if you'd come home with us like you were supposed to. I'm impressed that you were able to lose Cas so easily. Not many people could do that, and believe me, lots have tried."

I passed him a cup without replying and hoisted myself up onto the worktop, wrapping my fingers around the cup in my hands. "Out of interest, on a scale from zero to really pissed, how was he?"

Sam grinned at me and sipped his coffee. "Oh, I'd say he was absolutely fuming."

I smiled to myself and took a drink, watching Sam wrinkle his nose as he took another. "Sorry, I'd offer you milk and sugar, but I don't have any. I drink mine black."

He smiled at me. "Like the Italians?"

"Like my soul." I laughed as he spat out the sip he'd just taken. He wiped his mouth and set the cup down on the draining board.

"So, what do we do now?"

I glared at him. "I'm not going anywhere with Cas."

Sam sighed. "You really hate him, huh?"

"Understatement."

"What's with the furniture?" Sam asked, turning in the direction of the hallway.

I shrugged. "When I got home, someone had broken in. I locked the door again but wanted to take precautions in case they came back while I was asleep."

"What?" He stared at me in shock.

"What? It worked, didn't it? You couldn't get in."

He shook his head. "Faith, I'm a hundred and fifty pound surfer whose only skill is to get fluffier. There are magic users out there that could literally unlock your door and float the furniture away without breaking a sweat. If they'd have come back, you'd have been in serious trouble."

I stared at him. "I didn't think of that."

He sighed and stood in front of me. Taking my cup and putting it down on the side, he clutched my hands in his. "Faith, please come back with me. Forget about Cas, I get it, he can be an asshole. But I'll be there the whole time, and the other two guys we live with are sweethearts."

"Sweethearts, huh?" I arched one eyebrow.

"Wait until you meet them."

I took a deep breath. "Urgh, I just... *really* don't want to see Cas again."

"I get it." Sam moved forward, and I suddenly became aware that he was very close. His sky-blue eyes held mine. "On the other hand..." He laid his palms on my bare knees and gently pushed them apart, stepping between them. "I believe you said you wanted to see me again. That you wanted to continue where we left off." My lips parted involuntarily, and he leaned in, brushing his mouth against mine. I closed my eyes, feeling the hot flick of his tongue over my bottom lip. He pulled away, trailing his lips along my jawline to whisper into my ear. "I believe we were about here?"

"I believe you may be right," I answered. I slid my hands into his hair, pulling his mouth back to mine. His kiss was deep and sensual as he gently explored my mouth with his tongue, entwining it with mine. My arms snaked around his neck, and I shivered slightly at the feel of his hands stroking down my back. His scent and taste were intoxicating, and I pulled him closer, feeling him press against my core.

His kiss became more demanding. He pulled back for a moment, grabbed the hem of my T-shirt, and drew it over my head. His hands settled on my waist, then as he kissed me again, they travelled up my rib cage to cup my breasts. I moaned quietly and tugged at his shirt, not stopping to undo the buttons but simply dragging it off. He pulled me closer, and I relished the sensation of having his hot, smooth skin against me. He held me like that as his lips moved over the delicate skin of my neck, then he tipped me backwards, one arm sliding around my waist to support me. He dropped his head, and I moaned louder as I felt his mouth fasten onto one of my nipples. His tongue flicked back and forth over it, sending small waves of pleasure straight to the building heat between my thighs. His free hand found my other breast, and he teased and pinched my other nipple until I was panting heavily for him. I threaded my fingers into his hair and wrapped my legs around his waist.

He released my nipple and raised his head to crush his lips against mine again. Both hands fell to slide under my ass, and then he lifted me, pulling me hard against him. I moaned into his mouth as I felt the roughness of his jeans and the hardness of his cock rub against the thin cotton of my underwear. I dropped my hands to his belt, fumbling as I fought with the buckle. He shifted away slightly, breaking the kiss, and undid it himself, shoving both his jeans and his briefs to the floor. My eyes dropped to his rigid cock, and I ran my tongue over my lips. Sam grasped my chin, and he pulled it up to face him, his blue eyes boring into mine.

"I've spent all night thinking of you and me in that alley." Reaching between us, he slowly dragged his fingers across my cleft, spreading the wetness over my lips.

I took a deep breath. "Really? And what, exactly, were you thinking about?" His other hand brushed the hair away from my neck, and he leaned in close, his breath tickling my ear as his fingers tenderly moved back and forth, teasing me.

"I was imagining lifting you up, much like this, and pressing you against the wall."

His fingers increased their pressure, gliding back and forth over my clit before dipping into my entrance ever so slightly to dampen them. I was breathing heavily now, trying to concentrate on what he was saying. I felt a single finger slide deeper inside me, and I moaned, pushing against him in a silent plea. He chuckled softly and slid a second finger into my channel, moving in and out and curling up at just the right spot. He buried his face in my hair.

"I imagined you wet and moaning, just like this..." He curled his fingers again and again, and I bucked below him, crying out.

"Sam... Shit, Sam..." I could feel the climax rising within me, but suddenly, his fingers slipped away, and I almost growled in protest.

"Do you have any protection?"

I took a shaky breath and nodded, slipping my hand down to pull open one of the kitchen drawers where I knew I had a few stashed. I heard a quick rustle of a wrapper, and then I felt his fingers slide inside me again, his thumb circling gently over my clit in some kind of slow torture. It didn't take him long to get me going again, and I pushed my pussy against him, feeling myself slide over the damp worktop. For some reason, the thought made me hot as hell, and I felt the pleasure crest. He pulled his fingers away again, just at the last moment, and I opened my eyes in disbelief, only to feel the head of his cock pressing against my core. With one thrust, he buried himself inside me, filling me completely. The feel of him stretching me tipped me right over the edge, and I cried out his name as the release rushed through me. He slowly moved in and out all the while, never taking his eyes off my face, making it last as long as he could.

My eyes fixed on his as my breathing finally started to slow, and he smiled, bending down to kiss me gently. "That's kind of what I had in mind."

I laughed breathlessly. "Kind of? What else were you thinking?"

He grinned at me, still leisurely moving his hard cock back and forth. It was amazing and infuriating at the same time, and I wanted more. "I was thinking something along the lines of this..." He pulled my ass forward, so I slid straight off the counter. As my feet hit the floor, my knees started to buckle, but his arms wrapped around me, and in one movement, he turned me around and pushed my torso flat onto the worktop.

I felt the cold surface against my breasts, and I shivered until he pushed his cock into me again. His strong hands fastened onto my hips, and I gripped the edge of the worktop as I felt his weight press into me from behind. He moved slowly, filling me completely, and I pushed back against him. He gripped my hips, slowing me down, but I wasn't in the mood for delayed gratification.

"Something the matter?"

I could hear the grin in his voice, and he shifted his hips, changing the angle of his dick.

I inhaled sharply at the change in sensation. "I want..."

"What do you want?" he prompted, leaning in closer, his chest warm on my back and his breath hot on my neck. His whole body felt hot, as though he was burning with fever.

"I want... you to..." I gasped as his hand found its way to my clit and settled there, the heel of his palm rubbing gently against it.

"You want me to what?" He stilled. I released a frustrated sigh, tossed my hair over my shoulder, and twisted to look back at him. His cocky grin was still on his gorgeous face, even as he slid deeply into me again.

My eyes locked onto his. "I want you to stop pretending to fuck me, and just fuck me."

His eyes darkened, and his grin changed to a different kind of smile altogether. "Oh, baby girl, you've got it." He tangled his hand in my hair, gripping onto the strands and forcing my head down. I felt his fingers dig into my hip, and then he slammed into me with such force, I cried out. He didn't hesitate. Again and again, he drove into my core, his hand falling from my hair to caress my clit as he fucked me hard and fast. I felt the force as his body collided with mine, felt my thighs strike the cupboards in front of me. I knew I'd be bruised, but I couldn't have cared less. I felt the heat rising inside me again, driving higher at the feeling of him losing control, and I moaned loudly as I felt my climax approaching.

"Sam, Sam, fuck... Oh yes, fuck!" My words seemed to inflame something inside him, because he lost all restraint and pounded into me. I gasped, feeling myself tense around his cock, and he groaned.

"Oh fuck, baby girl... come for me." He slid his arm under my shoulders, pulled me up against him, and turned my head to take my mouth with his. The heel of his hand was relentless on my clit, and he sank his fingers into me, rubbing against his cock. With one more deep thrust, I came, screaming into his mouth with the force of my climax.

"Fuck!" He shuddered, thrusting harder as my muscles tightened around him. Sam gasped as he spilled his release. He took a couple of breaths, then turned me around and pulled me close to him, wrapping his arms around me and resting his chin on top of my head.

"Well," I rasped when I could get the words out, "maybe it's a good thing we didn't do that in the alley. We definitely would have been arrested."

CHAPTER SEVEN

CAS

She still slept on her front. Her face was buried into the pillow in such a way that I was always amazed she could breathe. I'd always found that odd, considering the fact that she hated small spaces, but I loved the way her red hair tumbled over her face and her bare arms stretched over the pillow to the top of the bed. The white shirt Sam had lent her earlier that night clung to her curves, and the sheets twisted around her like some endless toga, probably from her tossing and turning. I'd heard her call out a few times in the night, and I'd desperately wanted to get up and go to her, knowing she was dreaming. Memories had stopped me.

When we'd dated, I'd mentioned her nightmares a couple of times, and she'd brushed them off, obviously not wanting to discuss it. I'd tried not to mention it again, ignoring the nights she thrashed around in her sleep and I'd had to wake her. She started drinking heavily in the evenings, and when I'd mentioned that, she'd got angry with me. I'd even tried leaving a leaflet for the AA in her jacket pocket. *That* really hadn't gone down well. We'd fought, then made love, and she'd woken me in the night, tossing, turning, and moaning as if she were in pain. When she'd started to scream in a way that seemed to rip my heart out of my chest, I'd tried again and again to wake her, but I couldn't. She'd carried on screaming until finally, out of desperation, I'd slapped her across the face. She'd woken then, kind of. Her eyes opened and the screaming stopped. She'd sat up and drawn her knees against her chest, staring off into the darkness. I'd tried to make her talk to me, even look at me, but she wouldn't. Eventually, I sat next to her and wrapped my arms around her, keeping her close until the sun started to rise. When the morning sunlight fell on her face, she got out of bed, dressed, and left without saying a word or even looking at me. It was only a couple of weeks later when the shit had hit the fan, and everything was suddenly over between us.

That was five years ago, and now here she was, in my bed and my life again. Unable to stop myself, I knelt down next to the bed, setting the coffee cup on the bedside table. Black and unsweetened, just how she liked it. I reached over and gently brushed her hair away from her face, which was turned slightly towards me. Her emerald eyes fluttered, and I smiled at the smudged eyeliner that ringed them like some kind of cute yet deadly panda. I couldn't tear my gaze away, and I brushed more of her hair back. She started to stir, and her lips moved slightly, murmuring something I couldn't quite hear. She frowned, whimpering as though she was in pain. I put my hand on her arm, gently trying to shake her awake without startling her. She moved a little, and the sheets that were tangled around her legs tightened. Her emerald eyes flew open, and she gasped and strained at the sheets. I reached across and tugged them free. Her long, slender bare legs stretched out as she revelled in her freedom, then she looked up and seemed to notice me for the first time. Faith sat up quickly, snatching at the sheets to pull them over her legs.

"Cas! What are you doing in here?"

I grinned and ran a finger along her shoulder and down her arm, twisting a lock of her hair around it. "Don't worry, Peaches, I've seen it all before."

"Urgh, seriously, don't start calling me that again. And stop looking at me like that. What the hell were you doing in here this early anyway? Taken up perving in your old age, have you?"

I shrugged. "You never minded me looking at you before. In fact, I remember when you—"

"Okay, okay, don't remind me. Well, now that you've had a good look, you can just piss off back to... whatever you were doing. Or maybe you need to go and have some alone time with your right hand? Don't let me stop you."

My anger flared. Dammit, why did she always have to go for me with a nasty remark? My eyes dropped to her gorgeous lips, curved in a sneer. Flicking my wrist around, I fisted a thick wad of her hair and pulled her face close to mine. She braced her hands on my chest, and I felt my cock twitch at the feel of her hands on me.

"Ow! Leave off, you psycho!"

I leaned in closer to her. "Don't push me, Peaches," I growled in her ear. She stopped struggling and stared straight into my eyes, her green gaze full of defiance.

"Or what?"

I grinned, loving it when she challenged me. I brought my other hand up and ran my finger down one side of her face, enjoying the softness of her smooth skin. I imagined pressing my lips against her cheek and brushing them along her jawline and down her throat as she tipped her head back... This is a really bad idea.

"Or... fuck it," I cursed, and pressed my mouth to hers, slipping both of my hands into her hair and holding her in place. My tongue explored her sweet mouth as I pulled her close. I felt her melt against me, her soft body moulding to mine, and then I felt her stiffen and push against my chest, shoving me away. I stared at her, my heart racing, my breathing unsteady. I could see by the rise and fall of her breasts under her grey T-shirt that her breathing was just as rough. She stared back at me, and then she raised her hands. I flinched, expecting her to slap me, which I probably deserved, but she wrapped her arms round my neck and pulled me down to kiss her again. That was all the control she got. I pushed her down onto the bed, crushing her into the mattress. Her thighs parted to let me lie between them, and I pulled one of her ankles up, wrapped her leg around my waist, and pushed my growing hardness against the thin barrier of her panties. She moaned into my mouth, and the sound filled me with the need to touch every inch of her to remember every detail of her sinful body. I slid my hand inside her shirt, cupping the round softness of her breast and rubbing my thumb over her nipple. She gasped and pushed her hips against me, rubbing her core along my shaft. I dragged my mouth away from hers and trailed my lips along her jaw and down her throat, breathing in the cinnamon scent of her hair. I pushed away the thought that being with her again felt like coming home.

"God, Faith, I've missed you."

She froze instantly. What the fuck? She pushed me up, and I moved back, confused. As I did, she slid out from under me and climbed out of the bed, pulling her shirt down and spinning away from me.

"Faith?" I didn't trust myself to turn around.

"Sam will be wondering what we're up to. You should go, and I'll get dressed."

"Faith, what the hell—"

"I'm really not in the mood for any of your moves, Cas. Like I said before, I think you and your right hand could do with a bit of alone time."

"Bitch." She might as well have slapped me. I hated her like this. Hot and cold. I never knew where I fucking stood. I scrambled off the bed, and she turned around. Her eyes travelled down my body to my cock, which was still visible through my sweatpants.

"Yeah, a bitch you were trying to bed thirty seconds ago. Don't be so desperate, Cas, it's a real turnoff." She turned and walked into the en suite bathroom, locking the door behind her. I smiled bitterly at the thought that a lock couldn't keep me out. If I wanted to break down the door, it wouldn't take much of an effort to smash my way through it. As much as driving my fist into the door appealed to me right now, I wasn't in the habit of being violent towards women. I turned and stalked out of the room, suppressing the admittedly immature impulse to slam the door behind me in my temper, and headed towards the small gym on the lower floor. No, violence towards women was not something I entertained, but violence towards a punching bag, however, was exactly what I needed right now.

Chapter Eight

FAITH

Fucking bastard. Why'd he have to say that and ruin it? What happened to a good hate fuck when you needed some stress relief? I rolled my shoulders, trying to get rid of an annoying tingling sensation in my shoulder blades. They weren't the only thing tingling either, and I pressed my thighs together tightly, trying to rid myself of the feeling. Since the surprisingly good time I'd had with Sam last night, my libido seemed to have ramped up a notch. Hence the temptation to indulge myself with Cas, despite the fact that I still hated his guts. He might be an asshole, but he'd always been a damn good fuck.

Shower. Just have a shower, relax, and chill out a bit. Forget him.

I glanced around the bathroom, and realising there were no clean towels in here, unlocked the door and went back into the bedroom. There were a couple of clean white towels folded on a chair near the door and I went to grab one. As I did so, I saw a large cup on the nightstand near where Cas had been when I woke up. I picked it up, wrapping my hands around the china. Black coffee. He'd remembered. I shook my head in confusion and headed back into the bathroom, taking the coffee with me.

After our rather pleasant encounter in my kitchen, Sam had convinced me to come back with him. Despite not wanting to live in the same house as Cas, and a deep-rooted desire to do the exact opposite of what someone was trying to make me do, I'd given in. To be honest, I'd been fairly freaked out by the fact that someone had managed to break into my apartment and get through three deadlocks without any sign of interference or damage. After Sam's comments about magic users, I'd already decided that independence was still my thing, but the fact remained that I'd be a hell of a lot safer staying in a house with supernatural guys who'd been tasked to keep me protected. I was strong willed, not stupid. Sam had waited around while I packed a bag, and at his suggestion, I'd left my bike in the lockup with Sam's promise that he'd bring me back over to get it at any time.

Sam and Cas lived with the other two members of their team in a large house by the coast. According to Sam, the house belonged to Cas. Though the Concordia usually provided housing for its teams, Cas had amassed a bit of money over the years and had decided he wanted somewhere a bit more comfortable to live. Comfortable was an understatement. The house was down a private gravel drive, about half a mile from the main road. It was a large, modern barn conversion—half red brick, half dark stained wood siding. As we drove up, I had seen the huge two-story window in the centre of the front of the building. The day had been dark and overcast, and the golden light had flooded out through the panes, revealing the modern wood and glass staircase. Sam had given me the grand tour, seeing as no one was home, though he passed the guys' bedrooms, which I could have quite fancied a nosy in. The downstairs was huge, in some parts two storeys high, revealing the beautiful wooden beams which striped the high ceiling. The kitchen was in the centre, right in the part with the glass walls. Wooden units with a polished concrete top gave it a rustic but modern feel, and next to it was a snug, comfy study. Expensive looking built-in bookshelves lined the walls, and there was a long chesterfield sofa along one side. Another door led down to a large basement, which housed a basic gym, a laundry room, and a small home cinema that had a huge L-shaped sofa. On the other side of the kitchen was an open-plan living room with three squashy sofas, a woodburning stove, and a pool table. Not a bad home, to be honest, and a far cry from the dingy flat Cas had taken me to when I'd dated him. When I'd mentioned that to Sam, he'd shrugged it off, simply saying it was part of a cover for an investigation Cas had been doing at the time, but he told me no more, even when I prodded. The upstairs was smaller but still huge compared to my cupboard-sized place, with five bedrooms, all en suite, as well as a larger bathroom with a double walk-in shower and a bathtub that would easily take four people and looked like it had jacuzzi jets. I had made a mental note at the time that I needed to avail myself of that bath before I left.

This morning, though, I had simply taken advantage of the waterfall shower in my own en suite. The water pressure had far surpassed my own, and it was nearly an hour before I ventured out of my room. I had switched my T-shirt up for a Metallica one, and after gazing sadly at my torn bike leathers, picked a pair of ripped black skinny jeans and my normal biker boots. Not finding a hairdryer, I towel dried my hair, combing it through and leaving it hanging over one shoulder.

The bedrooms upstairs were all on one long hallway. Where the oak and glass staircase reached the landing, there was a lengthy balcony, allowing me to gaze down into the open-plan kitchen. Cas was sitting at the table with a cup of coffee, looking at his phone, but Sam was leaning against the worktop across from him, orange juice in hand. Deciding I could risk Cas's wrath with Sam there, I padded downstairs on my bare feet. Cas glanced up for a moment then looked back down, clearly deciding to ignore me. *Good. You do that.*

Sam looked up as I reached the kitchen and gave me a dazzling smile. "Hey, baby girl, how'd you sleep?"

"Fine. Good. I was exhausted. That shower is amazing though. I might have to take it with me when I leave. Oh, and thanks for the shirt." He'd lent me one for the night when I realised I hadn't brought anything to sleep in. In all fairness, I usually just slept in my underwear, but I hadn't wanted to mention that in case it gave him ideas to join me. I'd been exhausted and craving my sleep by the time we'd finally made it back to the house, stopping off on the way for a burger.

"No problem. It looked better on you than me anyway, and I usually have spares." Sam smiled.

Cas snorted without looking up from his phone. "Yeah, he wrecks loads by forgetting to strip before he shifts."

"Like you can talk. Yours are always covered in blood and guts and who knows what else, and we can never get the stains out." Sam laughed, but I could tell he was serious. I stared at Sam, not wanting to look at Cas. I'd forgotten in our little encounter this morning exactly how dangerous Cas could be. Sam winked at me. "Don't worry, baby girl. It's not usually his."

I cocked my head to the side. "What a shame. Now, you guys have anything passing as food here, or is it the bachelor breakfast of warmed up pizza I have to look forward to?"

"Nah, we actually eat pretty good here. The other guys will be down in a minute, and Amadi cooks a mean breakfast." Sam pulled out a chair for me. I hesitated, not particularly wanting to sit across from Cas but not wanting to offend Sam who was being so charming.

"Amadi?" It couldn't be.

Sam nodded. "Yes, we have two other housemates, but they work at Concordia too, so—oh, here they come now."

I looked up as Amadi and Alex came down the stairs. Alex nodded at me, but Amadi flashed me a grin. "Faith! Babe! I thought I was irresistible, but having a lover waiting in my kitchen for me is something new."

I blushed as I stood and took his proffered hand. Noticing with some small satisfaction that Cas had snapped his head up at the word "lover," I smiled prettily back at Amadi. "What can I say? I was hungry for more."

He laughed. "Talking of hungry..." He moved around the table and began opening cupboards. My eyes followed him as he moved. Breakfast was obviously quite a casual affair in this house, as he wore nothing but a pair of loose grey sweatpants. I was impressed to realise those swirling black tribal tats covered his chest as well as his arms, and the muscles had continued underneath as well, with every single one defined very clearly.

"You two have met, I take it?" Cas's eyes glittered darkly at me over the table, and I smiled innocently.

Wondering how long I could string this out, I began to answer, but Alex beat me to it as he slipped into a chair at one end of the table and opened a small laptop. "In the cathedral yesterday. We were there looking for... something... and we ran into Faith."

Cas visibly relaxed, and I sulked slightly. Alex was no fun. I looked over at him. He was much more formally dressed than his partner, wearing smart trousers and a pale blue shirt with one button open at the top. His glasses were perched on the end of his nose as his eyes flickered over the screen in front of him. As I watched, he raised his hand and absentmindedly ran his fingers over the stubble on his square jaw. I licked my lips.

"So, you guys all live and work together? That's... odd." They seemed a bit old for having housemates. Though, to be fair, I'd maybe consider one if I got to live somewhere like this.

"We're a bit odd." Amadi grinned. "But we're also a team who likes to work and play together." He leaned on the table next to me. "You a real woman, Faith?"

I was confused. "What?"

"You a real woman? You eat proper food, right? Or do you prefer bowls of leaves? Please don't tell me you're a salad and smoothie only kind of girl?"

Sam laughed. "Well, I took her for dinner last night, and she put away two burgers, a large fry, an ice cream, and most of the shared cheese melts. I'd say you're pretty safe, Amadi."

I shot Sam a dirty look, then turned back to Amadi. "Yes, I like real food. I dance for a living and I work out quite a bit, so I'm lucky to burn through it all."

Amadi straightened with an exaggerated sigh of relief. "Thank Hell. I was worried you were one of those girls who lived on salad. So, the full works?"

I glanced over to a load of bacon and sausages heaped on a chopping board next to the hob. "Hell yeah, Amadi. Load me up." Sizzling noises began almost immediately, and a lovely smell filled the air. My stomach growled slightly, so to cover the noise, I turned back to Sam. "So, what exactly do you all do? Do you... I don't know... sniff out demons or something?" Sam appeared horrified, while Amadi and Cas burst out laughing. Looking down the table, I could see even Alex was trying to conceal a grin behind his laptop screen. "What did I say?"

"No, we don't 'sniff out demons.' I'm not some kind of bloody spaniel!" He looked rather put out, but I couldn't help but grin at his hangdog expression.

"Aw, I'm sorry, I didn't mean to upset you. I'm just new to all this. I'm guessing you're more like the big bad wolf than a sniffer dog..." He looked slightly mollified.

"Well, yes, I suppose I am."

I nodded seriously. "I'm so sorry if I offended you."

He smiled. "It's okay, you don't need to apologise."

I sighed in mock relief. "Oh good. Just, when you gave me those puppy dog eyes..." Laughter exploded around me again, and I gave him an evil grin over the top of my juice glass. Sam rolled his eyes then reached out and poured himself some juice, pointedly ignoring me. "So, we've established you're not some kind of supernatural dog unit. What do you guys do?" Amadi slid a plate in front of me, and I looked down and groaned with delight. Bacon, sausages, eggs, beans, and even fried bread. My mouth watered, and I grabbed some cutlery, ready to dig in. My gorgeous chef placed another couple of plates on the table in front of Cas and Sam before sitting down with his own next to me.

"I don't know how much Grumpy and Puppy Dog have told you..." He winked at his housemates as they both slowly raised their eyes to send him death glares. "But, yeah, we've all worked together for... well, a while. In a nutshell, pretty boy Alex pretty much runs the Northeast Paranormal Science Department, and he's also the resident computer nerd. Cas and Sam are the cannon fodder patrol boys, also known as guardians, and I do all the hard work by training the guardians, so they don't get their asses kicked by rogue demons and other nasties. Oh, and I cook like a Michelin chef, dance like Patrick Swayze, and am a *demon* in bed. So, in summary, ignore Cas's brooding and Sam's fluttering eyelashes and stick with Alex and me."

I paused, a forkful of sausage and egg halfway to my mouth, and stared at him, watching him take a bite of toast. The others had stopped eating to stare at him too, so I glanced at them. "Is all that true?"

Sam shrugged. "Well, he's not a half bad dancer, and I'm not going to criticise the food, cause he's the only one who cooks, but I'm afraid I can't attest to his bedroom skills. Alex?"

Everyone looked down the table at Alex, who was still tapping away at his laptop. "Fair to middling," he answered, never taking his eyes from the screen or changing his typing pace. Sam and Cas laughed, and Amadi rolled his eyes.

Across from me, Cas's phone vibrated on the table. He picked it up and frowned as he read the text. "Hargreaves wants me to check in first thing. Sam, would you take Faith back to the house, and I'll meet you there in a bit? I'd like to give it another once-over in the daylight without hellhounds looking over our shoulders. You okay with that, Faith?"

"Me? Oh, yeah, sure." The conversation had brought me straight back to the events of the last night, and I suddenly felt tired. I leaned back against the chair, and Sam came to stand behind me. I could have moaned out loud when I felt his hands settle on my shoulders and start to rub firmly. Feeling his solid body against me reassured me slightly. *And did other things*, I thought, as I breathed in the scent of saltwater and fresh air.

"You think we missed something?" Sam dug his thumbs into a couple of knots in my back, and this time I did moan. Cas and Amadi glanced over at me, and even Alex lifted his eyes from the computer screen for a few moments. Cas cleared his throat, and Sam sadly removed his hands from my shoulders, taking the seat next to me and grabbing the plate Amadi shoved his way.

Cas shook his head. "I don't know, I don't think we'd have missed anything, but Faith mentioned a hidden room downstairs." He turned to me. "I want to see if there's anything down there that might give us an idea of what your mum was working on. It might give us a direction to go in. I think we need to follow any lead we can."

"Sure, no problem." I wasn't too enthusiastic about going back down to the creepy room, but he was right. We needed to investigate every lead.

"Great. I'll meet you two there after I've called in and seen Hargreaves."

Sam looked up, his mouth bulging with food. "Hssss erd sumfing?"

Cas shrugged. "He didn't say. Maybe. I'll fill you in when I see you later."

Amadi laid his knife and fork down and stood up to grab a coffee refill. "Fine, but I want you both in the gym by six tonight, or there will be serious ass kicking."

Sam groaned. "But Faith's here, I was hoping to..."

Amadi rolled his eyes. "And she'll be here a while longer, but you two already skipped this morning's session, and I'm not letting other parts of you grow soft just cause your dicks keep growing hard." Cas snorted, but I was very amused to see that Sam was blushing. "So six on the dot. Faith can always come and watch me kick the crap out of you both." He grinned over at me.

I cocked my head and pretended to think it over. Three hot guys working out, with a possible bonus of seeing Cas get his ass kicked? Hell yes! "Meh, might as well. Doubt there's anything else to do round here, if you're all still insisting on keeping me prisoner."

Cas got up from the table and started to clear the plates. "We are. Everyone finished?"

I glanced around the table as the guys began to get up and noticed Alex still tapping away. "Aren't you having any breakfast, Alex?" A hush fell over the table as everyone paused.

Alex looked over at me, his fingers finally halting on the keys. He stuttered, "Err... I'm a... uh..."

"He's a vegan," Amadi interjected smoothly, whipping the plate out from in front of me. "And I've stupidly run out of his vegan sausages. He said he's fine grabbing something at work."

"Oh, okay... sorry."

Alex smiled, visibly relaxing. "Nn... nn... no, it's fine. Th-thank you."

Amadi bumped his shoulder with his hip as he walked past. "Sorry, man, I know the vegan thing is a real turnoff for most, but I don't think you'd be able to hide it for long with her living here." Alex blushed and closed his laptop.

Sam stood up and held out his hand. "Ready to go, Faith?" I looked at his hand and then met his gaze, rolling my eyes as I stood and walked out of the door, glancing back to see if he was following. He was.

Chapter Nine

CAS

"You have got to be fucking kidding me!" Both of the men standing in front of me raised their eyebrows at my language. Hargreaves cleared his throat. "For fuck's sake, sir. Begging *your* pardon, I've got enough to do without babysitting one of these guys. Besides, he might get dirty, and we wouldn't want that." I glared at the guy in the white suit.

He glanced down at his attire, then met my gaze with a steely look. "I shall adapt my dress as per normal human customs, and I do not require babysitting."

I rolled my eyes and looked back at Hargreaves who was sitting forward in his chair, tapping his fingers together. "Cassiel, this is not a request. Lord Euriel has been assigned to us by the Heavenly Council for the time being, and he will need a place to stay and transport. You and Sam are not doing much at the moment, besides supervising Miss Matthews, and you have plenty of space. How is Miss Matthews doing, by the way? Settling in okay?"

I gave him a hard look. "She's fine. Sam's with her now. She's not going anywhere without our say so."

Hargreaves nodded. "Good. Even so, I have heard things from Rose that suggest she can be a bit of a handful, so another pair of eyes can't hurt either."

Euriel's silver eyes narrowed. "With all due respect, Sir Phillip, I am not here to deal with the sheep, I am here to investigate shepherds."

"Of course you are, my lord, and I shall endeavour to be of as much assistance as I can. I merely meant if our charge were to try and sneak out or something, another pair of eyes can always come in useful." He passed Euriel a smartphone. "I assume you've had experience with these before?"

Euriel took the phone from him. "Yes, I was here about eight years ago, though I shall need to do a little research into the newer technology."

Hargreaves nodded. "Well, one of your new housemates, Alexei Makarov, is our resident computer technician, and I'm sure he'll be more than happy to help if you need any."

"I wouldn't say he'll be happy," I muttered, kind of under my breath, but also kind of not. Euriel and Hargreaves both shot me a look.

"I'm sure they'll enjoy having such an esteemed member of the Heavenly Council to work with, my lord. Might encourage them to raise their standards a little. Don't you agree, Cassiel?" Hargreaves shot me a commanding look, and I fought the urge to say exactly what the angel could raise and specifically where he could raise it.

"Sir."

Hargreaves nodded and turned back to the new inconvenience. "Very well, it's arranged. If you check down at logistics, they'll sort you out some transport. Cassiel will meet you down there after we've had a few words about his current assignment."

The angel nodded and left, and I collapsed into the chair opposite Hargreaves, shooting him an exacerbated look. "An angel? *That* angel? Really? There weren't any other guardians you could have put him with?"

"He's investigating the other guardians, Cassiel."

I sat up straighter. "What? Why on earth would he be doing that?"

Hargreaves leaned back in his chair, tapping his fingers together. "The Heavenly Council has received some information regarding one or possibly more of our guardians. He won't tell me more than that, other than that person is suspected of committing a most heinous crime against both Heaven and Sheol."

I leaned back, frowning. "That would explain why they sent that jumped-up prick, but it doesn't explain why you stuck him with me. Come on, Hargreaves. An angel and a fallen angel working together? I'd rather be working with a sloth demon. At least you know you'll get to chill out, have a beer, and watch Netflix. I doubt that guy's taken a day off since time began."

"Look, Cassiel, I know it's not the best of situations, but I have the Heavenly Council breathing down my neck right now, and it's only a matter of time until the Infernal Council gets wind of what's happening and then they're demanding an agent be involved. He's investigating *my* guardians and won't tell me why or who. If someone or someones have committed an act this important, I want to know who and what before he does."

I grinned, finally catching on. "You want me to spy on him."

Hargreaves looked mildly shocked. "Of course not, I would never suggest such a thing. But if you were to see or hear anything regarding the actions of my guardians, I would assume you'd feel it was your duty to inform me so I could take action accordingly."

I stood up and stretched. "I completely understand, sir. And don't worry, I'll make sure *Lord* Euriel has a very enlightening experience earthside."

"I trust you, Cassiel. The others too. This is a very delicate situation."

I stopped smiling. "Sir, I have never let you down before, nor your predecessors. Your trust is well-placed."

He stood up and shook my hand. "Thank you, Cassiel."

Outside in the hallway, I paused for a moment and looked out of the window over the extensive garden below. If someone as high up in the Heavenly Council as Euriel had been sent to investigate instead of their regular agents, whatever the guardian in question had done had to be very serious indeed. I hadn't heard of it happening before in all the time I had worked for the Concordia, and that had been a good couple of millennia. I couldn't imagine what would be serious enough to merit it, nor what punishment would befall the perpetrator. I could only hope we discovered them before Euriel did.

Heading downstairs, I leaned into the doorway of the logistics office. Helena looked up as I did, her four pairs of eyes all swivelling to see me. Three pairs dropped back to her desk as she continued with her tasks, and one set of hands continued typing away at the computer while the other flicked through sheaves of paper. Euriel was seated on the low sofa by the windowsill, struggling to keep his ramrod straight posture as he sank into the squashy cushions.

Fighting not to laugh, I nodded a greeting to Helena. "Did you get him sorted?"

"I did indeed, though unfortunately it will be a few days before a vehicle that Lord Euriel can drive will be available."

I grinned. "Museum took a bit of bribing, did they?"

She raised her eyebrows at me. "The Bentley garage was unable to provide that particular model immediately and begged that we give them forty-eight hours to remedy it."

I looked over at Euriel who returned my gaze, saying nothing. "A Bentley, huh?"

"It's what I was provided with last time and what I am most comfortable driving."

"Hmm, I'll bet. Well, this afternoon should be fun. If you're all done here, we'll get going. I'll drop you at the house before I go off, and you can get settled."

Euriel stood up. "I believe I shall accompany you to your assignment. It will give me something to do and allow me to see the more recent generation of guardians in action."

I shrugged as I led him out of the house. "Fine by me. Here." I stopped by my bike and passed him the spare helmet."

He didn't take it and stared at it in horror. "What is that?"

"It's a bike helmet."

"I can see that. Why are you giving it to me?"

I slipped my own helmet on and climbed onto the bike. "Well, I know you're all powerful and everything, but trust me, even as divine beings, it really fucking hurts coming off one of these at speed." He stared at me. "It's this or you get a taxi." He exhaled strongly through his nose and snatched the helmet, sliding it on and getting behind me. I grinned as I felt his hands hesitantly grip my waist.

"You've been watching way too much TV, *my lord.* There's a grip handle behind you. Unless you have a deep desire to put your arms around me."

Euriel made a strangled noise in his throat as he immediately released me and reached behind him. "You disgust me, Cassiel, with your repulsive humour. And for your information, *you* are no longer a divine being. You gave up that honour when you turned against our father."

I turned my head, though I couldn't really see him. "Really? It's been millennia. Are you still holding that against me?" I felt him exhale with righteous indignation, and I smiled under my visor.

"You committed the ultimate sin and betrayed our father, our creator! I shall hold that against you for eternity."

I shook my head and started the bike, revving it slightly more than I needed to just for effect. I pulled away with a screech of my tyres, revelling in the yell that came from behind me. The next few weeks would certainly feel like an eternity, no doubt about that.

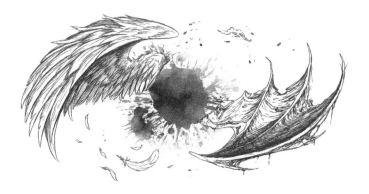

CHAPTER TEN

FAITH

I watched Sam's broad shoulders disappear down the stairs into the cellar, and I shivered. Sam must have noticed my hesitation, because he paused and looked back at me.

"Everything okay?" I smiled at him. He really wasn't that bad of a guy. Normally, I'd say he was a little too sweet for my taste, but in the current situation, it actually felt nice to have someone being nice to me all the time. Plus, he certainly wasn't sweet when it came to the physical side of things. I was still aching slightly from the day before.

"I'm fine. Last time I came down here I got a hell of a shock, that's all."

He put his hand on my arm and squeezed gently. "Yeah, I can imagine it's one hell of a surprise finding out your mother is a witch who keeps a secret ritual room below the house."

I stared at him, then realised what he meant. "Oh no, I didn't mean... I mean, yes, that was a shock. But when I came down here last, I walked through the door and got this huge electric shock. Knocked me off my feet and had me blacked out for a moment."

Sam frowned, then pulled me back slightly so he could go first. He ran his hands over the doorframe, then paused when he noticed the inscription above the door. "There's an enchantment on the door."

"On the door?"

"Well, no, not technically on the door, more on the space between the two rooms. Hang on..." He pulled his phone out of his pocket and poked at the screen.

"Hey, Cas, you far off? Ah, cool. No, it's just there's a spell on the door to the ritual room, and Faith got a nasty shock from it yesterday when she went through. Thought we'd be better off waiting to see if you could lift it before we went back inside." He went quiet, then nodded. I grinned at the sight. At least I knew I wasn't the only one daft enough to nod when the other person couldn't see me. "Great, see you in a sec." He hung up and put the phone back in his pocket. "They'll only be a couple of minutes. We'll just wait, I don't want to take any unnecessary risks."

I leaned back against the wall. "Who's they? I thought we were just meeting Cas."

Sam shrugged. "Apparently there's been another person assigned to our little group of investigators."

"Someone I've met?"

"No, I've not met him either. His name's Euriel. Somehow, I don't think Euriel and Cas are going to get on."

"Why not?"

Sam opened his mouth to reply, but then we heard Cas's voice at the top of the stairs. "Don't worry, I don't think it's *that* dusty down there. But you know, there's a great dry cleaner near my house just in case. Now, now, are you guys *allowed* to use that kind of language? Oh hey, guys." He came into view, and for a moment, he seemed bigger than normal, his enormous frame practically filling the hallway as shadows branched out behind him. My breath caught in my throat as he squeezed past me to the door, his hard body pressing against mine. He avoided looking at me though, and I turned to see the newcomer.

Holy hell... The man standing behind Cas was like no man I'd seen before. Taller than Sam, but still a good few inches shorter than Cas, he was slender and pale skinned. Even under the harsh fluorescent lights, his skin seemed to glow faintly with a light of its own. His hair was white-blond and long, falling in soft waves about his face, and when his gaze found mine, I felt any breath I had left leave me instantly. His eyes were insane. No words could do them justice. The pupils were black, but the irises were silver and gold and seemed to glitter and change as I stared at them, transfixed. He stared back, and he only averted his eyes when Cas moved next to me.

"This is Faith Matthews, the human daughter. Faith, this is Euriel. He's going to be working with us for a while and help us find your mother."

I nodded. "Sure, hi. Nice to meet you."

Euriel stared at me a moment longer, then he turned away without replying. Moving to Cas's side, he looked up at the inscription above the door. "A revelation spell. And a powerful one."

Cas nodded. "Agreed. Whoever put this here had some help, and a shit ton of magical strength. Not just when it was cast either. It's been added to over several years."

I pushed forward to squeeze between them. "Okay, enough of the magical mumbo jumbo, what are you guys on about?"

Cas put his hand on my shoulder, pulling me back from the doorway. "A revelation spell is designed to reveal any and every truth. It breaks other spells and enchantments as soon as you pass through it. It's almost foolproof."

"Plus, knocking you out too. No wonder it says, 'against enemy attacks,'" I scoffed. Cas stared at me, as did Euriel.

"You can read ancient Sumerian?" Euriel asked, his smooth voice sending a shiver down my spine as he fixed his glittery gaze on me once more.

"Yeah... my mother made me learn. Plus ancient Greek and Latin. I'm lucky, I find it quite easy to memorise words and phrases, but it wasn't great fun spending my Saturday nights reading ancient texts. There's only so much enjoyment to be had by reading about the kinks of the twelve Caesars." Cas smiled, but Euriel remained stony-faced, so I ignored him and turned back to Cas. "So, it was a spell to protect the room then? Maybe that means there's something in there my mother wanted to protect, something that might give us a clue as to why she was taken."

"Well, not exactly. Revelation spells aren't exactly known for knocking you out." He glanced at the doorway, then back at me and sighed. "Okay, look. I'll show you what it does, just don't freak out on me. I'm not as cuddly as Sam."

"Hey! I'm not cuddly! I'm terrifying and ferocious." We both laughed as Sam stood on his tiptoes to peer over Euriel's shoulder. Cas grinned, but it faded when he looked at me.

"The spell reveals what someone truly is, no matter what they are doing to conceal themselves. It's almost impossible to conceal your true nature. You'd have to be an insanely strong supernatural being to do that." He turned and stepped through the doorway and into the room beyond. The candles flared up all the way around the room, and the shadows seemed to grow and darken, flexing around Cas as he slowly turned towards us. My mouth fell open.

Standing a few feet back from the door, Cas seemed to grow in height. He towered above me, at least another foot taller than normal. His shoulders widened and his muscles, although already pretty impressive, swelled to bodybuilder proportions. As I watched, dark shapes formed at his back, spreading out and creating huge black wings, the ebony feathers gleaming like oil in the flickering candlelight. I raised my eyes to his, and they burned red. He held my gaze for a moment then looked away as though he was ashamed.

Forgetting about the doorway, I stepped forward. "Cas?"

He looked back at me. "Yes?"

I leaned closer. "I think you're starting to take the whole Harley Davidson logo thing a bit far now. The wings are a bit of an overkill."

He stared at me, his crimson eyes dancing, and behind us, I heard Euriel murmur to Sam, "Who's Harley Davidson?" Cas laughed, his eyes meeting mine, full of humour. I grinned, and moved past him into the room, turning to look at the spectacular black wings that grew seamlessly from his powerful shoulder blades.

"What are you? Other than... well... stunning."

Cas looked at me over his shoulder, that familiar arrogant grin of his reassuring the large part of me that was completely freaking out quietly inside. "You think I'm stunning?"

I smacked him on the ass. "Oww!" His body was as hard as stone. A devilish memory fluttered through my head as I recalled my fingers digging into those solid muscles as I pulled him towards me.

"He's an angel," Sam said, stepping through the doorway. I blinked, dragging myself away from my indecent thoughts.

"An angel? Shit. Hang on, how come you didn't change?"

"Because I was born human. Shifters can be born either as human or as their animal counterpart. It really depends on what form the mother takes for her pregnancy. My mother was human throughout, so I show up as human in this room. And it means that in here, I can't shift to my wolf form. Cas, however, was created as an angel, so he will always appear in his angelic form rather than his human form."

I looked back at him, my eyes drinking in the sheer size and power of him in this form. "I can't believe you're an angel," I whispered. "All that time..."

"Fallen angel." I turned back to the doorway at the sound of Euriel's voice.

"I'm sorry?"

"He's a fallen angel. One who betrayed his creator, who committed evil and unforgivable treason against Him who brought us all life. He was thrown down from Heaven and

condemned to spend his life on Earth and eternity in Hell."
Euriel's eyes glittered darkly, and he stepped through the
doorway. As he advanced towards us, he also grew in height,
and his skin glowed fiercely. Behind him, great wings unfurled,
not black or white, but a soft dove grey that seemed to shine,
and the two of them stood facing each other. Cas was breathing hard, and I could tell from previous experience he was
really trying not to punch Euriel in the face.

"That's one side of the story anyway," Sam muttered.

Euriel turned and glared at him. "There is only one side of
the story. His story."

Cas stepped forward, but I moved in front of him. "Okay,
guys? Let's calm it down a little. Kind of getting off topic here.
You obviously have your whole good and evil thing going on,
and that's cool, but can we focus please? Cas?"

He glanced down at me and his breathing slowed. "Yeah, no
problem. Some things are more important than arguing with
brainwashed idiots."

I glared at him, then swung around to face Euriel. "And you?
This is your job, right? Think you can maybe do it instead of
arguing like little kids over who broke Daddy's cup?" His eyes
narrowed, and my insides quaked a little. The guy was pretty
intimidating, but he was also arrogant as fuck, and there was
no way I was letting him know that he unnerved me. He gave
me a sharp nod and folded his wings behind him. A rustle at
my back told me Cas was doing the same. With their wings
folded, they were slightly less formidable. I stuffed my shaking
hands into my pocket and turned to Sam. "Okay, surfer wolf, if
this spell reveals truths, what the hell happened to me when I
walked through the door? I mean, the damn thing knocked me
out, and I felt like I'd been zapped at the mains. But this time,
nothing." I rolled my shoulders in irritation, my skin itching
against my bra straps.

Sam frowned, then leaned forward and nuzzled my neck. It
tickled slightly, but also sent a shiver of delight down to my
belly as his nose and lips brushed against the sensitive skin.

"Um, what are you doing?"

"Smelling you."

"Uh... why? I had a shower this morning, sniffer wolf!"

He drew back and grimaced at me. "Don't call me that! And, baby girl, you smell amazing. Like jasmine and sandalwood." I didn't know what to say to that. "But I was seeing if you still had any residual magic on you."

"What do you mean?"

Cas stepped forward. "He means that for the revelation spell to have had that effect on you yesterday, there must have been a very powerful enchantment on you. The enchantments on us that hide our true natures are small mind glamours to fool humans, nothing more. But the spell on you must have been extremely powerful." He took my face in his huge hands and bent down to gaze deep into my eyes. The burning red pupils definitely disconcerted me, and I tried to pull away, but he held me fast. "Wait, I'm just looking." I stood still, uncomfortably aware of all three men staring at me. Eventually he pulled back, looking confused.

"See anything?" Sam inquired.

Cas shook his head slowly. "No... but there's something else there, something I just can't place, but I can sense it. Just out of reach."

Euriel huffed behind us. "Clearly, her mother placed a powerful protection spell on her. It's common sense, considering where she worked. Can we please get on?"

Cas nodded and pulled away. "Maybe that's it. Maybe not. We'll drop by the Concordia later and get Deliah to take a look at you."

"Who's Deliah?"

"She's Hargreaves second-in-command. A powerful witch. If something has been cast on you, she'll be able to find out what."

I nodded. "Okay then,"

Sam walked over to one of the bookcases. "I guess we'd better get started."

We spent all day there going through my mother's things. I had never given much thought to how hard my mother worked. As a kid, I just hadn't been interested, and I had barely known her as an adult. I felt a pang of regret as I flipped through pages of notes in her neat, elegant handwriting. When this was all over, I was definitely going to make sure we talked. Pins and needles started to tingle in my legs, so I put the papers aside and stood up. I walked around the room, trying to ease my aching muscles, trailing my hand across the bare brick wall. At the end of the back wall, I paused. A slight draught had tickled my hand, and I looked up to see if there was an extractor fan or vent somewhere nearby. Nothing. I ran my hand back over that section and felt the draught again. I found it blowing in through a crack in the mortar between the bricks, and following it farther down, I realised it wasn't a natural crack.

"Sam? Can I borrow you for a sec?"

Sam glanced up from the leather diary he was skimming. "Sure. You found something?" Cas and Euriel looked up at me.

"Well, no, not exactly. Only, I think these bricks might come out. Maybe there's something behind them?" He leapt lightly to his feet and padded over to me. Taking his hand, I placed it over the crack in the wall. "There. Feel that? And it goes all the way down to the floor and up to the ceiling, I think."

Sam looked down at me, his warm hand curling over mine. "I think you're right." He glanced over his shoulder. "Cas, you're up. See if you can open this hidey-hole." He pulled me back from the corner to let Cas through, and I noticed he hadn't let go of my hand. The thought made me smile.

Cas stepped up and felt around the crack all the way up to and along the ceiling, which with his current height wasn't exactly a stretch. He stepped back and stared at the wall. "I don't think it's a hidey-hole."

"Oh?" Disappointment bloomed inside me. Hours of searching, and we were still no closer.

He shook his head. "No, I think it's a doorway." I watched as he placed his hands on either side of the wall and murmured something in Sumerian. For a moment, nothing happened, and then a section of the wall slid backwards and sideways out of view, and a gaping black hole appeared in front of us. I started forward, but Cas reached out his arm to block me. "Hold up, Peaches. It's pitch-black, and I haven't checked it for any more enchantments yet. You want to get knocked out again?"

"Fine." I leaned back against the wall, folding my arms. Yes, I knew I looked like a sulky child, but I was tired and cranky.

Cas ran his hands over the doorframe, muttering to himself. Eventually, he stepped back. "It's fine."

"Great." I stepped in front of him to go first.

"And how are you going to see? *Immaru.*" He opened his hand and a glowing ball of light appeared.

I looked at it, then up at his arrogant smile. "Impressive. But I can do that too."

He frowned. "What? No, you can't."

"Sure, I can. Watch." I slid my phone out of my pocket, swiped down, and turned on the torch, shining it onto the floor just beyond the doorway. It showed large, smooth flagstones on the floor. "See? Easy." Sam burst out laughing behind me, and I stepped into the room, grinning to the sound of Cas telling him to shut it. Stopping a couple of feet into the space, I lifted the phone and swung the torch beam slowly around the walls.

"Whoa."

"What is it?" Sam stepped through after me, and Cas stuck his head through the door.

"It's... incredible." It really was. The room wasn't huge, but it was still impressive. Huge tapestries hung on every wall. I stepped closer to the one nearest me and shone the torch over it. A beautiful garden was embroidered in exquisite detail. Hills covered in trees rose in the background, from between which glistening waterfalls tumbled and swept around into sparkling streams silver fish jumped out of. Every kind of tree you could imagine, bearing flowers and fruit, provided perches for colourful birds and small animals, and below, all kinds of animals wandered through the lush grasses and ferns. It was truly stunning.

"It's paradise," Cas said. He'd managed to squeeze into the room and stood behind me, his eyes running over the stunning designs.

"It really would be. How beautiful."

He smiled. "No, I mean it's a depiction of paradise. Look." He grasped my wrist gently and pulled me around to the far end of the room.

"Oh, God!" At the end of the room stood another altar, but instead of being almost empty, this was laden with all kinds of objects. Pillar candles of varying heights were intermixed with crystals and gemstones, river pebbles and pinecones. Cones of incense, partly burned away, gave off a lingering scent of sandalwood and roses. Hundreds of flowers had obviously covered the altar recently, but they had died and were starting to rot. A wide, wooden bowl held the remnants of rotting fruit and vegetables, an offering to the statue behind, I assumed. It was a simple female figure, pillar-shaped, with her hands coming around to support her generous breasts. Her eyes were beautifully carved, and her hair was in braids. In front of the statue lay a wooden plaque, inscribed with the words, *"Kima Parsi Labiruti."*

"Treat her in accordance with the ancient rites," I murmured to myself.

"Did you know?" Sam asked me, his hand on my shoulder.

"About all this? No."

"You didn't know your mother worshipped Asheran?" Cas interrupted.

I turned to look at him, his red eyes gleaming in the near darkness. "Cas, I have no idea what that even means." He took my phone from me and pointed it at the wall behind the altar. Another tapestry hung there, even more intricate than the others. It was a continuation of the garden, depicting a low hill with a beautiful tree. The tree's branches hung low, and it was laden with all kinds of fruits. Two naked human figures stood below, entwined in a loving embrace.

"Adam and Eve, right? So it really is paradise, or at least the Garden of Eden?" I asked.

"Look closer."

I did, moving around the altar to get nearer. "They have wings! But Adam and Eve were human, not angels." I touched the figures gently, running my fingertips over the embroidered feathers. Adam's were tawny, a range of browns and creams touched by gold, like an eagle's, but Eve's were the iridescent blue of the peacock, blue and green merging together like the sea. I looked back at Cas and Sam, confused. "What—"

"Oh, this is becoming utterly ridiculous. You are now telling me that the woman everyone so desperately wants to find just so happens to be a soulless, worthless heathen, and nobody knew?"

I spun around to see Euriel standing at the entrance to the room, looking around with undisguised disgust on his face. I'd had enough. Marching up to him, I slapped him hard across the face. "My mother was not soulless, and she's missing. For someone who is supposed to be an angel and full of God's love, you are incredibly insensitive, and, well, basically, you're being an arsehole. Grow up and stop being such a dickhead. In fact, I want you to leave." He glared down at me, his bright eyes causing my hands to shake as I felt the pressure of his stare. I stuffed them into my pockets and glared back at him.

"How dare you?" His voice was low and measured, but the power in it shook me slightly.

I didn't care. "I said leave. Now."

"You cannot order me to leave, you miserable little human."

"Yes, I can. This is my mother's house. As she is not here, being her next of kin, I am in charge of it, and I say you need to leave, or you will officially be trespassing."

He took a deep breath, and his wings spread out behind him. "You presume to order me? That your pitiful earthly laws apply to one such as I?"

"Fairly certain the Bible says that everyone should abide by the laws of the kingdom they are in. And yes, I presume, you nasty little sparrow. Now get out." He stared at me, his mouth gaping open like a fish. I held his stare, and he snapped his mouth shut, then turned and stormed out of the room. I relaxed slightly, letting out a breath I hadn't realised I'd been holding.

Sam came over and put his arm around my shoulders. "You okay?"

I nodded. "Yeah, I just feel awful."

"Don't," Cas said. "That asshole totally had it coming."

I turned and grinned up at him. "Oh no, not him. I just feel bad for insulting sparrows." They both looked at me for a second, then burst out laughing.

"Hell's bells, Faith, you are one fine woman!" Cas commented, wiping tears out of his eyes.

Sam nodded, a huge grin on his face. "That you are. Not many people could face down an angel like Euriel."

"That idiot? Why not?" Cas looked at Sam, then back at me, pressing his lips together as if trying to repress a smile.

Sam looked at me. "He... um... Euriel is... well, he's second-in-command over the Heavenly Host."

"He's what?"

Cas let out another booming laugh. "He's basically one of the highest angels you can get. He's second only to those in the highest Host of Heaven, and you..." He paused, gasping for breath through his laughter. "You just called him a dickhead. To his face!"

I stared at the two of them as they collapsed into giggles.

Oh fuck, I am totally going to Hell.

CHAPTER ELEVEN

FAITH

Putting a possibly pissed off dominion to the back of mind, I chose to concentrate on the matter at hand. My eyes scanned the obviously well cared for altar and fell on the stone statue at the centre. "So you were going to tell me, what's an Asheran?"

Cas sat on the floor, leaning back against the stone wall. I noticed he had managed to shift back to his human form and guessed that the enchantment must only reveal truths as the person passed through the doorway. He could have shifted back at any time. He had probably kept his angel form to let me get comfortable with it. I sat down on the opposite side of the room, and Cas waved a hand in the direction of a small console table against the wall he was leaning on. Several pillar candles on the tabletop flickered to life, and I gasped.

"Show off," Sam muttered as he dropped gracefully down next to me.

Cas grinned for a moment, then the smile left his face, and he grew more serious as he turned to me. "An Asheran is a follower of Asherah."

I frowned. "Is that some kind of a demon or something?"

Cas shook his head. "No, not even close. Asherah was... is... was a goddess."

"Like Artemis, Aphrodite, and Athena—that kind of goddess?"

"Yes and no. She was the Queen of Heaven and Consort of Yahweh. She helped Him create the Earth and the Heavens and all of the creatures in between."

Sam snorted. "Don't let Euriel hear that."

Cas glared at him. "Euriel is a pompous, brainwashed sheep, the same as the rest of them. He'll believe whatever his superiors tell him to and won't question anything."

"Are you telling me that God had a wife? Like the whole Jesus and Mary Magdalene thing? I loved that film. Knights and quests and legends..." I trailed off as Cas looked at me.

"No. This was a long, long time before Jesus made an appearance. I'm talking about Yahweh. Allah. God. Asherah was his goddess, his equal."

"Hang on a minute. I've read the Bible. Many times." I grimaced, remembering the many Bible study classes my mother had made me attend and quizzed me on afterwards. "There was no mention of a goddess in there. I mean, Christianity is not exactly well known for its sexual equality."

Cas jumped up and disappeared into the ritual room, reappearing a moment later with an old Bible of my mother's. "Actually, you'll find she's mentioned several times. Over forty times in some translations, in fact. Here." He flicked through, then leant forward to pass me the book. I looked down at the page he pointed to. "There, in 2 Kings. Solomon built a temple for Yahweh, and Josiah is reported as cutting down the statues of Asherah later on."

I looked up. "What? She had statues?"

"Statues, shrines, temples. Jewish women used to have shrines inside their houses where they would burn incense and leave small cakes as an offering to her."

"So... how is she not known now? Why isn't she in the Bible more?"

Cas sighed. "It's tricky. There's a lot you don't know. What's in the Bible and other holy texts written by humans are just snippets of stories. All know some things, and in some they agree, but none of them know everything."

"To be fair, even the ones who were there don't agree on everything," Sam added, stretching his long legs out. "Like I said, Euriel would be horrified by Cas telling a human this story."

"Heaven falls into three lots of angels. Those who question, those who don't, and those who refuse to take sides." Cas leaned back against the wall again, lost in thought.

"Why do I think you're on the questioning side?" I asked dryly.

He tipped his head forward and grinned at me. "The word 'fallen' should have given you a clue."

I stared at him. "You mean every angel who questioned something they were told fell from Heaven? That's barbaric!"

"To be fair, there's a bit more to it than that. I mean, there are these little things called the Wars of Heaven—huge, epic battles where fire and ice fell from the sky and rained down on Earth for generations. Let's just say the meteorite that killed the dinosaurs didn't come from space."

I was now gaping at Sam who returned my gaze with a deadpan expression, and for the life of me, I couldn't tell whether Cas was kidding or not.

"Anyway, that's a very long story for another time. The point is, if you believe... well, *my side*, as Sam would say, Asherah was a goddess who, with Yahweh, created the Earth and Heavens and all living beings. Some say that Yahweh created the masculine, and Asherah created the feminine, hence that passage in Genesis, 'Let us make man in our own image.' She was worshipped and adored by humans, and shrines and temples were erected to her all over Earth, often alongside those to Yahweh. At some point, something happened. There was a huge falling out between Yahweh and Asherah, and she was banished. No one knows where, or if she even still exists.

Commands were sent throughout the realms that any shrine, temple, or image of Asherah was to be destroyed." Cas nodded at the book in my hands. "Look up Deuteronomy, there's a passage in there that clearly states, 'You shall not plant any tree as an Asherah beside the altar of the Lord your God.' No more shrines, no more worship, no mention of her."

"What does it mean by planting a tree as an Asherah?" I asked, interested now.

"She loved trees, they were her love. So beautiful, so essential to life on Earth. She covered every space she could with them. They were sacred to her and to her followers. Her temples weren't usually built of stone, they were groves of trees planted in her honour. When the orders came, many groves of trees were burned. I remember the smoke column rising from Earth, it was heartbreaking." His eyes left mine and focused over my shoulder.

"You... knew her?"

Cas blinked and glanced back at me, then away. "From afar. I wasn't high in the hierarchy of angels, even before I fell. I doubt she knew my name. But I remember the day she was banished, and I remember her tears for her trees and for her people. It was probably the thing that tipped me into fighting on the 'wrong side.'" He cleared his throat. "Anyway, she is still remembered as an ancient Semitic goddess, and pagans all over the world worship her under many names, so that's some small comfort. Your mother was clearly one of them."

"All the things she taught me about the Abrahamic religions, and she never mentioned this. I wonder why, especially since she obviously had some pretty strong beliefs." I gazed around the room, my eyes falling on the flowers that had been placed on the altar less than a week ago.

"I assume she was trying not to draw attention to herself," Cas murmured. "The worship of Asherah is still officially forbidden by God, and Concordia exists as a balance, so its members aren't meant to take sides. Maybe she was worried she'd be thought badly of. I believe Phillip leans more towards the side of Heaven on this one, so perhaps she thought if he found out, her services would no longer be required."

Sam rose to his feet. "With that in mind, I suggest we check that there's nothing in this room that might help us and then close it back off again."

Cas started to get up to. "The white-winged wonder saw the room. I doubt we'll get him to keep quiet about it."

"Maybe he will, or maybe he won't see her as being important enough to worry over," I suggested, mentally crossing my fingers. "Anyway, I suppose this is the most secret place in the house. If she was going to hide anything, it would be here." I stood up and stretched. "Then can we call it a day? It's nearly five, and we've been here all day."

Cas nodded. "Yeah, we're supposed to be meeting Amadi in the gym at six. We should wrap this up."

Sam murmured his agreement, and we all started searching the room. Kneeling down next to the altar, I lifted the golden velvet altar cloth to see if anything was underneath.

"Score!" I called out.

"What have you got?" Sam crouched down next to me and took the cloth from my grasp, holding it up so I could reach beneath. I dragged out a large cardboard box and sat down to rifle through it. Cas began to ignite the candles around the room to give us some more light, though I noticed he didn't light any on the altar itself, even though there must have been at least twenty on there. I pulled out everything on the box and laid all the items on the floor.

"Hmmm... scrolls... some really old papers... portable hard drive?" I passed it to Sam, who glanced at it then stuck it in his pocket.

"I'll pass that on to Alex. He can have a look and see if there's anything useful on it."

Cas crouched down too and started looking through the ancient papers, touching only the edges.

"Anything useful?" Sam inquired, straightening up.

"Well, in that she's a biblical historian, no, but..." He trailed off, reading through the papers.

"But?"

"But we've already searched her office at Concordia and the university, and there's no reference to her ever having done any work at these particular locations... oh!" Cas shuffled the papers slightly and an envelope, considerably newer than the papers, slipped out and fell to the floor. It had my name on the front, and I grabbed it before Cas could reach it. I sat back and opened the envelope. Inside was a notecard card with a medieval looking painting on the front. My mother's neat handwriting filled the inside. I looked up.

"Can I have a moment, guys?" Sam looked at Cas, who nodded, and they left the room. Moving closer to a group of candles, I held the letter up to the light.

Faith,

If you have found this letter, or someone has passed it along, then something has gone very wrong, and they have found me. We haven't spoken properly for years, and I understand your anger at me for keeping the secret of your birth from you for so long. Please believe me when I say it was not out of choice, but out of necessity. The information I gave you when you were eighteen was inaccurate, and I fear your wrath from discovering this, but all I have done was for your own protection. I do not know the identity of your birth mother and father, as I told you, but your father and I did not adopt you from the local council.

I am sure by now you have encountered members of the Concordia and have discovered what I was—a witch of angelic lineage. I believe your mother was another of us. You were brought to us in the greatest of secrecy by a member high up in the Concordia ranks. She was a very powerful witch who bound your powers with an ancient ritual known only to a few and undetectable by most. The enchantment on the door will have removed certain elements of that binding, and some of your powers will start to manifest. You must learn to control them. That witch entreated us to raise you as our own, to say nothing of your birth parents, and to strengthen the binding each year so you could not be found.

More information was not forthcoming, only that there are some who seek to find you who mean you harm. Trust no one. Even without your powers, I hope the education and training I made you endure for so long will help you navigate this new world. You are strong and have powerful instincts, my darling daughter. Follow them. Trust no one and take great care. I hope beyond measure that we will see each other again, and that you can find it within yourself to forgive me.

Your loving mother,

Rose Matthews

"I'm not human," I murmured quietly.

Cas spun around and stared at me. "What?"

"Euriel was wrong. I'm not human. I'm a witch. Like she was." I leaned against the doorway. Sam stood up and was at my side almost instantly. He touched my face gently, brushing the tears away, then he took me into his arms as the tears began to fall faster. I tried to wipe them away angrily. I never cried, and I *really* didn't want Cas of all people to see, but the last few days were getting to me, and on very little sleep, very little caffeine, and now this... I had hit my limit. He wrapped one arm around my shoulders and one around my waist and held me close. Gently pulling the letter out of my hand, he skimmed through it then handed it to Cas, who did the same.

"Well, I guess that answers the questions I had about your reaction to the room's enchantment. That must have been one hell of a binding ritual." Sam took the letter back from Cas, folded it, and handed it to me.

I pulled away from him and slipped the letter into my pocket. "Can we leave? Please? I'm exhausted. I can't face any more of this right now. We can come back tomorrow."

Sam looked at Cas, who nodded. "Why don't you take her home, Sam? I'll tidy up here and lock everything. Plus, there's a dominion out there who's supposed to be bunking with us, so I guess I'd better track him down. I'll see you guys back at home."

"Sure. Come on, Faith. I'm seeing a hot shower, fish and chips, and possibly a couple of beers in your not-too-distant future."

I smiled up at his sky-blue eyes. "Beer?"

"If you behave. No more insulting powerful supernatural beings though, you'll get us all in trouble."

I wrinkled my nose. "I'll try, but I can't promise anything."

"Don't try too hard," Cas muttered in the background as we headed up to the kitchen.

I stopped just before the door that led out into the hall. It had been open every other time we'd walked through the kitchen, but now it was closed. Euriel must have shut it behind him when he left. Or slammed it in a temper. I smiled to myself, hoping it was the second. Hanging from the hook on the back of the door was my mother's everyday handbag. It wasn't that surprising, since she often took her nicer ones to conferences and such as this one was a bit battered. But it was her favourite, and she'd had it since I was little. I lifted it down from the door and raised it to my face to breathe in that soft, buttery leather smell laced with traces of her floral perfume. The weight of it told me the bag wasn't empty, and I unzipped it to look inside.

"Something wrong?" Sam asked, coming up behind me. He rested his chin gently on my shoulder, and my skin warmed at the affectionate gesture.

"My mother's handbag."

"Does she have a spare?"

"Yes, several actually. But everything is in here, look." I opened the bag wider so he could see the contents and rifled through the small container of chaos. "Her purse, passport, car keys. All here. The only thing missing is her phone. I guess that definitely proves she didn't go anywhere of her own accord. She was definitely taken." I leaned back against his solid chest for a moment.

"We've got a trace on her phone, Faith. If she, or anyone else, turns it on, we'll be able to pick it up," Sam reminded me. "Come on, let's go. You need a distraction and food." He pushed me gently through the door, the handbag held tightly in my arms.

I resisted for a second. "And beer. Don't forget the beer."

"Baby girl, one thing you should know about me—I would never forget the beer."

CHAPTER TWELVE

CAS

Snapping the top off the bottle, I lifted it to my lips and took a long drink, concentrating on the feeling of the cold bubbles sliding down my throat. I set the bottle on the nearby wall and leaned against the side of the house, looking out over the lawn and into the trees. I could hear the sound of squealing tyres and gunshots from the practically plotless action film they'd decided to watch inside. I'd sat through the first one, laughing and joking with the others as we'd tried to distract Faith from this today's revelations, but once the sequel had started, I'd made an excuse about needing the bathroom and had snuck out on my own. To be perfectly honest, I needed to come to terms with today's revelations as well.

Faith was a witch. And not only that, but if the effect that the releasing enchantment had on her was anything to go by, she must be a pretty powerful one to be under that kind of a binding spell. I briefly wondered which of the watchers she was descended from. With witches being descendants of the nephilim, it was usually possible to trace one's lineage back to a particular watcher. A large part of the witch society could get rather snobby about who was descended from whom, often deigning to arrange marriages for their children with others descended from the same watcher in the hope that it would increase their powers. There was no evidence it ever had, but they were still determined to try.

Not that I'd ever known many of the watchers personally. I mean, sure, I'd been around when they were sent to Earth, but I'd only really known a few, and they had been of lower rank. I paused, briefly remembering Arkas, Cambriel, and Kabaiel as they had been before I watched them descend to Earth, overjoyed in their new assignment. I'd never seen them again, and when I'd heard of their betrayal of our father, I'd hated them alongside the rest of them. Until, of course, I'd finally found myself on Earth and had seen true beauty and love for the first time. I'd seen what humans could feel for each other, and I'd been in awe of such emotion. I'd discovered the physical side of love and indulged freely. Since the fall of the watchers, our father had made sure that no nephilim could ever be created again. Angels had been forbidden from physical contact of any kind except fighting, and fallen angels were stripped of any ability to reproduce before they were cast out. Angels were created only by Him, and He had made sure of that. I smiled to myself wryly, thinking back to when I'd told Faith to make sure she was taking the pill so I didn't get her pregnant. It was normal for me to pretend I was taking precautions with women. It made them more comfortable. Funny, though, I remembered feeling slightly disappointed when I'd told Faith. She'd been young at the time, and there was no way we'd have wanted a child, but for the first time ever, I'd felt... sad... that it would never be an option for me. It was also another reason I had told myself we shouldn't be together. Plus, she was human, and long-term relationships between supernaturals and humans were definitely frowned upon. Of course, now, as it turned out, she wasn't actually human at all. She was a witch. I sighed. Not that it mattered. She still hated me for what happened all those years ago.

"Cassiel."

The quiet voice came from behind me, and I suppressed a groan as I turned around, forcing my face into a pleasant smile. "Euriel."

"It's Lord Euriel. I am still your superior, whether you work on Earth or down below."

"Of course, *my lord.*"

The sarcasm wasn't lost on him, but he chose to ignore it. "You need to have a word with your charge."

"My... oh, you mean Faith. Well, I would, but—"

"I will not be spoken to like that by a lower life form. You will inform her of my rank and my status, and warn her that should she speak out of turn, there will be consequences."

I cocked my head. "Will I? See, I would, but I think it would be much better if you told her yourself."

Euriel frowned. "You do? Why? I thought I might be too intimidating for the child."

I bit my lip and tried to look as though I was giving the notion serious thought. "Well, if I tell her, it won't go down well. She doesn't like me much."

"Can't imagine why," Euriel muttered.

I ignored him. "But if you told her..."

"What?"

"Well, we'd all get to see what she says when you tell her she's a lower life form and that she shouldn't talk to you that way. And I, for one, would not want to miss that," I added, grinning. His expression darkened, and I saw a pale blur as his barely suppressed frustration nearly caused his wings to form.

"You have no idea who you're talking to and what I am capable of. I suggest you ask around before you continue with your immature efforts to annoy me. If you continue this childish rebellion, there will be ramifications. For you and her." He turned to stalk away.

"Hmm, I don't think I'm that worried. I've been involved in childish rebellions before, and the last one worked out rather well for me."

Euriel whirled around, his face red with rage. "You dare... You will regret making an enemy of me, Cassiel. The crimes I am investigating hold significant and *long-term* punishments, and those found guilty will suffer as none have before."

"Which would worry me greatly if I had committed such a crime."

Euriel moved closer so that he looked me directly in the eyes. There weren't many who could do that with my height, but most angels were taller than humans. "Let me put it clearly, Cassiel. If you continue to enrage me, you might find yourself accompanying the damned to their punishments whether you committed the acts or not." He straightened up, his face returning to its normal sickeningly pleasant appearance, and righted his collar. "I suggest you relay to... *Faith*... that I am not someone to trifle with." And with that, he turned and went back inside, leaving me alone on the patio wondering what on earth was going on.

"Nice to see angelic morals haven't changed since I fell," I muttered to myself as I downed the rest of my beer and headed back inside to the others.

The film was still only halfway through, so I sat down between Faith and Amadi. Faith had her legs curled up on the sofa and her head resting on Sam's shoulder. I stared at the screen, trying not to remember those days when she would curl up with me like that and suppressing a twinge of jealousy. I couldn't deny that the overwhelming attraction I'd felt the first time I'd met her was still very much there. I still felt drawn to her, as I always had. That desire to make her smile, make her feel good, protect her, and to just be near her was still there. As were other slightly less savoury desires that involved feeling her nails raking down my back and her sinful mouth screaming my name over and over again.

Enough. She's clearly not interested in you anymore, and you're asking for trouble by trying to reignite that spark again. You're her protector, nothing more, I admonished myself. I stared hard at the screen for the rest of the film, trying my best to ignore her.

When the credits came on, I stood and turned to look at her. She stretched her long legs out in front of her. She changed when we'd got home, replacing her jeans and jacket with an oversized T-shirt, which I suspected was Sam's, and a pair of boxers I really hoped weren't. I held a hand out to her to help her up and pulled her straight against my chest. Stepping back immediately so she wouldn't feel my half hard cock through the flimsy clothes she was wearing, I moved towards the door. She leaned over and ruffled Sam's hair.

"I'm off to bed. Thanks for the distraction. And the beer."

He grinned at her. "Anytime, Faith. Sleep well." He caught hold of her hand and pulled her down for a kiss, brushing his lips over hers. She let him for a moment before pulling away and poking her tongue out at him. Turning, she headed for the door, but Amadi reached out and caught her, drawing her into his lap.

"What are you doing?" She laughed. "I really can't watch another one, I'm shattered."

"I'm just wondering why Sammy boy over there got a good-night kiss and we didn't," Amadi complained.

She mock sighed and pressed a kiss to his cheek. Scrambling out of his lap, she looked at Alex who was watching them. "You too?"

"Well, um... I'd not turn one down if you felt inclined..." If I didn't know any better, I'd swear the guy was blushing. I shook my head in wonder as she dropped a kiss on his forehead.

"Night, guys," she said, and moved towards the door. I held it open for her, and she walked past me into the hall, not giving me a second look. Following her up to her room, I caught her hand as she was about to open her door.

"What?" She didn't look too happy with me and tried to pull away. I didn't let her.

"I just wanted to warn you, Euriel's not impressed with how you spoke to him earlier."

Her eyes narrowed. "What a shame for him."

"Faith—"

"Tell me you aren't asking me to apologise."

I raised my eyebrows. "I'd never tell you to do anything you didn't want to, Peaches. I just wanted to warn you to be careful. He might look like a suit, but he's a suit that's packing."

She gave a frustrated sigh. "Fine, I'll try to restrain myself. Was there anything else? I'm tired."

"Well, nothing much, just..." I pushed her back against the door, pulling her hand up to wrap it around my neck and sliding my own into her hair. I brought my lips down on hers before she could refuse and felt her melt under me for a moment or two. She stiffened and pushed me away. Her mouth opened, but I stepped back and walked down the corridor to my own room.

As I reached it, I turned and grinned at her. "Good night, Faith."

She was still glaring at me when I shut my door.

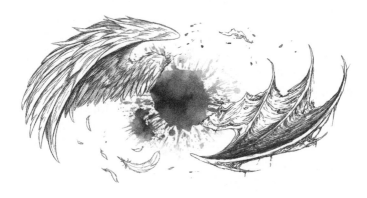

Chapter Thirteen

FAITH

Bloody, bloody man! Damn him. I hated the way he could get to me like that, even after everything that had happened. Fuck him. And fuck Euriel too. I got ready for bed, cursing the two of them under my breath the whole time. I sat on the edge of the mattress then stood back up and wandered around the room, unable to settle. I sat back down again, leaned back on my elbows, and tipped my head backwards, squeezing my eyes shut. I felt completely drained, physically and emotionally, but way too wired to sleep. The pizza and beer had made me feel a bit more alive, but now I just felt emotionally and mentally exhausted. Sighing, I dragged myself up and stuck my head out into the hallway to see if any of the guys were about. Dressed in only a cami and my underwear, I didn't want to run into any of them wandering the hallways. All seemed quiet, so I slipped out of the door and made my way as quietly as possible down the stairs.

Although beautiful during the day, at night, the large arched beams that branched over the main, open-plan part of the house reminded me all too much of the cathedral that kept appearing in my nightmares. I shivered slightly as I crept into the kitchen. Thankfully, all the cupboard doors were soft close, so they made no sound as I raided them. I leaned back against the workstop, frowning. Nothing. No alcohol of any type except the beer in the fridge, and they wouldn't knock me out. I glanced around the sitting area. Searching the oak sideboards didn't reveal any liquor stash either, and I was starting to think that strong coffee and a refusal to sleep was going to be the way forward until I saw blue light flickering under the door in the far corner.

Deciding I was desperate to risk running into one of the guys, even in my rather revealing attire, I pushed open the door. The library was dark, except for the blue light, which I assumed to be coming from the screen of the open laptop on a side table, as Alex had been working on it before Amadi had distracted him. On the sofa, Alex sat with his head tipped back and his white shirt pulled open to the waist. His eyes were closed, and he didn't see me as I moved into the darker shadows next to one of the bookcases. Amadi knelt between his legs, and I couldn't look away as I watched his mouth slide up and down Alex's very hard cock. That blue light was coming from Amadi. His tattoos were glowing with a pulsing cerulean light that lit up the surrounding area. The light threw his features into sharp relief and illuminated the curved horns that protruded from the top of his head. I bit my lip, observing as Alex slid his hands over Amadi's shoulders and behind his head, stroking through his hair until they reached his horns. Alex was moaning quietly, and I felt my panties grow damp as I watched the shine of his wet cock in Amadi's mouth.

Fairly sure they couldn't see me, I slid my hand into my panties, desperate to relieve the frustration Cas had begun in me the other morning. Dipping my fingers into my wetness, I began to circle my clit, mimicking the rhythm in which Amadi's head was moving. Fighting to keep my breathing as quiet as possible, I watched as Alex gripped Amadi's horns and pulled his head down so he could fuck his mouth hard. The sight turned me on immensely. Alex was so quiet, shy even, and yet here he was dominating Amadi, thrusting his long length deep down Amadi's throat. I closed my eyes briefly, imagining it was my mouth that his smooth hardness was sliding into with Amadi beneath me, his mouth on my clit. My breathing quickened, and I heard Alex moan louder. My eyes flew open, and I watched as Amadi sped up, straightening his neck slightly so he could slide all of Alex's length down his throat. My gaze travelled over Alex's toned chest, and I froze as my eyes met his. Unable to look away, I held his stare as he fucked his boyfriend's mouth. Two more hard thrusts and he groaned, spilling his cum into Amadi's mouth.

I slid my hand from my pants and turned to sneak back out and finish myself off in my bedroom, but Alex's voice stopped me. "Leaving so soon, Faith?"

I froze, then slowly turned to see Alex reclining against the back of the sofa and Amadi getting to his feet, his tongue snaking out and over his lips.

"I'm so sorry! I didn't mean to interrupt, I was just... I couldn't sleep, and I was looking for a stiff drink to relax me. I didn't see..."

Alex smiled. In the light from his laptop, his teeth seemed very white. The light from Amadi's tattoos had faded to a muted glow. "That's the thing with most supernatural beings, Faith. We're pretty good at seeing in the dark, and our hearing is above human abilities as well."

Heat flooded my face as I realised Alex must have seen me as soon as I came in, and they both would have heard what I'd been doing.

Amadi moved over to me, seemingly indifferent to the fact he now had horns and glowing blue markings on his skin. He ran a hand down the side of my face. "Don't worry, beautiful. We're certainly not adverse to an audience." He brought his face close to mine, his dark eyes falling to my mouth. Tilting his head to one side, he leaned into my neck and inhaled deeply. Having him this close was extremely disconcerting.

I could feel my heart hammering away, and my breathing picked up as I felt his lips brush my skin. Alex's gaze never left mine.

"Well, well, well, it seems you weren't particularly offended by what you saw," Amadi murmured.

Alex slowly got to his feet. "I think she was rather enjoying herself," he remarked. He clutched my hand and lifted it, taking my index and middle finger into his mouth. I gasped as he ran his tongue over them, tasting my juices. He had seen what I was doing. I didn't think I could have blushed any harder.

"Is that so?" Amadi whispered against my neck, trailing a finger down over my collarbone and my breast before circling my nipple which stiffened at his touch.

Alex pulled me over to the sofa, his tongue still dancing over my fingers. Unable to breathe properly or even form a coherent thought, I followed him.

"Maybe we can help you relax," Alex offered.

Amadi sat down on the sofa and pulled me onto his lap. Tilting my chin back, he placed his mouth on mine. His lips were warm and smooth, and his tongue danced over mine, exploring my mouth. I could taste a lingering tartness from Alex's cum, and the thought thrilled me. Nudging me around so I straddled his legs with my back against his chest, Amadi slid my tank straps down over my shoulders and tugged the cami below my breasts. He cupped my breasts in his hands, stroking them gently and brushing his thumbs over my nipples, making them rise to his caress, and then he whispered Alex's name. I moaned as Alex knelt in front of us, fastening his mouth on my nipple as his lover massaged my breasts with his hands. Positioned where his boyfriend had been only minutes before, Alex ran his hands up my bare legs, pulling my knees wider apart. He began to kiss up the inside of my thigh, and I could barely breathe. His lips teased the edges of my panties, his tongue dipping just slightly underneath, and I squirmed, desperate to feel his mouth on my core.

Amadi broke our kiss, dropping his mouth to my neck, where his kisses grew rougher. He began to suck on my skin and graze his teeth against the column of my throat. It distracted me for a moment, so I didn't feel Alex push my panties to the side.

"Fuck!" I moaned as he slid a long finger inside me, then a second.

Slowly thrusting them in and out, he lowered his head, and I cried out when I felt his mouth fasten on my clit, his tongue flicking it lightly in exquisite torture. The sight of Alex being pleasured by Amadi had already turned me on, and it wasn't long before I felt my climax building inside me. I could feel how wet I was, and my hands slid down to tangle in Alex's soft brown hair, pulling his mouth harder against me. When Amadi felt me shift against him, he pressed his cock into me, and I rubbed against it. He groaned loudly.

Alex slid his fingers out of my core and trailed his hand up my belly. Amadi grabbed it and swiped his tongue over Alex's fingers. I wavered between feeling embarrassed as he tasted me and totally turned on. Alex's mouth clamped down on my clit and sucked hard, and I fell apart as my climax tipped me over the edge. Amadi's mouth sank onto mine as he captured my cry with his lips.

Alex withdrew slightly, and I thought he was done, but he pulled me to the floor and turned me over so I was on my knees, facing away from him. Realising what he was doing, I grinned up at Amadi and slid my hands up his legs to tug on his boxer shorts. His cock was already hard, and I bit my lip as I released it. He was huge. Not only slightly longer than Alex, but thick as well. My eyes flicked up to see him watching me, so I leaned forward and swept my tongue over the tip. He sighed, stroking my hair gently as I flicked my tongue up and down the underside of his impressive shaft. Behind me, I felt the warmth of Alex's tongue sliding into me. I closed my eyes and engulfed his boyfriend's hard cock with my mouth, enjoying Amadi's gasp as I did so. I took him as deep as I could, using my hands to grip his base as I ran my tongue over him. Alex slid his fingers inside me again, and I moaned.

Amadi did, too, as he felt my voice vibrate his cock, and I began to hum quietly. His fingers tightened in my hair as he pulled me closer. I let him, loving the feel of his thick cock sliding down my throat. I started to move with more of a rhythm. His hips found it too, as he began to thrust gently into my mouth. Alex was obviously watching, because he slid a third finger into me. I moaned, and he began to fuck me with his fingers, faster and harder.

I felt another orgasm begin to build, and I pushed back against him, begging him wordlessly. His thumb rubbed my clit, and I held onto Amadi's thighs as he thrust harder. I could feel Alex's hard cock against my ass, and my eyes flew open as I panicked for a moment. Amadi was watching him, and I realised by Alex's movements that he was using his other hand on his own cock. The thought made heat flood between my legs, and I slipped slightly, grazing my teeth against Amadi's shaft. He emitted a loud groan, so I did it again. He seemed to lose control, forcing my head forwards and shoving his length down my throat. I scraped my teeth over him once more, and I felt the saltiness of his cum spilling into my mouth. He began to pull out, but I held him still as my tongue laved his skin, licking up every drop.

Using my hair, he pulled me towards him, and his mouth closed on my nipple, sucking hard as Alex moved closer behind me. Dropping my hand from Amadi's shoulder, I wrapped it around Alex's cock and began to stroke him. I could tell he was close by his breathing. Amadi trailed his hand down to my pussy, and I gasped as he pushed two fingers inside me, sliding slickly against Alex's in my channel. Feeling both of them finger fucking me was enough, and I felt the wave build. Alex brushed my hair from my neck and ran his lips over my skin before biting down hard. The jolt of pain went straight to my pussy, and I screamed as I came. A muffled moan came from Alex, his teeth still locked on my skin, as his cum spurted from his shaft. Exhausted, I collapsed forward onto Amadi's chest, and he pulled me into his lap. I lay my head against his shoulder, feeling his heartbeat against my cheek as my own fought to slow down. Alex climbed onto the sofa next to us, and I felt him cuddle up behind me, stroking my hair. Surrounded by two pairs of strong arms, I gave up my fight against sleep and fell headlong into it, not caring about the possible consequences.

I was lying on the floor again. I could feel the smooth, cold stone against my skin, and when I opened my eyes, I could see the pew legs stretching on and on into the cathedral. Something seemed wrong this time though, and with a sick feeling, I realised it felt wrong because there was no pain. I climbed slowly to my feet, almost expecting the agony to assail me as I moved, but nothing came. The cathedral stood silent and empty as before. It was evening outside this time. There was no afternoon sunlight streaming through the stained-glass windows, and the colours appeared dark and muted. A familiar rumble sounded deep in the earth below, and I recognised the rustle of dust in the shifting stonework. I faced the opposite end of the cathedral, and I could see the ornately carved, dark wooden font opposite the main doors. I took a step towards the doors, then stopped. I had the strongest urge to turn around, and the tiny hairs on the back of my neck stood on end. It was not a sense that I was being watched, just a really strong compulsion to whirl around and run like hell without looking back. I took another step, and then half of another before I couldn't fight the urge anymore, and I turned.

The cathedral was empty, but no longer silent. The rumble and groans beneath me grew louder, and the floor rocked under my feet. Without knowing why, I walked steadily towards the altar, pausing with my hand on the stalls to steady myself as a violent tremor shook the building. Dust drifted down from the vast arches, but the walls seemed as solid as ever, and I continued towards the altar. It was as bare as it was during my previous visit, with only the gleaming metal cross atop its snowy white cloth. I stepped right up to the table, searching for the small symbol at the centre. I reached out then drew my hand back again, knowing what would follow. The compulsion was too great for me to resist, and my fingertips grazed the indentation.

"Faith." I spun around as my name was spoken in a voice I knew well.

"Cas?"

He stood at the bottom of the steps. He wasn't naked like me, he was wearing a white suit like the one Euriel had been wearing when I first met him. "Faith," he whispered, his eyes dropping to something behind me.

I turned, following his gaze, and breathed in sharply as I saw the blood dripping down the white cloth to the floor below. I spun back to Cas, who just stood and stared at me as the blood kept flowing. I looked around wildly, wondering why I wasn't waking up, but consciousness did not return and the cross kept bleeding. I felt the crimson pool reach my bare feet and start to trickle down the steps towards Cas. He stared at me in horror, backing away.

"Cas! No, please! Don't leave me!" I ran towards him, leaving bloody footprints on the pale stone floor. He moved away from me, shock and disgust on his face. I reached for him, and his black wings burst from his shoulder blades, wrapping around him to form an ebony wall.

"Cas!" I cried out, trying to pull his wings apart, but the feathers grew hard and sharp like steel knives, slicing my hands into ribbons. I screamed, and the wings drew apart, but Cas was no longer within them. A figure as black as coal stood inside their circle. It was humanoid in shape, but bore no features at all—except for eyes. Eyes of silver that burned white like magnesium.

He looked deep into my soul, and I felt like he knew every dark, twisted thought or desire I had ever had. Desires I had never admitted, even to myself. I was frozen, unable to tear my gaze away. He reached out and wrapped his fingers around my throat, and my skin crawled from his touch. Hot pain sliced down my shoulder blades, burning like my skin was on fire. I felt the hot stream of urine on my legs as my insides liquefied from fear. He raised his other hand and drew a fingertip down my throat, moving slowly between my breasts, across my belly, and down to the slit between my legs. His gaze dropped from mine, and I followed it, unable to control my own body. Where his finger had touched, my skin split and started to peel back. Blood flowed, and I felt my organs begin to slide from their positions. I snapped my head back up in shock to find his face inches from mine, those eyes boring into my skull, and the pain exploded through me. I finally closed my eyes against his silver stare and screamed and screamed.

"Faith! Faith! Wake up!"

My eyes flew open, and for a moment, I thought I was still dreaming as I stared into dark eyes inches from my own. I gasped and shrank backwards away from him. Cas's face darkened, and he pulled back just as Sam, Alex, and Amadi rushed into the room.

"Is everything okay?" Amadi asked.

Sam flopped onto the bed next to me. "You okay, baby girl?"

I took a deep breath and nodded. "Sorry... I'm so sorry. It was just a nightmare. I didn't mean to wake you all."

Amadi moved forward to stand just behind Cas. "No worries, sexy. We just wanted to check that you were okay. Some of us were already awake." He smiled.

"Maybe we should let her get back to sleep? It's still a few hours until dawn," Alex murmured from the doorway. "Can I get you anything, Faith? Something to help you sleep? Umm... milk, or..."

"Whisky if you have it, Alex?"

He nodded and disappeared into the shadows of the hallway.

"Is that a good idea?" Cas asked softly. My irritation spiked, and I ignored him.

Sam wrapped his arm around my shoulders as I leaned against the headboard, and he looked from his friend to me. "You often drink whisky to get to sleep, baby girl?"

I wondered if Cas had mentioned anything about my drinking when we were together. I looked up to see Cas still watching me, saying nothing. "I... sometimes... it helps knock me out, so I don't dream."

Sam hugged me close, and I laid my head on his shoulder, exhaustion starting to take over again. "Do you dream a lot?"

I sighed, my weariness leaving me no energy for lying. "Every damn night."

Alex stepped through the door with a bottle of whisky three quarters full and a glass. Bless him, he'd even brought ice cubes. I reached over and took the bottle from him, ignoring the glass, and brought the neck to my lips, closing my eyes as the fiery liquid made its way down my throat.

"You ever thought of sleeping pills? Cheaper, easier, and much less likely to fuck up that gorgeous body of yours." Sam took the glass from Alex and set it on my bedside table.

I lowered the bottle. "I've tried. They work for a while, but after a few weeks, they start to be less effective at keeping the dreams away, and the doctors were getting suspicious when I kept showing up for new prescriptions."

"Didn't you tell them what was going on?" Amadi perched on the dressing table and leaned back against Alex.

"Not a chance. They'd have thrown me in the loony bin. Looks, it's fine. I just get bad dreams is all. Whisky helps."

Cas took my hand gently in his and stared at it as he ran his fingertips over my skin. "How long have you had them?"

"A while." I pulled my hand away, taking another drink.

"How long?" He raised his eyes to mine, and for a moment, I thought they sparkled slightly. "When we were...?"

I nodded, and he looked down, exhaling hard.

"So the drinking... the whole time it was because you were having nightmares." He looked back up at me, and the anger in his eyes made me recoil slightly. "Why the fuck didn't you tell me? All those times we fought about how much you were drinking, when I was pestering you to go to a meeting, get help... For fuck's sake, Faith!" He paced about the room, his face thunderous. "The whole fucking time! Faith, why the fucking hell didn't you trust me? I could have helped you!"

I'd had enough. Damn this man and his temper tantrums! I kneeled, the covers falling from my body, and he turned to glare at me. "And what the hell would you have done? Would you have even fucking believed me? I told you I wasn't addicted, that I didn't have a drinking problem, but you didn't believe me. You didn't trust me either, so don't go ranting your pretty martyred head off here, you hypocritical bastard!"

He stared at me, breathing hard, then turned. I thought he was going to storm out of the room, but instead he strode to the nearest wall and planted his fist into the plaster, twice.

"Hey, man..." Sam straightened up, his arm tightening around me. Cas ignored him and went to hit the wall again, but Amadi got to him first and caught his fist.

"Cas, calm down." Cas wrenched his hand from Amadi's and stamped out of the room without looking back. Amadi and Alex followed him, catching Sam's eye as they left. He nodded at them. Clearly, he was my designated driver. I grabbed the whisky again, chugging a few gulps before Sam tipped it away from my mouth.

"Do you really need to?" He looked sad. I could see my fight with Cas had shaken him up. Well, maybe it was time he learned what his friend was really like.

I shook his hand off and took another drink. "Yeah, if I want any sleep."

"I wish you guys would sort out wherever it is between you. I've not seen him that angry for a long time."

I took another drink and stared at the bottle. "Nothing to sort out. He's a dickhead, I'm not interested in being friends. He can just stay away from me."

"Faith, don't be like that."

I glared up at him. "Like what?"

"So mad at him. He's just angry you never told him. He could have helped."

"Sam, Cas would never have helped me. And don't buy into the caring bullshit. Not that it's any of your damn business, but he's a fucking bastard, and this whole protector thing he's got going is just a pile of crap. He fucked me over once, and I am never, never going to let him do it again. Now, if you don't mind, I'd like to get some sleep before we carry on with this shitshow tomorrow." He regarded me for a moment, then reached out and touched my face. I jerked away from him. *Not in the mood, idiot.*

He sighed. "Fine, I'll leave you to it, and I'll see you in the morning. I hope you get some proper sleep."

I ignored him, taking another long drink of whisky before sticking the bottle back on my nightstand and curling up under the duvet. I squeezed my eyes shut. He didn't say anything more, and I heard the door click behind him before the sound of his footsteps faded down the hall. Only then did I let the tears fall.

Chapter Fourteen

FAITH

I opened my eyes and glanced around the room. Empty. I considered getting up, but instead I lay there, staring at the ceiling and cringing as I thought about the night before. My stomach rumbled, since I could hear a frying pan sizzling and cutlery and crockery crashing together in the kitchen below me. Light filled the room, pouring over the tops of the curtains. They'd obviously let me sleep in. Dragging myself out of bed, I grabbed a towel and headed to the bathroom for a quick shower. I let the hot water stream over my face as I thought over what had transpired with Amadi and Alex. A part of me was horrified at my behaviour. I mean, I'd had one-night stands before, but two guys at the same time was new for me, and the fact that they were a couple was throwing me. I closed my eyes, hoping it wasn't going to be awkward with all three of us in the house. They had both seemed up for it. Very up. I grinned as I rubbed the shampoo through my hair. To be honest, it was exactly what I'd needed to clear my head and at least let me fall asleep without worrying. It was just a shame the feeling hadn't lasted. I sighed and leaned against the tiles. I really, really wished they hadn't all overheard me screaming during my nightmares. The memory of them all standing around my bed and looking down at me made me cringe. I supposed it was best they knew how nuts I was before we all got friendly. Rinsing off my hair, I stepped out of the shower, grabbed my towel, and rubbed it gently over my hair. A familiar, painful, banging sensation was forming behind my eyes, and I briefly wondered exactly how much of the whisky I'd downed before passing out. A lot, it would seem.

Heading back to my room, I pulled out some clothes. Someone had been in and had hung all my clothing up in the wardrobe. I deliberated what to wear for a few moments. Nothing too fancy, just jeans and a T-shirt. I didn't want to look like I was trying to attract anyone. Okay, okay, I might have been trying a little. I mean, come on. There were four hot guys downstairs. Five if you counted the arsehole I knew was in the house somewhere, even if I hadn't seen him recently. I braided my hair in a long tail down my back to keep it out of my way, and pulled on fresh underwear and my favourite worn blue jeans. The rips in them showed a decent amount of leg, and they were so old and soft they felt like a comfort blanket.

My back was itching, so I reached behind me, trying to scratch it, but it was right at that point where I couldn't reach no matter what strange positions I got into. I decided to corner Sam when I got downstairs. He'd be happy to help. I smiled at the thought that Sam was always trying to touch me. Not in a sexual sense, necessarily, he just seemed to love physical contact, whether it be holding my hand, having his arm around me, or even just brushing his hand against my lower back as he walked past. I had thought it might get annoying, but so far, I loved it. It made me feel... cared for. I grabbed a T-shirt and pulled it over my head. Glancing in the mirror, I tucked the front into my jeans and slipped a black leather belt around my hips. I smiled at my reflection. The shirt was one of my favourites—nothing like Iron Maiden to get you in a good mood for the day.

Padding quietly downstairs on bare feet, I headed for the kitchen. I took a deep breath and walked in, expecting them all to stare at me. I'd had similar reactions in the past when people witnessed my night terrors, but I wanted these guys to understand and not think I was crazy. I paused in the doorway. Amadi was standing by the cooker, busying himself, and Alex leaned against the worktop next to him, his hands wrapped around a mug. Alex glanced up and smiled as I stood there, and Amadi turned to see me and did the same, holding up a dripping ladle. "Hey, Faith! American pancakes today. Do you want a couple?"

I smiled back, relieved they weren't giving me the freak stare. "Well, it depends... Do you have any syrup? Please don't tell me you're those weirdos who only eat it with savoury stuff like bacon!" Amadi stood back to let me see the pan of bacon sizzling on the hob, and I groaned.

"What's wrong with pancakes and bacon?" he asked, turning to flip the pancakes in the larger frying pan. "The Americans eat them that way all the time."

"And they're welcome to, but for me, pancakes should be sweet. I mean, really sweet, sweet like you get a rush from that amount of sugar."

Amadi laughed and gestured for me to take a seat. "There's syrup on the table, Faith. Knock yourself out, but I've got some extra crispy bacon just in case you want it."

I grinned and took a seat at the table. Cas was already sitting there, scrolling through his phone. Part of me thought about sitting as far away as possible, but the other part still wanted to act as if nothing had happened, so I took the chair next to him. His eyes flicked up as I sat down.

"How did you sleep?" His voice was more gravelly than usual, and he had dark rings under his eyes. His normal get-up had been abandoned in favour of a white T-shirt and grey sweats. He looked exhausted. I felt a pang of guilt for keeping him awake so long. Actually, no, I didn't. He'd been an arsehole last night, he deserved to be tired.

"Much better, thanks. The whisky really helped." I winced. "Got a thumping headache this morning though. Lost my tolerance from relying on sleeping pills." He smiled and raised his eyes to the door behind me. I turned to see Sam walking into the kitchen. Even with a hangover, I could still appreciate the sexiness of a man in ripped jeans and an open shirt, especially with that body underneath. He pulled out the chair next to Cas and threw something across the table at me, narrowly missing the jug of orange juice and the bottle of syrup. I put my hands up automatically, and by some amazing feat of reflex, I actually managed to catch it. Glancing down, I laughed. It was a box of paracetamol. I looked up and grinned at him.

"Thanks, Sam, you're a star." I poured myself a glass of orange juice and took a couple of the tablets. The juice was fresh and sweet and cut through the fluffiness of my mouth brought on by the hangover. I set the empty glass down on the table and looked up at his baby blue eyes.

"Sam, would you be a sweetie and scratch my back for me? It's really itchy again, and I just can't reach it." I smiled as his eyes lit up, and he put his own glass of juice down.

"Anything for you, baby girl."

Standing, I tugged my shirt out of my jeans at the back. His warm hands slid up my spine, and I shivered slightly, loving the feel of his hands on me. "A bit farther up, just round my shoulder blades. Left a bit... Ohh..." I closed my eyes and groaned as he raked his nails gently over my skin, relief spreading through me. He scratched a bit more, then moved his hands up to rub my shoulders, and I leaned back against him, not wanting to miss a moment as his fingers dug into my muscles.

"Um... Faith?" Amadi's voice cut through my bliss, and I opened my eyes to see him standing across from me holding a plate of pancakes, wearing a grin. His eyes were not on my face, however, and I dropped my gaze to see that Sam's ministrations had managed to drag my T-shirt up. I was now giving the entire room a view of my breasts. I silently thanked providence that I was wearing one of my nice lace bras rather than a sports bra, but quickly dragged my top back down again.

Cas cleared his throat and passed me another glass of juice. "Here, we've got plenty, and it'll bring your sugar levels back up. Make you feel less nauseous."

I nodded and sat down, wondering exactly when the aliens were bringing the real Cas back. He was being disturbingly pleasant. As if he read my mind, he smiled and glanced back down at his phone. "Sam, are you okay to do patrols with Amadi again today? Hargreaves wants me in, probably to babysit the pigeon upstairs."

Sam rolled his eyes. "You need to cool it with Euriel before you get us all into trouble with Upstairs, but yeah, that's no problem. Are we checking out that club in the West End?"

Cas nodded, still staring at his phone.

"Not a problem for me," Amadi added, placing a plate of fluffy American pancakes in front of me. "The only training sessions I had today were for Max and Iladiel, and they've sworn off due to injury. Bloody wolves."

Sam glanced up. "Wolves?"

Amadi slid a plate to him. "Yeah, not your lot though. Just a few youths trying to throw their weight around." His brown eyes flashed back to me and he grinned. "Big fuckers, them wolves, but rather cocky. Didn't think they'd get their asses handed to them by a vampire and an angel." He chuckled and turned to pour a new batch.

I stared at his back, then looked over to Sam who was tucking into his pancakes. The uncultured swine was having bacon and syrup. *Weirdo*. "Um... vampires? They're real too?"

Alex, who was pulling out the chair next to me, paused. "They're real." He pushed the chair back in and headed towards the doorway.

"Is everything real? The whole garlic, crosses, and wooden stake thing?"

Sam looked up from his pancakes. "Nah, garlic won't do squat. Crosses, well, it depends. Your average two bits of wood nailed together won't do anything, but a cross used and blessed by a priest might prove uncomfortable, especially to younger vampires. Wooden stake... I guess most things would die if you shoved a piece of wood through their hearts."

I nodded. "That's... fair enough. And they don't really..." I looked down at my pancakes.

"Don't really what?" Cas asked, looking up from his phone.

"Um... it doesn't matter." I could feel myself reddening.

"No, what were you going to ask?" Sam pressed.

I looked up at him, and the grin on his face made me blush harder. Looking around, I could see all the guys staring at me—even Alex had stopped on his way out of the room and was watching me intently. "Fine. Umm, I was going to ask if... they... um... could go in sunlight and if they could... if they..." I paused.

"Go on," Sam urged, his grin getting wider. I let out my breath.

"I was going to ask if they sparkled." They'd strung it out long enough that I was expecting the explosion of laughter that filled the room. My face flamed, and I took a big bite of pancake drizzled in syrup, ignoring the surrounding noise. Cas leaned back in his chair, roaring with laughter, Amadi was chuckling away, and Sam was actually crying. Git. Wasn't that funny. I glanced over at Alex. He wasn't laughing, but if looks could kill, the other guys would have turned to ash on the spot. He grabbed the chair next to me and pulled it out, sliding into it gracefully.

"Pay up!" Sam croaked at the head of the table. To my horror, Cas and Amadi pulled their wallets out of their pockets and passed over twenties. Sam made a big show of checking for forgeries before folding them into his own wallet. I busied myself with my pancakes, ignoring Sam as he sent a gleeful look my way. Alex sighed, and the next thing I knew, Alex was passing across his own twenty.

I put my knife and fork down and glared at him. "You too?"

He shrugged. "Hey, I bet you *wouldn't* be dumb enough to ask."

I opened my mouth to retort but reconsidered. It had been a pretty dumb question.

He watched me take another bite before adding softly, "In answer to the first question—which wasn't dumb at all—whether or not a vampire can go out into the sunlight depends on how old and strong they are. A newly made immortal won't even be able to stand the slightest amount of daylight at first, whereas an immortal who is much older, say a few hundred years, can go out on an overcast day and be fine. I haven't ever met an immortal who is comfortable in strong sunlight. I think they'd have to be ancient and extremely strong to bear that."

"That makes sense. But it must be awful to never feel the sun." I took another bite. "I mean, I do relate. My skin is so white it practically glows in the dark." Alex's gaze seemed to darken, and I felt his eyes drop, lingering over the pale skin of my throat and arms, and I shivered slightly, remembering those beautifully curved lips trailing up my thighs to—

"Faith, is that okay with you?" Cas's voice interrupted my thoughts, and I turned to see him watching me.

"Um... sorry... you lost me." I took a last mouthful of delicious sweetness.

"He asked if you were okay with me taking you into Concordia today to meet with Deliah, since everyone else is busy," Alex interjected smoothly.

I looked over at Cas and swallowed my pancake. "Who's Deliah again?"

"She's Hargreaves' second-in-command. Another witch. Very powerful. Some say she's more powerful than Hargreaves himself," Amadi said, sitting down with his own pancakes. No bacon. Not too weird then, horns and glowing blue tattoos aside.

"Yeah, she's a serious player. Mind what you say to her. You don't want to piss her off." Sam stood and started loading the dishwasher.

Cas snorted. "She's a real sweetheart, don't listen to them."

Sam turned and rolled his eyes. "Yeah, she is when you're her favourite. The rest of us cower in fear."

Cas grinned and shrugged. "What can I say? She loves me."

I glanced down at my empty plate, chasing a smear of syrup with my finger, trying to ignore the slight twinge of something that definitely wasn't jealousy. "So why do I need to meet her if I already met Hargreaves?"

"It was my idea." Amadi slid the plate out from under me and passed it to Alex. "I thought she might be able to find out something about your dreams. Deliah's pretty good at reading people and tapping into the subconscious. If they've been bothering you this long, and if it's taking heavy sleeping pills and a lot of alcohol to knock you out enough to sleep through the night, there's definitely something not quite right there. From what we now know about you, it might be a side effect of the spell that was on you for so long, and she might know how we can stop the nightmares from happening again. That's what Cas meant last night when he said he could have helped you."

"Oh, I see." I didn't dare look at Cas. The idea of never having the nightmares again had me excited, but I was somewhat concerned at the idea of some woman poking around in my head. Especially a woman that seemed to like Cas immensely. Not that I was bothered about that.

Alex put his hand on my leg in a comforting gesture. "Don't worry, Deliah is powerful and slightly intimidating, I'll admit, but Cass is right—she is a sweetheart, and I'm sure she'll want to help."

I smiled at him. "It's fine, bring it on. Anything to get rid of these damn nightmares. Besides, she might even be able to show me how to use some of these powers I apparently have."

All four guys looked at me as I said that, and I laughed at the identical expressions of panic on their faces. Alex stood up again. With a smile and a wave at the others, I followed him outside. A large gravel driveway led up to the house. Cas's bike stood to one side, and Sam's VW camper on the other. Alex led me around the camper, and I whistled quietly.

"Nice," I murmured, fully approving of the sleek black Jaguar E-type. He smiled, clearly happy with my appreciation.

I grinned at him. "You should smile more."

He opened the door for me, gesturing for me to get in. "Should I?"

I slid onto the cream leather seat. "Yes. You're pretty damn cute when you smile."

Alex stared at me. "Cute?"

I laughed. He closed the door, walked around to the driver's side to climb in beside me, and started the engine, which came to life with a gorgeous rumble.

He shook his head again as he pulled away from the house. "I can't believe you called me cute."

I sat quietly for a bit, slightly unsure how to act around him. I mean, we shared a pretty intimate experience together, but then his... boyfriend? Partner? Had been there too, so where did that leave us?

I must have been quiet for some time, because Alex glanced over at me. "You okay?"

"Oh, yeah, I'm fine."

He smiled, though he kept his eyes on the road. I noticed he was much more of a careful driver than Cas. My gaze drifted down his navy shirt to where his hands rested on the steering wheel. His fingers were long and graceful, his nails well-manicured. He seemed very different to Cas and Sam and even Amadi, who were all very physical. Cas and Amadi had the bodies of men who loved being in the gym lifting weights.

Sam was more slender, and I knew his six pack and beautifully sculpted arms came from practically living in the sea with his surfboard. Though maybe the wolf thing had something to do with his physique—wolves were usually very lean. Alex, on the other hand, was slim, though just as toned as the others. I guessed he wasn't as physically active as the rest of them. His hands were more used to computers than weights, though they were definitely skilled. I shivered, remembering the feel of them dancing over my clit...

"Are you sure you're okay?"

I flicked my eyes up to his as he glanced over at me. "I'm fine, really. Why?"

"Well, it's just... you're very quiet. And you're breathing kind of hard, and your heart is racing. Are you worried about being alone with me?" He stared straight ahead, but I noticed his hands gripped the steering wheel tighter.

"Oh, no. No, nothing like that. Why would I be worried?"

"I mean, I get it. We barely know each other, you're finding out all this stuff about yourself and your family. I imagine it's hard to know whom to trust right now. Getting in a car with a complete stranger..." He genuinely sounded concerned.

I shifted in my seat so I was angled towards him and placed my hand on his thigh. "You're sweet. I am totally fine with being in the car with you. Maybe a little... shy after last night, is all. It was rather unexpected."

He glanced down at my hand and smiled. "I guess it was."

"I'm not usually... I mean, I have... with guys... just not two at a time. I don't usually get like this, but with you two being a couple, I don't want to cause problems, and I guess I'm feeling a little uncertain."

"About what?" He glanced in the mirror and pulled off the motorway onto the slip road. I shifted forward, feeling embarrassed.

"Well, about what that makes me."

Alex looked over at me, then suddenly spun the wheel so we veered to the side and pulled up in a small layby. Two cars whizzed past, blaring their horns at his sudden manoeuvre. Alex ignored them and turned to me. "Did you enjoy last night? Honestly?"

I toyed with the zipper on my jacket. "Yes, very much."

"Did you feel like you had to go along with it, or did you feel like you could stop any time you wanted?"

I looked up at him in surprise. "No, I never felt pressured or anything."

He took my hand in his. His skin was cool, and his thumb stroked my palm gently. "Then it was three adults having a good time and enjoying themselves. I think, as much as last night was seriously hot—well, for me anyway—you needed to know you weren't alone. And that makes you a beautiful woman who enjoyed having two men pay her exactly the kind of care she deserves."

I nodded and smiled, feeling slightly better. "You're right. And I never usually get like this, just with everything changing, finding out I'm not who I thought I was, it makes me question everything."

Alex slipped his hand into my hair and made me look straight at him. "I haven't known you long, but I can tell you that finding out you are capable of more than you thought doesn't change who you are. You are still the Faith you were a week ago."

"Just more kick ass."

He laughed and turned forward, starting the car up again. "Definitely more kick ass. I, for one, can't wait to see what you can do."

I grinned as he pulled back out onto the road, more slowly than he'd pulled in. I cocked my head, still watching him. "Alex, what exactly do you do? I know they said you were a science whizz, but what does that mean? I wouldn't have thought science had much of a place with the whole Heaven and Hell scenario."

He smiled. "You'd be surprised. Science is still very real. The discovery of how the universe was formed and how it works is still an ongoing quest, even if you believe some greater being started it all off. That being said, my job is actually pretty boring to most people. I oversee the labs for Concordia Northeast. We have several scientists who work on everything from supernatural biology to magical chemistry, plus studying things like the effects of electricity on someone's ability to perform magic, and using equipment like heat scanners to locate magical sites that are currently undiscovered. Even theological archaeology, like your mother."

"You knew my mother?"

"I've run into her a few times. I don't work in the lab much, I'm more of a computer nerd, but I saw her a few times when she came to use the facilities here rather than causing mayhem at the university."

"Why would she cause mayhem at the university?"

He grinned. "Can you imagine taking a dagger forged in Hell, made of metals currently undiscovered by humanity, to be carbon dated at a regular university lab?"

I raised my eyebrows. "Fair point."

He looked over at me. "I didn't really know Rose. She seemed nice. I helped her use a machine once, and we exchanged pleasantries when I saw her in the hallway. That's all, I'm afraid."

"No, that's fine. So what else do you do? You said you were usually around computers, right?" I tried to bring the conversation back to him, not wanting to think about Rose right now.

"It's kind of mundane. I basically do tech help for every department. If they need information dug up or are acquiring from more ... tricky places, if they need data recovered from hard drives they've found, or tech wiped to remove evidence that could reveal the Concordia, that kind of thing. Plus, I like to tinker with little tech gadgets too." He pulled into the driveway in front of Concordia.

"So you're a hacker?"

"Well, if you want to put it like that..." He turned off the engine.

"That's illegal... you seem way too well-behaved."

"The Concordia has contacts everywhere. We've infiltrated every official government and military organisation in the world. We kind of have immunity to most human laws."

I unclicked my seatbelt as he did. "So you guys *are* like secret agents? Except instead of investigating terrorists and arms dealers, you go after demons?"

"Well, Cas and Sam are more like your stereotypical secret agents. I'm more like... Q." I laughed, and he grinned at me. "And we only go after some demons. Others are quite amenable."

His tongue darted out and swept over his lips, and I realised he was thinking of Amadi. My thoughts went straight there too, remembering the glowing blue tattoos over his dark skin while Alex held onto Amadi's horns, pulling his mouth farther down his cock...

My eyes met Alex's, and he took a breath. "Don't do that."

"Do what?" *Damn, what is he? Can he read minds or something?*

"Whatever you were thinking about."

"Why?" *He's definitely reading my mind.*

He leaned over and brushed his lips over mine, trailing them across my cheek to my ear. "Because I can hear your heartbeat and your breathing speed up, and I can feel you growing warmer." His lips moved over my neck, and I felt his hand gliding up my thigh and slipping between my legs. I moaned softly as his fingers pressed against my core through my jeans. "I can smell your wetness from here, and it's driving me crazy knowing I have to go into work right now when all I want to do is kneel between your legs and taste it."

His mouth fastened on mine, and I was lost in his kiss. I didn't care who saw us as I slid my hands into his hair, pulling him closer. His fingers pulled away, and I growled in frustration until I felt him undo my belt and slip his hand inside. He didn't waste time teasing me, instead sliding two long, graceful fingers into my pussy and using the heel of his hand to rub circles around my clit. His lips broke away for a second.

"Alex..." I pushed my hips against him, and he slipped a third finger inside me.

"There's about to be a guard change in a few minutes, Faith, so I need you to come quickly. Can you do that?" he murmured in my ear.

"I... I don't... know..." I closed my eyes, my head tipping back as I felt his fingers slide back and forth in my wetness. I could feel the sensation building. His lips still tickled my ear, and his voice was soft and low, even as his fingers moved faster.

"Maybe you wouldn't mind if they came out now. I mean, you seemed to be pretty turned on last night watching Amadi and me. Maybe the idea of them standing outside the car watching would turn you on even more." My breath caught in my throat, and I opened my eyes, staring straight into his. He grinned. "I think you'd like that. Yes, you definitely like that idea, don't you, Faith? You're so wet. Maybe next time you surprise Amadi and me, we'll switch places. I'll let him stand back and watch your pretty lips slide over my cock. Can you imagine that? Him standing there, his cock in his hand as he watches you pleasure me?"

I moaned, twisting against him, unable to keep still. "Alex, please... please..."

"Or maybe we'll just have a repeat of last night, and we'll invite Sam and Cas to watch us. I love the idea of them standing there wanting you so badly, yet having to watch me lick your dripping wet pussy, knowing they won't even get a taste..." He lowered his mouth, slipping his tongue over my neck as he gently bit down. I could feel the climax building within me.

"Alex, please..."

He hooked a finger into my t-shirt and pulled the neckline down over my shoulder. "Looks like the door's opening, Faith.

You'd better be quick. Come for me, beautiful creature." He slid his fingers out of my pussy, pinching my clit hard as he bit down on my shoulder, just above my collarbone, and the sharp sting tipped me over the edge as I completely fell apart. I turned my face into his chest, trying to muffle my scream. He held me tight, his tongue moving over my skin, before he gently pulled his hand from my jeans as the waves subsided.

As my brain started to clear, I snapped my head around to the front door. It was open. A man and a woman stood in the doorway chatting, completely unaware of the two of us in the car. Shaking, I redid my belt and ran my hand through my hair. Alex watched me, a strange smile on his lips. I turned to him and he slid his fingers into his mouth, licking my wetness from his skin.

"Fuck, Alex," I breathed.

"Shh." He leaned forward and kissed me. I could taste myself on his lips, and I sighed.

Pulling away, he twirled a curl of my hair around his finger. "Don't tell Amadi. He'll get jealous."

"Oh, my... I'm so sorry, I didn't think!"

Alex laughed and adjusted his trousers. "I meant he'd be jealous of me getting you to myself. He thinks you're hot as hell, or didn't you get that?"

I blushed. "I just can't get used to the idea that you're a couple and yet..."

"We've been together a long time. Sometimes it mixes things up to have new playmates. Besides, you'll find the 'couple' thing isn't as common amongst supernaturals. It's actually more common to have groups of beings sharing each other than just two."

I stared at him. "Groups of beings?"

He opened the door and started to get out. "I mean demons, vampires, shifters, that kind of thing. Though they usually stay with their own species. Amadi and I are unusual like that."

I opened the door and got out, looking at him over the roof of the car. "Amadi is a demon." It wasn't really a question. The horns and glowing skin had kind of given it away, but Alex nodded anyway. "So... what are you?"

He smiled at me, reaching into the car to grab his laptop bag then locking the car and heading towards the door. The two guards had left a couple of minutes before with a nod to Alex and a curious glance at me as they passed. I followed him, and he held the door open for me.

"Well, according to you, I'm cute, sweet, and well-behaved." He reached down and pinched my bum as I walked past him. "That'll have to do for now. Deliah's waiting."

Chapter Fifteen

FAITH

After Alex knocked on the door to Deliah's office, I shifted my weight nervously from foot to foot, my confidence waning now that we were standing outside the door of a very powerful witch who descended from angels.

Alex touched my hand. "It'll be fine. Deliah doesn't bite."

I looked at him in shock. It suddenly occurred to me that considering the amount of supernatural races showing up in my life, she might actually have been the type that *did* bite. When the door swung open, the woman standing in the doorway was not what I had been expecting. Having witnessed Cas's obvious admiration for the woman that morning, I had formed a picture in my head of what Deliah would look like—sultry, sexy, confident, tall. At the sight of a small elderly woman wearing cream twinset and pearls with her silver hair pulled back in a bun, my mouth fell open in astonishment.

"Ah, Alexei, how delightful to see you again." She extended her hand, and to my surprise, Alex didn't just take it, he pressed his lips gently to her fingers.

"Deliah, a pleasure, as always," he murmured. She turned to me and took my hand in hers.

"And this must be Rose's daughter."

Alex nodded, stepping back slightly. "This is Faith. Faith, this is Deliah Trowbridge."

"Nice to meet you," I said with an overwhelming urge to curtsey. This woman felt... strange. I could see why the guys were slightly intimidated by her. Power rolled off of her in waves, as though her size was merely an illusion.

There was a strange look in her pale blue eyes that I couldn't quite place, although she smiled at me. She turned back to Alex. "Thank you, Alexei. I'll send for you if we need you. Faith and I have much to discuss." Well, that sounded ominous. Alex nodded and smiled at me before turning and striding off down the hallway. Deliah stood back from the door. "Come in, my dear. Tea?"

"Um, that would be lovely, thank you." She pushed the door closed behind me and walked over to an ornate tea trolley that stood in the corner to our right, bearing a china teapot and teacups and saucers. I stood and looked about the room. As with Deliah's appearance, I had been expecting something more... witchy. I wasn't sure what, a cauldron maybe? Instead, the room was light and elegant. A tall white marble fireplace dominated the wall to our left. The alcoves on either side were shelved from floor to ceiling and were filled with books with worn leather spines. The windows that stood opposite were also tall and draped with sheer white voiles, framing a seating area much like Hargreaves had in his office. In the centre were two ornate sofas and a glass and mahogany coffee table, which held a huge vase of gypsophila. To my right was a large mahogany desk, which was clearly used regularly but as neat and tidy as the rest of the room.

"Have a seat on the sofa, my dear." Deliah moved past me, carrying a tray with our cups on it. I followed her and took a seat on the nearest sofa. She placed the cups on the table, as well as a plate of biscuits. Normally, I'd have grabbed a couple, but I was feeling way too nervous, and my stomach flipped at the thought of eating right now.

Delian took a seat opposite me, tucking one ankle behind the other. "How are you doing with all of this? I imagine the revelations you have been subjected to came as quite a shock."

"You think?" That came out wrong, and I cringed.

Deliah leaned forward and picked up a cup and saucer, adding a drop of milk to the cup before pouring in the tea. "I imagine you have a lot of questions. I hope to be able to answer at least some of them." She passed me my cup and poured another for herself.

I sighed. "I just... can't understand why my... why Rose didn't tell me anything about this. That she was a witch."

"Rose studied under me as a young witch, as did your adoptive father. They met in my class and went on to get married."

I raised my eyebrows. "My father was a witch too?"

Deliah nodded and sipped her tea. "Yes indeed. Neither of them were particularly powerful, but both were extremely intelligent and wanted to serve in Concordia, therefore they were perfect to slip into human organisations. When they discovered they couldn't have children, they were distraught. It took them a good few years before they decided they wanted to adopt a child. When you started showing signs of being a witch, they were..."

"Surprised? I was under the impression witches were fairly rare." I took a sip of my tea. It was still too hot, but I felt the warmth spread through me so fast that I gave the liquid a suspicious look.

"Extremely surprised. The Concordia keeps records of all registered witches and their offspring. You had somehow slipped through the net, and nothing on the register showed any witches who had recently had a child."

I stared at her in surprise. "The Concordia keeps tabs on everyone?"

She nodded. "It tries to."

"But you knew?"

She set her cup down in its saucer and met my gaze head-on. "Yes, your mother confided in me early on. She asked me to keep it a secret and to help protect you from the supernatural world, and I did. What did Phillip tell you about witches exactly?"

I frowned, trying to remember. "Something about how there were only a few of you with any real power, and you were descended from angels who came to Earth and slept with human women."

Deliah set her cup down on the table and moved over to the bookcase nearest to us. She skimmed over the titles until she found the one she wanted. Drawing it out, she came and sat back down next to me. Flicking to a spot a little way in, she glanced up at me. "This is the *Book of Enoch*. Enoch was the great-grandfather of Noah. He describes the angels that came down from Heaven. Listen." She began to read, running her gnarled finger along the lines of text, which were written in a language I didn't recognise.

"And it came to pass when the children of men had multiplied that in those days were born unto them beautiful and comely daughters. And the angels, the children of heaven, saw and lusted after them, and said to one another: 'Come, let us choose us wives from among the children of men and beget us children.'"

She looked up at me. "The angels fell in love with women and married them. They had children, families. But God was not happy about this. The children being born, half human, half angel, were so powerful, he believed they would destroy humanity."

"So what did he do?" I questioned, listening with rapt attention.

She looked down and began to read again.

"Then said the Most High, the Holy and Great One spake, and sent Uriel to the son of Lamech, and said to him: Go to Noah and tell him in my name 'Hide thyself!' and reveal to him the end that is approaching: that the whole earth will

be destroyed, and a deluge is about to come upon the whole earth, and will destroy all that is on it. And now instruct him that he may escape and his seed may be preserved for all the generations of the world."

"Noah! So the deluge, that was the great flood, with the ark and all the animals?" I stared at her in shock. That story had always struck me as fairly disturbing, and this new information just added to it.

Deliah closed the book and laid it down gently on the table, well away from the teacups. "That was the reason. God and the angels were afraid that the hybrid children would cause the downfall of humanity. The angels that were sent to Earth to watch over humans had become far too involved. They were called the watchers, but they couldn't bear to just watch. They had taught them knowledge and skills that God had not intended his mortal children to possess."

I leaned back against the sofa. "So he drowned them all? Even the bad angels?"

Deliah smiled sadly. "The immediate children are known as the nephilim. The angels that had sired them had committed sins so terrible that God ordered for them to be cast down and imprisoned in the Pit for eternity. By this point, many had grown up and had children and grandchildren of their own. The flood was sent to wash them all away."

"The Pit? Is that Hell?"

Deliah laughed. "Oh no, dear. Think of Hell as a continent, and the Pit is just one high security prison."

I blinked, then shook my head. "I'm sorry. This is all... I mean, I've seen the effect spells have on people, so yeah. I've seen Sam turn into a wolf, and I've seen... demons, but the whole Heaven and Hell being a real thing, I just can't..."

Deliah glanced down at the slender gold wristwatch she was wearing. I half expected her to tell me our time was up, but instead she stood and crossed over to a coat stand by the door. Pulling on a tweed jacket, she gestured for me to rise. "Come with me, dear. This might help you, it might... not. But we'll see what you are made of." She walked to the fireplace and beckoned me over. The white marble was ornately carved, and I could see words engraved just above the hearth. I traced the words as I read them.

"Abandon hope, all ye who enter here." I looked at Deliah with a flare of panic, and she chuckled.

"Yes, I'm afraid Azrael has a wicked sense of humour." She turned to the fire and spoke some words loudly, stretching her hand over the small fire that was crackling merrily away. The fire flared up until the fireplace in front of us was a curtain of sheer flame. I stepped back, but she took my hand. "Trust me, Faith. Nothing will harm you while you're with me." I stared at the blaze, feeling the heat searing my face.

"Deliah, who is Azrael?"

She smiled at me, the flames throwing odd shadows over her face. "Why, he's the Devil, dear." And with that, she pulled me into the flames.

I blinked as the glare faded away, eventually revealing the inside of a cave. Turning to look back the way we had come, I saw a stone archway rising up out of the rock floor. A heavy oak door stood closed inside the arch, with iron hinges and studs. It reminded me uncomfortably of the door at the cathedral, and I shivered. A long tunnel stretched ahead of us, though it looked well lit with flaming sconces.

"Deliah, where are we?" As I asked the question, I got the strong feeling I didn't really want to know the answer.

"We are currently between places. Come now, we have a little walk to reach our destination." She stared down the corridor, and I followed slowly.

"And what exactly is our destination?"

She glanced back and gestured for me to hurry. "Well, my dear. I am taking you to visit Hell. Come on now, don't dawdle."

Hell was not what I had expected. I had assumed it wasn't going to be full of pillars of fire and screaming tortured souls, but I hadn't expected this. I stood next to Deliah on a concrete lane. Around us, cars passed by, their horns blaring. Other pedestrians pushed past, some in a hurry, while others ambled along, chatting. Shops and restaurants lined the streets, some with flower boxes in the windows. Groups of twentysome-things could be seen through the window of the coffee shop next to them, talking away. The only difference from Earth was that the grey stone most of the buildings seemed to be constructed of was shot through with red, giving me a slightly disconcerting feeling that the buildings were alive with blood running through very visible veins. I looked up at a sky that seemed completely overcast with dark red clouds. No sun or light source was visible.

"This is... it reminds me of..."

"New York."

"Yes, that's it. Deliah, why does Hell look like New York?"

"Don't mention that to the higher-ups, dear. Technically, New York looks like Hell. Though this isn't all of Hell, it's just the city of Pandaemonium. Let's just say certain demon architects went earthside around the time New York was in its infancy. I guess they made it feel like home."

"This is weird. So Hell is just people carrying on with their lives like nothing happened?"

"Not exactly, dear. Look closer."

I looked again and realised what Deliah was getting at. Of the group of twenty somethings in the coffeeshop, only two were obviously human. One man had hair that looked more like bright orange tentacles that fell down his back like dreadlocks. A woman sitting next to him had pale blue skin and tiny white horns that protruded from her carefully blow-dried white hair. A man hurrying past in a business suit, talking loudly on a mobile phone, was completely hairless, with moving tattoos that covered every inch of skin I could see. "They're demons."

Deliah nodded. "Yes, a lot of them are. Demons and humans live together. Just like up on Earth, really, but here everybody knows about it."

"But what about the whole punishment and torment thing?"

Deliah stepped forward and held up her hand. A red taxi pulled up, and Deliah gestured for me to get in. "That's where we're going next, dear. After you."

The taxi ride was surreal. The driver, a demon named Malael who appeared fairly human except that he had three pairs of eyes, chatted away the whole time, complaining about something called the Infernal Council and the problem of immigration. A photo was tucked into his visor, and I could make out a woman with long green hair and a small girl with four eyes smiling up at the camera. Deliah paid the driver with coins that shone red gold, and she seemed to tip him generously as he gave us a big grin and wished us a good day before he drove off. I was too busy staring at the building we had stopped at to say goodbye.

It towered above us, taller than any other building around. A huge palace that stretched out in either direction as far as I could see, it reminded me strongly of the Louvre in Paris I had once visited on a school art trip—except this structure looked as though it had been carved from a massive piece of black granite. The lower windows were stained glass, and the colours stood out vividly against the black stone. Soldiers or security guards—I wasn't sure which—stood at attention in black and red uniforms on either side of the door. They didn't blink as Deliah led me straight past them and into a cavernous hallway. Inside, an ornate staircase rose up in front of us, branching to the right and left, leading up to the floors above. The black and white tiled floors stretched down vast hallways on either side of them. People milled around in the corridor, mainly in suits and ties, while others came in and out of rooms in the hallways talking, tapping on phones, or hurrying past. Grand gold picture frames hung on the deep red walls, bearing paintings with fashions dating back hundreds of years, but tending to depict demons and angels in formal poses. The walls rose to high, ornate ceilings hung with huge chandeliers. In front of the stairs stood a mahogany reception area manned by a demon woman and a man with red suits and ties.

I followed Deliah over to the desk and watched as she pulled a large, open, leatherbound book towards her. She scribbled down our names and passed it back with a smile. The demon woman took it from her, then glanced up at me. "First time?"

I stared at her. "Here? Um, yes."

"Hand please."

"Sorry, what?"

"I'm sorry, dear, I forgot to warn you. They need to take some ID. For security reasons." Deliah smiled reassuringly.

I shrugged and held out my hand, wondering if she was about to fingerprint me. "Ow!" I snatched my hand back at the shock of pain. The demon woman looked up at me coolly. *Yeah, I don't care if you have really cool cat eyes, that hurt, bitch!* She held out a small piece of absorbent paper. Deliah took my finger and squeezed a drop of blood from the pin wound the demon had just made onto the paper. The demon nodded and slipped it into a small electronic device. After a moment, it flashed green.

"That's fine, you can—" The machine started flashing again, green then red then white, over and over in quick succession. The demon looked confused. She pulled the paper out, and the flashing stopped, but when she reinserted it, it started flashing again.

Deliah frowned. "Is there a problem?"

The demon stared at the machine for a moment, then glanced up. "No, no, I'm sure it's fine. I think the machine might be acting up. There was no warning, so it should be fine. Witch, I take it?"

"Yes, angel descended. That might be what's confusing it."

The demon nodded again, though she still looked a little confused. "Yes, yes, that's probably it. Okay, you can go through."

"Thank you, dear." Deliah took me by the elbow and ushered me around the desk towards the stairs. We started to climb. The stairs were wide, and the marble was worn. They were also deceptively shallow, and as we climbed higher, I started to slow.

"Where are we?" I asked, trying not to breathe too hard as I tried to keep up with the older woman. *I really must work on my cardio.*

"I'm giving you the official tour of Hell. Just, in a slightly more comfortable way than Dante experienced." She winked at me. I wasn't sure if she was kidding or not, but the reference to Dante suddenly made me realise what she'd meant about the quote on the fireplace. Wicked sense of humour indeed. "These are the Halls of Stygia, home to the Infernal Council. It is the centre of Pandaemonium, built by the angels that were cast down after the War of Heaven. You were asking about punishment, well, this is where it is decided." She fell quiet for a few minutes, and I was too out of breath to ask any more questions.

Deliah led us to the very top of the building, and I had lost count of the number of floors we had ascended. At the uppermost landing, I doubled over, trying to catch my breath. When I straightened, I leaned over the ornate balustrade then stepped back quickly as I realised how far up we had climbed. No wonder I was so knackered. How the hell was she still going strong?

"This way," Deliah said quietly. She gestured to a heavy wooden door. An engraved gold sign on the door was set to the words, "Not in session." I frowned and looked over at Deliah, then with a reassuring nod from her, I turned the elaborate gold handle and pushed the door open.

It was dark inside the room at first, and it took a few minutes for my eyes to adjust after the brightness of the hallway. The room, if you could call it that, reminded me of a circular lecture theatre, except it was colossal, more like a stadium. As I looked far down into the centre, I understood why Deliah had chosen to have us climb to the top. The effect was incredible. Rows and rows of red velvet seats lined the funnel-shaped chamber. The handrails and armrests were gold, as were the stair rods on the red carpets lining the stairs. I slowly descended down the nearest flight of steps, struggling to take in the sheer size of the place. Deliah followed just behind me.

About halfway down, I paused. "*This* is a council chamber? How big is the council?"

"At last count, about a quarter of a million."

"*A quarter of a million?*"

Deliah sat down in one of the chairs and indicated for me to take the one across from her. "Just after the creation of mankind, there was a great war in Heaven. A rebellion, led by a powerful angel called Azrael—you would know him as Satan, dear—was defeated by the Hosts of Heaven. Azrael faced his brother Michael alone, and Michael cast him and his followers down to Hell. I believe the number sent down was around a hundred million. Banished from Heaven, and forbidden to reside on Earth, Azrael begged Samael to be allowed to stay in Hell. Samael permitted it, and Pandaemonium was built. Azrael was angry and resentful, however, and he found a way to Earth. I'm sure you know the story of Adam and Eve."

"Yes, of course. Satan tempted Eve to eat the fruit from the Tree of Knowledge of Good and Evil, and then she tempted Adam. God said they couldn't remain in the garden because they had sinned, so He threw them out."

"And that is one of the biggest misunderstandings you humans have about where you come from," a deep, gravelly voice interjected suddenly from my right, and I leapt into the air. A man stood not three feet away, robed in grey. How he'd got so close in the silent theatre, I had no idea. His face was handsome, but not overwhelmingly so, with dark hair and a closely cropped beard. He towered above me, and though his appearance was unassuming, power radiated from him in huge waves that made it difficult for me to catch my breath.

Deliah stood and bowed her head. "My Lord Mahazael. It is an honour."

He smiled. "Deliah, descendant of Saphiliel. It has been some time. I gather you are instructing another recruit?"

"Yes, my lord, though she is one of the descended, she has not yet been recruited by the Concordia. An oversight meant that she grew up away from the organisation and with human parents who knew nothing of our existence. I am merely filling in the gaps in her knowledge."

"What did you mean about the biggest misunderstanding?" I inquired.

Deliah shot me a quick look, raising her eyebrows, but I ignored her. Lord Mahazael turned to me, and I gasped before I could stop myself. While one side of his face was smooth and ageless, the other was blackened and cracked with glowing embers beneath, like charcoal burning in a fire. He chose to ignore my reaction but fixed his eyes on mine. One was green like my own, but the other burned red. I couldn't tear my gaze away. It was like I couldn't move, like he was holding me in place.

"The Tree of Knowledge of Good and Evil. It was a fallacy. Knowledge of Good and Evil was simply a term in an ancient language of your world meaning 'everything.' Eating the fruit gave his children the potential to learn, to understand. Until that moment, although they had free will, they had no choice. Azrael was the first to give them a choice, and they chose wisdom over ignorance."

"Oh, I see..." Well, kind of...

"Do you? They began to notice things and think about themselves, the animals, plants, and other things around them in the garden. They started to ponder where they came from and what would happen to them. They began to think about each other, and they thought about all of that instead of thinking about God."

"They began to ask questions," I surmised, realising what he was getting at.

He nodded. "Exactly. Questions He couldn't or didn't want to answer. And that is the difference between Heaven and Hell. One wants humans to be ignorant and innocent with blind faith and trust. The other believes humans should have real free will and real choice."

"So you're saying Satan was doing the right thing?" This was not what I'd been taught in religious education lessons, and my head was starting to spin.

"Lord Azrael loved humans, as did we all. He wanted to help and protect them, but saw no reason to bow down to creatures that, at the time, were much less developed than we were. Many agreed and would go on to agree throughout the ages."

"But that would make all demons the good guys."

To her surprise, Lord Mahazael threw his head back and laughed. I looked at Deliah, who appeared stunned. "Yes, young one, we are most definitely the good guys." He bowed his head slightly and began to move back up the stairs. When he reached the nearest doorway, he paused and looked back at us. "Of course, there's only one problem with that concept."

"And what's that?" I asked.

"You're assuming good and evil are real, and not just the likes and dislikes of a demanding deity." He turned without waiting for a reply and left as silently as he had appeared. I stared after him.

Next to me, Deliah took a breath. I looked over at her.

"He was an... interesting... man." Taking a breath myself, I sat back down.

Deliah perched next to me and laughed. "*He* was the Eternal Judge of Souls."

"He was *what?*" My mouth dropped open.

"Yes, dear, the 'man' you were just talking to was an angel of the highest order of Heaven before he supported Azrael in the rebellion and was cast down to Hell millennia ago. A seraphim. Now he is the one who sits down there and passes judgement on each human soul that has ever existed."

I gaped at the door he had left through, my mouth falling open, then I eyed Deliah, who looked suspiciously like she was trying not to laugh.

"So... I've just been chatting about Satan with..."

"Lord Mahazael, Eternal Judge of Souls, and one of the four crown princes that rule over Hell."

"Well, shit." Fuck, fuck, fuck, I really needed to learn to keep my mouth shut.

Deliah stood up. "Maybe we should get home, dear, before you try to insult any more demonic royalty."

"That's probably a good idea."

CHAPTER SIXTEEN

FAITH

FAITH

When Amadi found me, I was curled up on one of Deliah's sofas, hastily scribbling notes from a large, leatherbound book onto a lined, refill pad like I used to use in school. He approached so quietly I didn't know he was there until he sat down next to me and reached for my notepad. I gasped and jumped several inches off the sofa cushion.

"Now that's an interesting sight. I didn't take you for the bookish type. Alex will be over the moon." He grinned as he looked down at me, and I glared at him.

"Remind me to hang a bell around your neck. Do demons not make noise?"

He laughed, revealing his white teeth which were slightly sharper than your average human's. "Not the demons who are trained in stealth."

"You were trained in stealth? Why? By whom?"

He ignored me, leaning over to look at my scribbling. "What are you making notes on? Trancework? Really? That's all she has you working on? I thought you'd be throwing fireballs by now."

I shrugged, ignoring the fact he'd dodged my question. For now. "She thinks if I have more control over my mind, it'll help with the nightmares. I might be able to take control of my subconscious and control the dream."

He passed the notebook back. "Well, anything that'll help. They sound awful."

I looked down at the book in my hands. "They are. The fear and the pain are just... but the worst thing is how powerless I feel. And I'm used to feeling that way in my dreams, but now, in real life, I'm just as powerless."

He reached over and took my hand, rubbing his thumb gently over my knuckles. I noticed how the swirl of his tattoos danced over his fingers. I was about to ask him about them, but he leaned forward and tenderly brushed his lips against mine. "You are a strong person, Faith. Your whole world has been rocked, and not just by your mother's disappearance, but all of this on top of that. However, you aren't powerless." I nodded, not quite daring to look him in the eyes. "Come on." He stood up suddenly and pulled me with him.

"What? Where are we going?"

He pulled me towards the door. "To my office."

Five minutes later, we stood in Concordia's basement. I looked around the room. "Nice office," I commented with a smile.

It was perfect for Amadi, but as far from Deliah's office as you could get. Three walls were completely mirrored, and the floor was covered with firm pads that would cushion a hard landing. One wall was taken up with weight machines, but there were several cross trainers and treadmills as well. The wall that wasn't covered with mirrors had punching bags suspended a couple of metres from it, and the rest of the room was a large open space that was obviously utilised for various activities. Amadi slipped his hoodie over his head and draped it over a nearby machine, revealing his beautifully sculpted arms displayed to perfection by a black, sleeveless T-shirt.

He glanced about the room and nodded. "Thank you, I like it. Now strip."

I blinked. "What?"

He grinned. "You heard me. I'm going to put you through your paces, and it's going to get hot in here, so strip."

I stared at him, realising he was serious. He was still grinning at me, and it occurred to me he didn't think I would. Keeping my eyes on his, I slipped my jacket off and placed it on top of his hoodie. His grin faded slightly as I unlaced my boots and slid my jeans down and off my legs, and as I stood up to face him, I could feel his eyes moving over my bare skin. Pulling the hair tie from my wrist, I pushed my locks up into a high ponytail, pretending not to notice how his gaze lifted to my breasts as I raised my arms above my head.

"So what do you want me to do?" I asked.

"Huh?" His eyes flicked up to mine.

"What do you want me to do?"

He blinked a couple of times and stepped back. "Oh, um... yes... well, seeing as you mentioned you liked to train and workout, I thought that might be something you'd be interested in doing? Bit of stress relief? Cas said you used to have weapons training as a kid, so I thought you might like to refresh your memory."

"Sparring? Sure. Though I might be a bit rusty, it's been a while."

He turned and pushed against one of the large mirrors on the wall. It opened with a click, and he slid it to the side, revealing an impressive display of weaponry. For the two of us, though, he selected wooden training swords, which although couldn't exactly kill you, could still deliver a nasty bruise if you didn't move fast enough. He threw one to me as he turned, but I was expecting him to, so I caught the hilt as it reached me.

"Okay, if you're rusty, we'll start with some training drills then move on to sparring patterns. You okay with that?"

"Sure, let's go." I twirled the sword in my hand. It was weighty, but feeling the hilt in my hand brought back a rush of familiarity, and I remembered how much I'd enjoyed this part when I was younger. He came at me in a basic attack, and I fell back on muscle memory to react. I was right. I was rusty, and not only that, but my fitness level seemed to have dropped considerably, as I was sweating like crazy twenty minutes in. I guessed dancing hadn't really maintained my fitness level like I'd thought. Making a mental note to start working out more, I tried to keep pace with Amadi, concentrating on the weight of the sword in my hand rather than the developing ache across my shoulders.

"You never said where you trained for stealth." I brought the sword forward in a low strike to the left and then the right, keeping my wrists flexible.

"I was in the military." He blocked me easily.

"Really? When? For how long?" I dropped back into a guard position.

"Oh, it was a while ago, can't remember how long exactly. I was in for a few centuries, not that long really."

I stared at him. "Amadi... which military were you in?"

He paused and looked at me. "The Tears. I made lieutenant colonel, but it wasn't really for me. Too many rules, and the food was awful."

I shifted my grip on the sword, leaning the blade back on my shoulder. "What are the Tears? Normal human upbringing here, remember?"

He smiled. "Right, sorry. The Order of Tears is the formal military force of Sheol."

I frowned. "Is Sheol in the Middle East?"

"Not exactly. Sheol is what the locals call Hell." He leaned on his sword and watched my reaction. I forced myself to respond with only polite interest rather than the *holy fuck* that was actually going through my mind.

"Okay, but I thought it was called Pandaemonium?"

He shook his head. "Pandaemonium is only one city. Think of Sheol as the continent."

"Oh, yes, that's what Deliah said. So there are other places in Hell... Sheol?" He nodded then beckoned me to follow him. Opening another mirrored door, he revealed a fridge underneath a wooden bench. Opening it, he passed me a bottle of water and took one for himself as well. I tipped it up, trying not to drink as fast as I wanted, and ignored the droplets of water escaping down my throat and into my cleavage. I lowered the bottle, noticing Amadi was well aware of the track the escaped water had taken.

He saw he'd be caught staring and grinned. "Sheol is a vast place. It wasn't always though. Originally, it was just supposed to be a prison for one archangel."

I nodded. "Lucifer."

Amadi laughed. "Ah, humans. No, way before Lucifer there was an archangel called Samael. He was condemned to live alone in Sheol, but then the War of Heaven broke out and it had to be made bigger."

He sank down to the floor, resting his back against the wall, and I did the same. "I thought only a few angels rebelled?"

"Well, 'a few' is relative. I think it was about three million."

I gaped at him, open-mouthed. "Three million?"

He nodded. "So I've heard, but I wasn't there. Anyway, after that came the watchers. You've heard of them, right? Okay, so there was a whole other section built for them, and Samael wouldn't have it anywhere near the cities, so Sheol became even bigger."

"So there are more cities? And a prison? But you said Sheol was a prison for Samael."

Amadi sighed. "Yeah, I'm really not the person you should be asking about this. There's another city called Dis. That's where I'm from. The watchers' prison is called Tartarus. They are the only beings imprisoned there. Samael, that's a long story, but he's basically one of the four rulers of Hell. The others are Mahazael, Azrael, and Amaimon." I sat up at the mention of Mahazael, but Amadi didn't seem to notice. He took another drink and continued, "Azrael—that's the guy you know as Lucifer or Satan—is the Commander of the Order of Tears. Hell's army."

"And you were part of it."

He shrugged. "For a while, yes."

I cocked my head and regarded him. "Why did you leave?"

He was silent for a few moments, staring off into space, and I wondered if he'd even heard me. "It's not like a human army. Well, not in Britain anyway. Soldiers also act as palace guards and police. There are a lot of powerful demons in Sheol, and some of them have their own private armies. Although, technically, the four princes rule all of Sheol, they need to keep the archdemons happy, keep them subdued. An uprising could be catastrophic. It just got so political, and no one knew who to trust. Eventually, I quit. I bounced around a bit, managed to work my way earthside, and then I met Alex."

I smiled, watching his whole face soften at the mention of the handsome Russian. "He means a lot to you, doesn't he?"

Amadi took a breath. "Yes, he does."

I took a breath myself. "And it doesn't bother him that you're a..."

"Demon? No, it doesn't bother him." Amadi smiled then glanced down at his watch. "We'd better get going. I think we could both do with a shower when we get in, and then we can catch a ride back with Alex if we're quick."

I got dressed swiftly, grimacing as I pulled my jeans on. There was definitely a shower in my near future. Between my little interlude in the car with Alex that morning and training with Amadi this afternoon, I was concerned about the car ride home. I pulled my jacket on and felt a strong pair of arms circle my waist. Amadi's breath tickled my ear, and I could smell his exotic, spicy scent as he pulled me back against his hard body.

"We all have pasts, Faith. Some much, much longer than others, and things aren't always as black and white as they are for humans. I don't open up about mine much. I'm not sorry I told you, but it might take the others longer to trust you with theirs."

I relaxed back against him and turned my head to meet his gaze. "Thank you for trusting me," I whispered, and pulled his mouth down to mine.

I stared down at the symbol I'd drawn in the sand between my outstretched legs, trying to work out where I was going wrong. Deliah had given me a list and asked me to practice at home so I could memorise them. Each sequence could invoke the elements or summon demons, so I was only allowed to draw one symbol at a time, making sure I erased it completely before drawing the next. Summoning a horde of water demons on a freezing beach in Northumberland was not something I was quite ready to do. However much my sparring skills and general fitness had increased in the last couple of weeks, my magical abilities still seemed mediocre at best. As for memorising things... I traced back over the symbol with my finger. The others I'd drawn correctly had all glowed faintly as I completed them, but this one hadn't.

"Hey, Faith, you fancy a spar?" Amadi yelled from slightly farther up the beach where he was putting Cas through his paces. These guys trained hard, getting up at five every morning to put in a couple of hours before work and spending most of their free time making sure their fighting skills were the best they could be. I shivered. After some of the stories I'd heard over the last couple of weeks, I wasn't surprised they worked so hard, knowing what they could be up against. It had definitely inspired me to return to my own training regime. I tried not to think about all the fights I'd had with my mother over having to train when other kids were out hanging around the cinema or having sleepovers. I really wished I'd kept it up during the years since I'd moved out, but I was determined to make up for lost time.

Just come back, Mum. Whatever there was between us, we can work it out.

I turned to look over my shoulder at the two guys behind me and shouted, "No, I'm good, thanks. I really need to learn this lot by tomorrow for Deliah."

Amadi nodded and turned back to Cas. I watched them for a minute as they circled each other, waiting for a chance to slip in and deliver a well-aimed punch or kick. They didn't hold back. If the other wasn't quick enough to get out the way, it was his own faul—or so Amadi had told me after Cas had walked in one night sporting a black eye. They weren't as cutthroat with me, though my skin did bear several bruises from them when I made daft mistakes. Amadi had continued to train me, both with the sword and mixed martial arts, and I had completely forgotten the peace I'd gain from practicing the patterns and drills, almost like a dance or a meditation. It had definitely helped with the anxiety that was increasing every day as Hargreaves' agents repeatedly came back with no new information about Rose.

To my surprise, Cas had offered to help train me as well, both in martial arts and firearms, though our sessions were not as fun as the ones with Amadi, which usually had us mucking around and making each other laugh, and often ending with a steamy encounter in the mini sauna. Cas was professional and to the point with very little small talk, for which I was grateful. I had no intention of getting friendly with him, despite how he'd acted when I first came to stay with them, but it was hard not to appreciate his physical form right now.

Both men had stripped to the waist, and I was definitely enjoying the sight. Cas was taller by at least six inches, with broad shoulders tapering down to a slender waist. His tats covered his arms, shoulders, and back. Large, black angel wings hung down on either side of his spine. Rather fitting, now that I knew what he was. Between them, a dragon crawled up the centre of his back. His arms bore a large wolf and a lion, then they were filled with entwined animals, birds, and plants. Looking at them now, they reminded me of the tapestries depicting paradise hanging in my mother's secret temple to Asherah. He'd bound his dreads up to keep them from swinging into his face as he fought, and I could see the gorgeous muscles along his shoulders. Guys might fall between liking breasts or bums on girls, but I was an arms and shoulders woman all the way.

I moved my gaze to Amadi, who was similarly stripped to the waist. His tribal tats covered every inch of his body, but were barely visible on his dark skin. I had seen the ones on his face and arms glow on the night I watched him and Alex, and I really wanted to see if they did that all over his body. His muscles were just as defined as Cas's, and I ran my tongue over my lower lip. A thought danced through my mind that if Alex and Amadi were willing to share, Cas might be too, and I knew from experience just how good he was between the sheets. The memory jarred me back to reality. Sex god or not, he was still the cruel, cold sack of shit that had abandoned me all those years ago. It would be a cold day in hell before I ended up in bed with him again.

I looked back down at the sand, pushing Cas out of my mind in place of demon summoning sigils. Where was I going wrong? One line down, crossed by two others. A crescent underneath and another line intersecting that and... oh, that was it. I traced a small line intersecting the end of the crescent on the left, and the symbol glowed red. I grinned. Nailed it. The glowing symbol sizzled suddenly, and steam rose from it. I frowned. That wasn't supposed to happen. A drop of icy water landed on my head, and I gasped and looked up. Sam was leaning over me, regarding the symbol with interest.

"Ah, Adramalech. Hmmm... nasty."

I hastily scrubbed out the symbol with my foot. The glow disappeared, and I turned to eye the blond hunk behind me. "Nasty? Why?"

"Aside from the fact he's a demon?" Sam raised his eyebrows.

"But Amadi's a demon. I thought they were mainly good."

Sam shrugged. "Some are. Some are downright evil. Like humans, really, and angels."

"How can angels be evil? You mean fallen angels?" I glanced over to Cas.

"No, angels can be pretty cruel and heartless. A lot of them are... well, imagine fundamentalist humans. Now imagine them with evidence that proves certain things about their beliefs with immortality and a major holier-than-thou complex."

I cringed, remembering Euriel. "Yeah, I can see where you're going with that. But what's so bad about Adramalech?" I glanced back down at the sand where I'd drawn the symbol, all kinds of horrible possibilities flooding through my warped mind.

Sam wrinkled his nose. "He's just... well, I don't know how to put this really. He's just such a little bitch. He loves spreading gossip, and Satan forbid you wear a Hawaiian shirt."

I stared at him. "So you're telling me this demon is nasty because he hates your style?"

"Exactly. Who wouldn't love my style?" He shook his head, and a spray of water droplets flew all over me.

I squealed. "That's cold!"

He grinned, grabbing the towel he'd left next to me, and dried his hair. "Nah, it's not that cold. It's October. That's when the sea's at its warmest. You should come in with me."

I glanced out at the rolling waves and shuddered. "No, thanks. I'll pass."

"Right, you and deep water. Sorry. Maybe we should try to beat this fear of yours before it really starts affecting your life? This would be an ideal time."

I looked at him incredulously. "So my mother has been kidnapped, I find out she's a witch and the entire world is not what I thought it was, I'm living with an evil ex who just so happens to be a fallen angel, plus a demon, a werewolf, and a computer geek, and I'm trying to learn how to summon demons, and you think this is a great time to try to defeat a fear I've had for over ten years?"

He bit his lip, appearing abashed. "Yeah, I guess. Sorry. Another time maybe." He grinned, his blue eyes lighting up.

I sighed. "What now?"

He dropped to the sand next to me, his clammy wetsuit brushing against my jacket. I moved it out of his way. "I just love the fact that you equate Alex being a computer geek with a werewolf, a fallen angel, and a demon."

I grinned back. "Well, he hasn't told me what he is, and something tells me he isn't human, so computer geek was all I had."

Sam snuggled closer to me, snaking his arm around my waist. I started to push him away, then realised how warm he was. "Alex isn't very comfortable with what he is. He's a very private guy anyway, and I think he really likes you. You're the only other person he's ever shown an interest in aside from Amadi, and he's been around a long time."

"Really?" I laid my head on Sam's shoulder. "Then why doesn't he trust me?"

He brought his hand up to twirl a lock of my hair around his finger. "I think he's afraid of how you'll react. Of what you'll think of him. He's got a past, Faith. We all do."

I looked at him. "That's what Amadi said."

Sam smiled a little sadly. "Well, it's true. We've all done things in the past that we worry will colour how you think of us. You're starting to fit in really well here, and I guess none of us want to ruin that."

My eyes fell on Cas and Amadi as they walked towards us, pulling their shirts back on. "Yeah, well, I know all about Cas, so I guess he doesn't have to worry. He knows what I think about him."

Sam frowned. "He's never told me what went on between you two, only that you used to date, but from what you've told me, I think you really need to talk to him about it."

"Oh, really?" I sat up and glared at him. "And why is that?"

"Because I can't imagine Cas ever wanting to intentionally hurt you, baby girl. And now that you know what he is, he might be able to explain things better."

"Forget it, Sam." I pulled out from under his arm and stood up, brushing the sand off my jeans.

"Faith—"

"I said, forget it." He nodded and jumped up, picking up his surfboard and carrying it over to the van. My eyes met Cas's as he and Amadi headed towards us. Neither of us smiled, and I looked away, climbing into the back seat.

No, Sam, he would never hurt me. He would just get other people to do it for him.

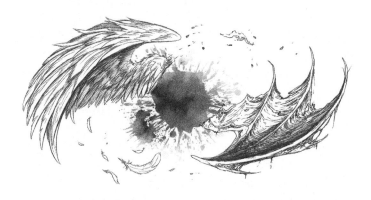

CHAPTER SEVENTEEN

FAITH

We'd stopped on the way back for pizza and beer—a regular occurrence on a Friday night—so it wasn't a surprise to find Alex waiting for us in the living room when we got home. What was a surprise, however, was that Euriel was sitting with him.

He never joined us for meals, preferring to make his own from supplies the "demon spawn" hadn't contaminated with his touch. I had thought Amadi would be insulted until he quietly shared that he found it hilarious to watch Euriel glower at him over our roast beef with all the trimmings while he played with a bowl of kale salad. Euriel couldn't cook to save his life. I watched the next time and realised Amadi was right, so I took great pleasure in visibly enjoying every bite and constantly complimenting Amadi on how good it was. It made me happy to observe Euriel getting more annoyed with every meal. He'd gone on much as he'd started. Avoiding everyone as much as he could and barely being civil when he was forced to speak to us. It was very clear he saw himself as far above our stations, and he was furious he was being forced to slum it. I got the feeling he *really* didn't like me, because I kept catching him staring at me with a strong expression of loathing on his face. I wondered what I'd done in a past life to make him hate me so much.

At least he was dressing better. Today he'd downgraded his three-piece suit to a light blue shirt and chinos to try to fit in a bit, and he perched on the edge of the sofa as he spoke with Alex. Geez, didn't this guy ever just sit back and relax?

Alex looked up as we all traipsed through the door, and I swear he mouthed the words, "Thank God!" as we did. "Hey, guys. Can you sit for a bit? I've got some news."

All thoughts of showers and hot coffee were forgotten as I plonked down on the sofa next to him. Remembering what Sam had said about Alex worrying about what I thought of him, I scooted closer and laid my head on his shoulder. Opposite us, Euriel scowled at me. Alex lowered his head, resting it gently on top of mine for a moment before straightening up. The other guys perched on the arms of the sofas, with Sam collapsing fully into the squashy armchair.

Looking uncomfortable at being the centre of attention, even though he had instigated the conversation, Alex cleared his throat. "So, um... I've not heard anything back from Hargreaves, but I've been doing a little digging on my own, and thanks to Faith, I may have found something. It's not huge, but it may be a tentative lead." I sat up straight. He leaned forward and pulled a card out of his laptop case and handed it to me. "The letter from Rose. I found the painting."

I took it from him, running my eyes over the depiction of the crucifixion. "You did? Did it mean something?"

"Well, not exactly. The painting itself is pretty standard. It's a print of a fresco, one of many found in a religious complex in Italy. The thing is, when I went through your mother's handbag, among the items were her passport and these." He handed me a pair of plane tickets.

"Rose Matthews. Return ticket to Florence, Italy." I looked at him. "These are from two weeks before she disappeared.

So she went to Florence and then left me a letter written on a card from a refectory there?" He nodded.

"Does the painting have any special significance for us or Rose?" Cas queried.

Alex shook his head. "Not that I can see so far. I haven't been able to hack into that portable hard drive yet, so there may be something on there that links it—or it could be a complete coincidence. She went to Florence, stopped off at a refectory, not unheard of for a theologian, and bought this card. When she wrote her letter to you, that was what she had at hand. It's just..."

"What?" I prompted, running my fingers over the image.

"The plane tickets," he answered.

I glanced down at them, then realised what he was saying. "There are two sets," I said slowly. "She didn't go to Florence alone."

"Then who did she go with?" Sam asked, leaning forward.

I turned the other set of tickets over and read the name on them out loud. "Phillip Hargreaves." I looked up at the other guys. "But he said he didn't know her that well. Isn't it strange he didn't mention he went on a trip with her just before she disappeared? Why would my mother go to Florence with Hargreaves anyway?"

Cas stood up. "I don't know, but I think we should find out. Let me have a quick shower, and we'll head into Concordia and ask him ourselves."

An hour later, we were pulling up in front of the stone townhouse on Cas's bike. I unzipped my leather jacket, revealing the black crop top I wore underneath, and pulled my helmet off, leaving it on the seat for when we came back. Cas did the same. For some reason, it felt strangely like the first time I had come here with him. I glanced over at him. He was watching me, his dark eyes fixed on my waist. I scowled when I realised what he was looking at. He stepped closer to me and brushed his fingertips over the scar that was still visible.

I pushed his hand away. "Admiring your handiwork?" I snapped.

His eyes jerked up to mine. "That's not fair, Faith. I didn't do this."

"No, you just got your lackeys to do it instead. I thought you didn't mind getting your hands dirty. Do the other guys know you get thugs to do your real dirty work for you, or don't you like to talk about beating women over pizza and beer?"

His eyes glittered, and he took hold of my arm, his fingers biting into the flesh, even through the thick leather. Cas leaned down into my face. "You don't know what you are talking about, Faith."

I wrenched my arm away from him. "Yeah, actually, six weeks in a hospital gives me a pretty good idea of what I'm talking about."

"Six weeks?" He looked shocked, and I wondered why.

"A broken arm, four fractured ribs, a concussion, and internal bleeding, not to mention three stab wounds and two blood transfusions. So six weeks, yeah." I spun and walked towards the front door. I reached it and turned to see Cas still standing where I'd left him, staring off into space. His normally generous lips were squeezed tight, and I could see his fists were clenched at his sides. Boohoo. "Look, I want answers from Hargreaves, I'm not wasting time rehashing the past. We have to work together on this, and when it's done and we've found Rose, I'll leave, and we'll never have to see each other again."

His eyes met mine for a brief moment, though I couldn't tell what he was thinking or feeling. He'd always been one for keeping his feelings locked away. Did he regret what he'd done? Maybe. To be honest, I couldn't give less of a fuck. I turned and waited for him to head up the steps and tap in the passcode for the door. He held the door open for me, and I marched in, ignoring him. I wasn't as nervous as I had been two weeks ago, and with Cas at my heels, I stalked up the stairs and along the hallway to Hargreaves' office door. Without knocking, I turned the door handle and walked straight in, ignoring Cas's protests behind me.

Hargreaves sat behind his desk, leaning back as though relax-ing. Another silver-haired man sat in front of him. He didn't seem that old, but his face was so gaunt and drawn, part of me wondered whether he was seriously ill. He stood up and turned as I walked in. Hargreaves did the same.

"Miss Matthews, I know you are new here, but it is common courtesy to knock on a closed door."

I cocked my head to one side. "Is that so? Well, where I come from, it's common courtesy not to lie to someone's face about something important."

He stared at me for a moment, then turned to his visitor and reached out to shake his hand. "Check in with me in three days. Sooner if you manage to glean any new information." The visitor nodded, and picking his coat up from the arm of the chair, he made his way towards the door. I stepped aside to let him by, but he paused and looked down at me. His eyes were dark, a bit like Cas's, except there was something strange about them. I wanted to say that they were soulless, like a shark's lifeless orbs, but it wasn't that. There was a malevolence behind them that I could feel boring into me. I took a step back, and he smiled. I really wished he hadn't. A cold shiver ran over me, and I felt bile rising in my throat. Who was this guy? He looked back towards Hargreaves.

"Have a good evening, sir." His gaze swung slowly back to mine, and I swallowed as he picked up my hand and brushed his mouth over the back. His lips were warm, but my skin crawled at his touch. He released my hand without averting his gaze and smiled again. "Pleasure to meet you, Miss Matthews." He left through the door, and I leaned against the doorframe for a moment, concentrating on not throwing up.

"You okay?" Cas put his hand on my arm, concern all over his features. Fucking hypocrite. I shoved his hand away.

"Fine." I turned to Hargreaves and moved to stand in front of him. He didn't offer me a seat, and I wouldn't have taken it if he had. "You lied to me." He leaned back in his chair again, pressing his fingertips together, and watched me shrewdly.

"About what, Miss Matthews?" I put both of my hands on the edge of the desk and leaned over it.

"You told me you barely knew my mother. But I know that two weeks before she disappeared, she went to Florence with you." He opened his mouth, but I cut him off. "Oh, nobody else knows. Apparently she told her co-workers she was going alone, and your secretary was under the impression you were at a conference in New York that week."

"How did you... Oh. Alexei."

"Right. Did you really think you wouldn't be caught? You teamed me up with some of your best agents and didn't expect us to find out you lied?"

He sighed. "Well, to be honest, Miss Matthews, from what I'd heard from Rose, I figured if I put you in a house with four rather attractive young men, you'd be too busy to do any snooping of your own. But I see you're more intelligent than your mother gave you credit for, and you've used your... skills... to convince my agents, as you put it, to put their jobs second to your own desires."

The large desk between us was the only reason I didn't reach out and slap him across the face. Or punch him. "My mother said nothing of the kind about me."

"Oh, I assure you, she did."

"She was professional. She wouldn't have spoken about me like that at work. You're lying to me again." I hit the desk with the flat of my palm and felt a small spark of vindictive from joy seeing Hargreaves jump.

"But she wasn't at work, was she, sir?" Cas came to stand next to me. He put his hand over mine, and I wanted to pull it away, but curiosity kept me still.

Hargreaves glared at him. "I don't know what you're getting at, Cassiel. I see this young woman has managed to convince even the most committed of soldiers."

"Well, as you said, she has her temptations, and, as I am starting to realise, so did her mother."

I twisted around to look at him. "What are you talking about?" I hissed.

"Yes, Cassiel, do spit it out. I am most intrigued." Hargreaves sounded almost bored, and the inclination to break his nose returned.

Cas watched him calmly. "Her mother wasn't being professional, because the two of you weren't on a professional trip together. It was personal."

"What?" I turned back to stare at Hargreaves. "You were... together?"

He glared at me for a moment, and then it was like the fight left his eyes and he slumped down in his chair. "We were," he murmured quietly. "I didn't tell you because she wasn't ready to tell you yet. In fact, we hadn't told anyone."

Cas sat in the chair the creepy visitor had just vacated. "You hadn't applied yet."

Hargreaves shook his head. Standing, he went over to a small, ornate side table and poured the three of us a finger of brandy.

"What do you mean, applied?" I glanced back and forth between them, still reeling from the surprise.

Cas shifted uncomfortably in his chair. "Well, Concordia exists to keep the peace on Earth between Heaven and Hell and the residents thereof. Certain rules apply to certain places and species. Angels, for example, are completely forbidden from forming any kind of romantic relationship, and having sex is punished by condemnation to Hell. Well, Hargreaves told you about the watchers and the nephilim." I nodded and took a drink of the brandy—definitely top-notch stuff. Cas did the same, then he continued, "Rules apply to other species as well. The Concordia is in charge of enforcing those rules. Supernatural creatures are not allowed to have relationships with humans. Sex is permissible, but the overarching rule of humans never finding out about the truth exists above all. Between supernatural races, other than angels, it starts to get really complicated. With witches, well, it's more of a snobbery thing. Sorry, sir, but it is."

Hargreaves sat down and propped his elbows on the desk. "What Cassiel is getting at is that witches are of different lineages, usually traced back to a particular family, and thereby a particular angel. However, there was often a lot of interbreeding between families to try to strengthen the angelic power in their descendants. This resulted in a so-called Court of Witches, which is similar to a mediaeval royal court, I suppose, but the families squabble over whose descendants are more powerful. Descendants of a more formidable family are expected to make matches with other powerful families. Your mother's lineage, though not low, is not as high as my own, and it would have caused... trouble for us both."

"So you kept it a secret," I said slowly. "And your trip to Florence was..."

He smiled sadly. "A romantic getaway. Rose had been working so hard, I wanted to treat her." Cas leaned back in his chair with a rather annoying self-satisfied smile.

"Florence is an odd choice though," I remarked, turning back to Hargreaves. Cas sat up and looked at me. "I mean, if you work for a major religious organisation, it's a pretty religious city. Surely there might have been people there who would have recognised you, if not her?"

Hargreaves took a drink, watching me over the rim of his glass. "It was her idea. She'd mentioned she wanted a few days off to visit Florence, so I thought it would be a nice trip for both of us."

"No, of course. I mean, for a theologian like her, I bet wandering through those dusty churches and refectories was the perfect date for her."

Hargreaves smiled. "Actually, we didn't visit anything like that. We took a trip to a lovely village on the wine route and did a wine tasting, then the next day we strolled around the city, spending most of our time at the Cattedrale di Santa Maria del Fiore. I bought her ice cream at a nearby gelato."

I smiled warmly at him. "That sounds lovely, and it does sound like my mother was very happy. But weren't you worried someone would see you?"

He shrugged. "I arranged a meeting in Rome for our last day. Business as usual, chatting to a few of my contacts and strengthening some relationships. Rose spent the day on the beach. It was unseasonably warm, I remember, though I don't believe she went swimming." He smiled for a moment, then it faded and he looked at me. "Will you believe me now when I tell you I am doing everything I can to find your mother?"

I nodded and stood up. "I believe you, and I'm sorry I doubted you. Please forgive me for barging in like that. I'm just so on edge with her disappearance."

He stood up and took my hand in his. "Of course, my dear, but please do keep this to yourself. It isn't common knowledge and could cause real problems for both myself and Rose."

"My lips are sealed, Sir Hargreaves." I gave him a sweet smile as we made our way out of the room.

To his credit, Cas waited until we were outside of the building before grabbing my arm and turning me to face him. "Okay, what gives?"

"What do you mean?"

"There's no way you just accepted what Hargreaves told you."

I looked at him blankly. "It sounded plausible to me."

He glared at me. "I don't mean the part about him and your mother, I mean the part where he pretty much called you a slut and you let him." I shrugged. "Faith!" he growled.

I beamed. "Fine, fine. He said when they were in Florence, my mother spent her last day on the beach, right?"

"So?"

"My mother adored the sea. She used to live near the coast and only moved farther inland when she and Dad adopted me. Her favourite thing was going for a swim in the ocean every morning, no matter the temperature. Even when we used to go to the beach as a family, she was in the water more than she was out of it. There is no way she spent an entire day at the beach and didn't go swimming. Even if it was freezing."

Cas looked at me, and then I saw him comprehend what I was getting at. "She didn't go to the beach on her last day."

"No, she didn't." I took out the card she had written to me and held it out for him to see. "She went to a refectory. And what's more, she lied about it to her lover and boss."

Cas looked at the painting, then back up at me. "If she was working on something, why did she lie to Hargreaves?"

I tucked the card into my pocket and zipped up my jacket. "She was already planning to go to Florence on her own. I think she wanted to go to this refectory, and she wanted to go alone. For some reason, she didn't want Hargreaves to know about it. So when he went with her, she had to lie about where she was. There's something we're missing about that refectory, Cas."

He turned and put his helmet on. "Okay, so Rose was up to something she didn't want Hargreaves to know about, even though she was dating him. And it has something to do with that painting and that refectory. What do you want to do?"

I took the spare helmet from him and slid it over my head. From behind the visor, I grinned at him. "What else? I want to go to Florence."

Chapter Eighteen

Faith

I dropped onto a low stone bench outside of the hotel with a groan. These boots might be made for many things, but walking long wasn't one of them. Sam grinned as he put my bag down on the floor and perched on the bench next to me.

"Alright there, baby girl?"

I glared at him. "I don't see why we couldn't have taken a taxi."

Cas dumped his own bag onto the ground but stayed standing, leaning against the wrought-iron fence as he answered, "Because the hotel was only a ten-minute walk from the station, and public transport is traceable. I'd rather no one knew where we were staying."

"I thought that was why we flew to Rome and took the train here? In case we were being followed?" I was whining and I knew it, but my feet hurt.

"Always pays to be careful," Amadi commented, walking up with Alex and Euriel at the rear. With grim pleasure, I realised Euriel hadn't relished the walk either. I supposed he was used to flying everywhere. He set his bag down and glanced up at the hotel.

His face visibly brightened, and I saw the first glimmer of a smile on his normally disapproving face. "We're staying here?"

Cas nodded. "That okay with you? I thought the Grand might be a little public." I caught the faintest tone of sarcasm in Cas's tone, but Euriel didn't seem to notice.

"No, it's fine. I've always wanted to visit here." We all stared at him.

"Why?" I asked.

He turned to look at me, and for once, his expression was not confrontational. "I've been to Florence a few times, but never visited here. The garden is famous for housing a school of art and sculpture where Michelangelo came at the age of fourteen to learn to sculpt under a student of Donatello."

"You like art? Created by lowly humans?" I cocked my head to one side as I regarded him.

"There are a few among your species that excel whom I have much admiration and respect for. Painters, sculptors, and musicians all possess some gift of creativity not granted to our kind."

"Shall we check in?" Alex inquired, glancing at the sky. I looked up. It had been grey and miserable when we arrived, but the clouds were parting now, and though it was still chilly, large patches of blue were starting to appear. Alex slid off the bench and picked up his bag, so I did the same. He'd graciously carried my bag when I started hobbling—stupid boots—but I could manage inside.

The interior of the hotel was lovely. It was modern and stylish, but still bore gorgeous features like polished marble floors and wrought-iron stair bannisters. I smiled as I looked around. Check in was pretty quick since Cas seemed to speak fluent Italian. As we made our way up to the rooms, I nearly asked him about it, but then I decided to keep quiet. It was becoming far too easy to fall into casual conversation with him, and I really didn't want to seem like I was being friendly. At the top of the stairs, he handed out the keycards. Alex and Amadi had a room to themselves, and Cas and Sam were sharing a twin, but Euriel and I had our own rooms. Opening the door, I put my bag on the floor and looked around. A large, king-sized bed sat in the centre of the space, with your standard wardrobe, desk, and little sofa. The room was minimal but stylish, with a cream colour scheme. Sticking my head in the bathroom, I squealed at the roll-top bath and waterfall shower. The brown and black marble formed a striking contrast against the cream walls.

A knock sounded on the door, and I went to open it. The guys stood outside, so I stepped away from the door and let them file in before dropping onto the end of the bed to unzip my boots. Stupid boots. I had wanted to feel more put together and stylish wandering around Florence, but my feet were against me. Luckily, I had my comfy biker boots with me for later.

"So what's happening?" I asked, rubbing my feet. Sam sat down next to me and pulled my feet into his lap, where he started rubbing them. I moaned in pleasure and relief and reclined on the bed.

"Um, Faith?" Cas sounded a little exasperated. I held my hand up, but kept my eyes closed.

"I can hear you, shoot."

He sighed impatiently. "Fine. I thought we should maybe split up this afternoon and make the most of actually being in Florence on a nice day. Looks like the sun's coming out. The gallery we want isn't open until tomorrow, and Sam and I would like to drop in on a friend here in the city."

"Afraid I'm going to be boring and stay here with my laptop," Alex inserted, leaning against the wall. "I'm still trying to crack open that hard drive. Whoever protected it did some pretty serious work on it."

I pushed myself up on my elbows. "What, like encryption stuff?"

He nodded. "Yep, all your standard digital protection, but there's also quite a bit of magical protection on it too. I could maybe do with a bit of help..." His gaze drifted to Amadi, who grinned back at him.

"Well, I've been to Florence before, so I'm happy to stay and... help." I smiled at how cute they were, then sent a death glare across the room to Euriel as he made a noise of disgust in his throat.

Cas did the same. "We'd appreciate it if you could keep your prejudices to yourself."

Euriel turned a hard stare on him. "Well, I will if they could keep their degenerate behaviour to themselves. Their perversion is a sinful mockery of a gift from God. I realise they have no hope of ever ascending to the hand of my father, but I have no desire to have it paraded in front of righteous beings and humans like the child there who may yet be saved." He'd been skating around the issue for the last couple of weeks, obviously trying to refrain from commenting, and he'd apparently given up.

The small room exploded. Amadi went for Euriel, only to be held back by Alex, and Sam leapt off the bed to grab Cas, causing me to roll onto the floor with a rather hard bump.

"You've got some fucking nerve," I growled over the incomprehensible yelling from Amadi and Cas in languages I didn't recognise. Euriel's icy eyes fixed on me as I pulled myself up, rubbing my backside. "They've let you stay with them, fed you, even clothed you, and you still spout this shit."

"They are—"

"They are two of the nicest men I have ever met. They are a gorgeous couple who obviously adore each other. If you don't like it, I suggest you fuck off to wherever you came from."

He glared at me and took a step forward. "It is *your* soul I am trying to protect, you foolish child!"

"Well, I'd rather you left my soul alone, thank you very much, if it means you hurting people I care very much about. And enough with the 'child' moniker please, it's offensive." I stood in front of him, glaring right back. Granted, he was quite a bit taller than me, but there was no way I was backing down from this asshole.

His chest seemed to inflate as he puffed up. "I was created before humanity even existed. I am quite entitled to refer to you as a child, an infant even, as is Cassiel." I glanced over at Cas who had calmed down slightly, though Sam was still hanging onto his arms.

Cas grinned at me, but I could still see the rage simmering in his eyes as he faced Euriel. "Don't include me in that, mate. If there's one thing I can tell you, Faith is definitely all woman!"

Euriel let out a huff. Turning back to me, he stepped closer and actually took my hand. "My dear, I can save you if you'll let me. Harlotry will be forgiven by the Lord Almighty if you repent."

I tilted my head to one side, making my eyes look wide and innocent. "Really? I'd be forgiven?"

He nodded earnestly. "Of course. You just need to repent."

"So I'd be forgiven for having slept around since I was eighteen?"

"Well, yes, if you—"

"And would I be forgiven for sleeping with two men at one time?"

He looked shocked. "Two—well, er, yes, I—"

I smiled sweetly, ignoring Cas and Sam whom I could see grinning behind Euriel's back. "That's good to hear. So the other night, when I crept into the library looking for a drink and caught Amadi with Alex's cock in his mouth, would I be forgiven for touching myself while I watched?" Euriel dropped my hand and stepped backwards, his eyes still locked on mine. "Would I be forgiven for sliding my fingers between my legs as I viewed Amadi's mouth slide over Alex's shaft? Or for kneeling and taking Amadi's cock into my mouth?"

This time, his eyes dropped lower, and he swallowed. "I—"

I couldn't tell if he was furious or turned on. I slowly swiped my tongue over my lips, my fingertips trailing along the low hem of my top. "Would I be forgiven for loving how his skin felt under my tongue, for getting wet when he pulled my head down so he could push deeper into my mouth? What about when Alex came up behind me and—"

"Enough!" Euriel roared and stormed out of the room, slamming the door so hard the walls seemed to shake.

I looked over at Amadi and Alex. "Hmm... I guess forgiveness does have its limits." Cas and Sam burst into laughter, but Amadi came over and took me in his arms. Alex followed, his long arms encircling both of us, and pressed a soft kiss to the top of my head. I snuggled in, smirking at Cas and Sam who were giggling behind us.

"Did you see?" Sam wheezed. "He totally had a hard-on when he stormed out!"

I twisted away from my guys. "No? Did he really? Ha!" I wasn't sure if I was flattered or disgusted, but I was definitely amused.

As the laughter faded, Alex and Amadi released me from their arms. Alex softly ran a finger down one side of my face. "Thank you, my sweet one. You didn't have to do that."

I looked up into his gorgeous green eyes. "Yeah, sorry I kind of spilled the beans on that night."

I glanced guiltily at Sam. Cas looked away, and something tightened inside me. Sam, however, wandered over and slid his arms around my waist, pulling me back against him. I turned my head to see him smiling down at me.

"And what, exactly, were you saying about Euriel?" I inquired, feeling Sam's hardness press into me.

"Hey, he's an angel, he should have better self-control. You know, since he's been around since before humanity was created." Sam rested his chin on my shoulder, and I laughed. "I, however, am a red-blooded man—okay, man wolf, and I have no such qualms. Besides, I'd like to see anyone imagine what you just described without getting at least marginally hot around the collar."

Amadi grinned at him. "You should have been there, man. Definitely more than marginally hot watching her on her knees!"

My mouth dropped open, and I smacked Amadi on the arm.

Sam chuckled, but the look he shot me was anything but comedic. "Well, if there's an open invitation to share, let me know the time and place. I'll be there howling at the door." He gazed down at me. "If I'm welcome, that is?"

My lips parted, and I could feel my heart thudding against my chest. I searched for something to say that didn't make me sound dumb or like a sex maniac. Cas, however, came to my rescue, though I doubt that was his intention.

"Shall we get going, Sam? It'll take an hour to get there." His humour had vanished, and he was back to being a grumpy sod again.

Sam sighed. "Sure, let's go. Let me grab my jacket from the room. Catch you later, baby girl." He dropped a soft lingering kiss on my lips then left.

Amadi and Alex followed suit, leaving me alone with Cas. He glanced over at me. "So what plans do you have for the afternoon?"

I raised my eyebrows. "Well, since I didn't know you were all going to abandon me, I guess I'll have to make some of my own."

He nodded and, to his credit, looked slightly guilty. "I'd take you with us, but it's really not the type of place I want to take you."

My interest piqued, I sat back down on the bed. "Really? Why? Top secret?"

"Nothing like that. Just, the demon we're going to see has a special talent for reading minds, and he's not particularly subtle about commenting on what he finds in a person's subconscious. I guess I wanted to spare you the embarrassment. I figured you'd had enough people poking around in your head. Besides, the meeting is mainly because if he found out Sam and I were here and didn't go see him, he'd be pissed. And whereas, I, too" —he stood up straight, put his hand on his heart, and looked up to the ceiling— "was created before humanity even existed..." I giggled in spite of myself at his pious impersonation of Euriel. He smiled at me and took his hand away. "Let's just say this is one powerful demon no one wants to piss off."

I nodded. "Fair enough. You aren't going to make me stay in the hotel then?"

He looked confused. "Why would I do that? No, no one knows we're here. Go and have a wander. We're in Florence, it's a beautiful city. Maybe we could all meet up for pizza somewhere tonight?"

I stood and opened my bag to grab my biker boots. "Pizza sounds good to me. Just text me when and where."

"Great, it's a date." He hesitated as he put his hand on the door handle as if he were going to say something else, but then he shook his head and left the room.

I perched on the end of the bed to do up my boots and opened the browser on my phone to find a decent street map of the city. The idea of finally having some time to myself without any of the guys around was quite exciting.

Several hours of sightseeing and snacking later, I stood outside of the Cattedrale di Santa Maria del Fiore, gazing up at the huge bronze door in front of me. It had long since turned green, but the beautiful jade colour contrasted wonderfully against the white stone. Pulling out my phone, I took a couple of photos, then flipped back through the ones I had already taken of the front of the cathedral from farther back to check they were in focus. The piazza wasn't busy. Maybe it was due to the time of year, but I was glad it had kept them away. Even with the cold, the clouds had dissipated, and the cathedral was beautifully framed in azure blue. I smiled to myself and wandered towards the smaller bronze door to my left where they were still letting people in to have a look around. Staring down at my phone, I became absorbed in the tourism website I was skimming through and didn't see the tall form in front of me until I collided with it. I stumbled backwards, losing my balance, but a long arm shot out and wrapped around my waist, pulling me in tight against a hard frame.

Regaining my balance, I looked up. "Oh, it's you."

Euriel's arm tightened around my waist, pulling me firmly against his body as he viewed me with his normal scowling expression. "You ran into me. I was merely trying to prevent you from falling."

"Right, yeah. Sorry," I mumbled reluctantly.

"Actually, I wanted to apologise as well," he said rather stiffly.

I looked up at him in surprise. "Really?"

"Yes, well, I realise I may have acted out of turn in the hotel room."

I rolled my eyes. "Yeah, you reckon?"

He scowled down at me. "I did not appreciate your attempts to seduce me, however—"

"Whoa, hang on a sec there. My attempt to what?" I gaped up at him.

"To seduce me. However, I should have maintained better control over my temper and not left the way I did until we had resolved the situation."

I raised my eyebrows, and then I couldn't hold it in any-more. I began to laugh.

He frowned. "I do not understand what you would find amusing about my apology."

"Well, for starters, I did not try to seduce you."

"Everything you said was a deliberate attempt to make me desire you sexually, was it not?"

"Well, yes, but—"

He shrugged. "Well then, it is logical to assume that your desired outcome was to seduce me, as you have done with the other male members of our current group."

I suddenly became uncomfortably aware that his arm was still around my waist and I was pressed up against him. I could feel the hard lines of his body under his expensive shirt and trousers, and I could feel desire burning inside my belly as those intense blue eyes gazed into mine.

Annoyed with myself as well as him, I put my hands on his chest and pushed him away. He let go immediately. "Euriel, let me set your mind at ease. I have absolutely no desire whatsoever to seduce you. In fact, the thought of being in bed with you makes me feel physically sick. What I did was merely to demonstrate that you might be all high and mighty in the way you speak, but you still have a body like everyone else, and it will react just as everyone else's does. Which it did, and which everybody noticed, much to their amusement." His lips pressed together in a thin line, and I saw a deep flush begin to creep up from his collar. "As for your apology, I refuse to accept it."

"You... refuse?" He stared down at me, clearly lost.

I nodded. "Apologising for simply walking out of a room, when you had greatly insulted me and two people I care very much about, is just crazy. When you want to apologise for how you spoke to me, and especially to them, then I might listen."

He appeared genuinely confused. "But what I said... What they do..."

"Is none of your business." I shook my head. "I don't get how you can miss so much, how you can't see what I see. You've lived with them as long as I have."

He cocked his head to the side. "Tell me."

I looked up at him. "What?"

He took my hand and guided me over to a nearby bench where he sat down and motioned for me to do the same. The wooden seat was cold through my jeans, and I eyed the other tourists walking into the possibly warm interior of the cathedral with envy. He took my hands in his then glanced down. "You're cold." He folded them into his own. I was surprised to find he had a warm touch, considering what a cold, insensitive bastard he was. "So, tell me."

"Tell you what?"

He leaned forward. "Tell me what you see when you look at those two sinners."

Oh.

I leaned back and looked up at the sky. "I see... the way they look at each other across the room when they think no one is watching. I see the way Amadi ruffles Alex's hair when he passes him. I see little touches, like Alex putting his hand on Amadi's back when he's cooking, just for a moment, to let him know he's there, or Amadi touching the back of Alex's hand when he starts to stutter, just to reassure him. I see the way they snuggle up together when they watch a film. I see Alex wandering around the farmers' market looking for just the right fruit and veg because he knows the best will make Amadi happy." I stopped and looked over at him. He was staring at the ground, his face impassive. "You know what all those things add up to, Euriel?"

He glanced up at me. "What?"

I smiled. "Love. Pure and simple. Yes, there's sex, but it's love making. It's making the other person feel amazing with just your touch, with the feel of your body against theirs. It's a deep, physical connection with another person that you sometimes just can't say with words." His blue eyes were locked on mine, and I saw his beautiful lips part slightly. For a second, I was tempted to kiss him, but then I remembered he was an asshole. But hey, at least he was listening to me. My mouth suddenly felt dry, and I ran the tip of my tongue over my own lips. His gaze immediately dropped to watch my mouth, and I realised he wanted to kiss me too. "Euriel..."

He looked up, blinked, then straightened and averted his eyes. I watched his defences raise again. "Angels are not permitted any kind of physical touch unless they are fighting or healing. It is hard to understand this connection as anything other than satisfying animal instincts that are forbidden by the Lord." I looked down at our hands, still wrapped around each other. He smiled wryly. "There are some rules I struggle with, and I find it hard to apply when I am on Earth. Like a simple touch for comfort. We are not permitted to touch humans, but I have found that humans often respond well to touch if it comes from a place of compassion. I have not been here often, and many of those times I did not interact with simple... with humans. It is like being thrust into an entirely different world where you can watch from a distance, but you do not have the personal experience to easily navigate it. I think you might understand this?"

His glorious eyes fixed on me, and I nodded. "Yes, that's exactly how I'm feeling. Everything around me is the same, and yet everything has changed and I'm not sure how to deal with it."

"I am in the same position. I must be among humans, and I was trained to interact with them, with you, but I get here, and it is so different than what they prepared me for. From the looks of it, your mother did her best to train you, to educate you, in the hope that if you did get pulled into this world, you would have enough training to cope. Compared to Cas and his team, however, you do not have the personal experience yet. That can only come with time."

I sighed. "I know, it's just hard. I feel like I'm back at school and the dumbest kid in the class. Not a good feeling."

Euriel nodded. "I am trying to learn by watching, listening, and experiencing. But my training and my conditioning are strong, and I have no reason to doubt most of what I have been taught. I do not agree with your viewpoint on the union between males of your species. The Creator teaches us that sex should be a godly expression of love between a man and a woman joined before him in marriage in order to conceive children. Anything else is sinful and wrong. I just don't think we're going to see to eye to eye on this."

I made a noise of frustration. "I guess not. But can you at least, just leave them alone and hate them from a distance?"

He nodded solemnly. "I appreciate the experience you have shared with me, of how you perceive it, and I realise that I may need to adapt my reactions to it. You've given me a lot to think about. Thank you." He squeezed my hands, stroking his thumb over the backs.

"For what?" I asked.

"For showing me a little of what it is to be human. For letting me in. And for trusting me with something important to you. No one has ever taken me into their confidence before. It feels... good."

"Um... you're welcome." I smiled at him, rather unsure of this unseen side of him, but the cold had finally got the better of me and I shivered.

Euriel frowned. "You're cold. Come on, let's go into the cathedral. I can show you around."

"What, were you a tour guide in a former life?" I teased as we made our way towards the door, and hopefully, warmth. He looked down and actually grinned at me. Something danced inside my stomach and my breath caught.

"No, but I was kind of hanging around when they built the place, and I have a pretty good memory." My mouth fell open, and he laughed.

"Fine, but afterwards I'm taking you for ice cream," I insisted. His outdated and frankly brainwashed ideals aside, this was a much nicer side of Euriel than I'd seen before, and I was rather interested to see how much I could get away with before he reverted back to his normal asshole self.

"Ice cream? You're freezing!" He looked completely confused.

I grinned. "Yes, but around the corner is apparently a gelato that sells the best chocolate ice cream in the world, and I don't care how cold I am, I am definitely not missing that!"

He shook his head. "Humans. You really are strange beings. Are all human women as confusing as you are?"

I laughed. "It's been said."

Chapter Nineteen

Cas

It was late by the time we all got back to the hotel. We ran in from the taxi, hurrying to escape the downpour that had started minutes before. Alex and Amadi made their goodnights and disappeared fairly quickly, hand in hand. I guessed Florence was living up to the reputation of being a romantic city. I'd been unnaturally quiet throughout dinner, which I'd realised after half an hour of Amadi and Sam trying to get me to join in the conversation that flowed along with the wine.

The table had been outside on the street under the stars, though the patio heaters placed nearby kept us warm in the autumnal air. The pizzas were freshly made and tasted amazing, and the wine was local and one of the best I'd had recently. Everyone else seemed to be chatting away, and even Euriel had joined in now and again without annoying anyone. I hadn't been in the mood. I spent the night drinking my way through my own carafe or two of wine and watching Faith across the table. I couldn't take my eyes off her, though I tried to be as subtle as I could. The light from the candles had lit up her face and made her eyes sparkle, and the wine had brought a warm flush to her cheeks. She was just... beautiful.

As we made our way up the stairs, I heard her laugh at something Sam said, and I could feel the jealousy sitting like a sickness in my belly. She'd repeatedly said she wasn't interested in me, that whatever was between us was in the past, but I'd felt her body respond to me without hesitation when I'd kissed her. I'd felt her heart race, her breath catch in her throat, and her body press against mine, wanting more. I'd tried to hold back, tried to ignore the pull towards her that I couldn't describe. I'd thought she was interested in Sam. She certainly had given that impression, and it was clear he returned her feelings. I'd never seen him so hung up on a girl before, and I'd seen him date plenty. But then this morning, she'd completely thrown me when she told Euriel she'd been with Amadi and Alex. That had shocked me and brought home how little I knew her now. When I'd met her, she'd been shy and inexperienced. She'd been spirited for certain. It had been one of the many things that had made me fall for her. But she'd been innocent. I felt a slight pang of guilt for being the one who had corrupted that innocence. I'd meant to take her on a few dates, but the pull between us was magnetic, and I hadn't been able to resist. As we reached the top of the stairs and I glanced across at her, I could still feel that pull that made me want to turn around, take her in my arms, and push her up against the nearest wall and kiss her like she'd never been kissed before.

Euriel gave me a civil nod as he wandered towards his door. I deliberately hung back, waiting for Sam to say goodnight. He tried to linger for a few minutes, and I could tell he was annoyed with me, but I didn't care at this point. Faith and I had been skirting around the events that triggered our breakup years ago, and I was done guessing what she was alluding to. Some of the things she'd let slip out the other day had really shocked me, and I was determined to get to the bottom of it. It was probably a bad choice of timing, considering the amount of wine we'd both had, but my inhibitions had dropped with the amount of Barolo I'd drunk, and I was hoping hers had too. Tonight, I needed nothing less than honesty from her. Sam disappeared into his room with a sulky glare in my direction.

Faith gave me a quick glance before she opened her own bedroom door. "Goodnight, Cas," she murmured, stepping through and moving to close the door behind her. I refused to be dismissed that easily and pushed my way into the room, gently but insistently.

"You and I need to have a talk."

She shut the door firmly and turned to face me. "*You and I* were over years ago, Cas. I don't *need* to do anything with you anymore." She stared at me defiantly, but I could see a slump to her shoulders and dark circles under her eyes. She was tired and worried about her mother. I wanted to take her into my arms and tell her everything was going to be okay. Fighting the instinct to reassure her, I leaned back against the desk. I watched her emerald eyes trail down my body, taking in every inch of me, and the attention made my heart beat a little faster. I could see the heat in her eyes, and it took her a few seconds to remember that she was mad at me. "Cas, what the fuck is this about?"

I took a breath, trying to play it cool. My heart was in my throat, and I felt on edge. I didn't want her to know that though, I really didn't want her to have any idea of the effect she still had on me after all these years. Not when she was more interested in pretty much anyone except me.

I stared back at her and straightened. I was sick of feeling like I was constantly cocking up with her. "It's about the fact that I really can't take this shit from you anymore, Faith. You're flirting with every guy in our vicinity. For fuck's sake, you were even fluttering your eyelashes at Euriel tonight!"

Her eyes flashed. "I don't flutter my eyelashes at anyone, you patronising tosser, and certainly not that stuck-up pile of feathers. And what the hell do you care?"

"I don't care. It's not fair to Sam." I cursed myself as I said it.

She smiled at me, raising an eyebrow. "Sam? Really?"

"What you did with Amadi and Alex wasn't fair when you've been leading Sam on. And you even described it in detail in front of the poor guy. It's fairly obvious to everyone he has feelings for you. Why would you rub it in his face like that?"

She frowned. "What I did with Amadi and Alex is none of your damn business. Sam didn't mind at all. In fact, he even asked to join next time. I think it's you who has the problem, and I can't figure out why. It's not like you ever really gave a shit, so why now?"

I couldn't reply, I just stared at her. I wanted to yell at her and call her out on her bullshit, but she was right. The silence seemed to stretch on for ages. My breathing grew ragged, and I couldn't form the words I wanted to say. Her breathing was uneven too, I could hear it from where I stood, and I honestly couldn't tell if she was angry with me or wanted me as badly as I wanted her. That thought was all it took, and before I knew it, I was striding across the floor. I reached out and grabbed her arms, pulling her hard against me, and felt her breath catch with the force of her body slamming into mine. Fire flooded my veins as I crushed my mouth to hers, and she didn't resist as I claimed her with my kiss. Everything seemed to pour out of me in the moment, all the frustration and anger and desire, and I realised she was kissing me back the same way.

She bit down hard on my lower lip, and I groaned, gripping her tighter before I slid my hands down to her hips. I felt her hands slide up over my chest before wrapping around my neck to pull me down into the kiss, and my skin burned under her touch. In that moment, she was everything. She was all I could think about. All I could taste, touch, smell, hear, see, and taste. My hands slipped farther down to cup her ass, and I pulled her against my growing hardness. She moaned, and I moved back slightly, breaking the kiss to look at her. Her face was flushed and her eyes were dark and sparkling with desire. Her lips were red and swollen, and I couldn't resist kissing her again, sliding my tongue between them, demanding entrance.

The thought that this wasn't what I wanted, that I'd desired to sit and talk to her danced through my head. I wanted her to tell me what the hell had happened all those years ago, to fill in the pieces that I was obviously missing, but my mind had given up, and my body couldn't hold back from her call. I grabbed at the hem of her t-shirt, yanked it out of her jeans, and slid my hands over the smooth skin of her hips, belly, and lower back. She did the same, raking her long nails down my back, eliciting a mixture of pleasure and pain that made me shiver with delight.

"Fuck," I swore, pushing her against the dresser behind her and pressing myself against her. Her heat poured into me, and I felt like I was holding a fucking firebrand in my arms. I needed more. I tore my mouth from hers, trailing kisses down her neck, nipping and sucking, wanting to taste every inch of her. She ground against me, and I could hear her soft moans in my ear and feel her sweet breath on my neck. Pulling away, I jerked her towards the bed, dragging her shirt over her head. I wrapped her long red tresses around my fist and tossed the fabric away before pulling her close and holding her tight while I devoured her mouth. My other hand fumbled with her bra strap, and I eventually managed to tear it away, flinging it across the room in my haste. Breaking the kiss, I pulled back a little so I could look at her. My eyes roamed over her face, her neck, her arms, and her breasts. She'd filled out a little since I'd last seen her like this, and I could tell she was working out a lot less. Her mother had insisted on a strict physical training schedule. Now instead of a sexy shredded six pack, she was soft and smooth, though still strong and fit. I cupped her breasts together.

"Fucking hell, Faith. It's a damn good job I've already fallen. You'd corrupt an angel," I murmured as I bent down to take one of her nipples into my mouth. She made a soft growling noise in the back of her throat and tipped her head back, arching against me.

"Cas..."

I bit down, loving the sound of my name on her lips. Before the night was over, she'd be screaming it. She moaned again, tangling her hands in my dreads to pull me closer. I ran one of my hands over her other breast, gently massaging her and rubbing my thumb over her nipple. My arm snaked behind her back to support her as I felt her knees weaken.

"God, Faith... you're just so..." I couldn't finish the sentence, my brain wouldn't let me form coherent words. All I could think about was wanting her so badly, wanting to be so deep inside her, that I couldn't tell where I ended and she began.

I pushed her down onto the bed, and she dropped eagerly, pulling me down on top of her. I braced my arms on either side of her head, looking down into those fiery green eyes. She met and held my gaze until I lowered to graze my teeth along her jawline and press my hardness against the heat between her legs. Her eyes closed, and she arched up against me, a low growl of need in her throat. I bit down on her neck, sucking at her soft skin and inching down over her collarbone. Detouring slightly, I took one of her nipples in my mouth, rubbing my thumb across the other until she moaned. But I wanted to taste more. I slid down the bed, kissing and licking my way across her belly, already loosening her jeans and tugging them open—and then I froze. I leaned back and touched my fingers to her skin, tracing the three deep scars that criss-crossed her lower belly.

Pulling the flap of her jeans open, I stared in horror at the mess of scars across the tops of her thighs and mound. "Faith... what the fuck?"

She shifted under me, pulling herself up into a sitting position, her arms around her knees. Her eyes flashed with anger, but I was in too much shock to respond. I couldn't do anything but stare at her. My heart was pounding in my chest, but no longer from desire. Horror and fear flooded my veins, and I felt sick as I started to put two and two together. I had visited her in the hospital, but it had been a few days after her attack. I'd needed some time to put certain things straight, and I hadn't counted on her reaction to me when I'd finally walked through the door. She'd been sitting up in bed, her normal fiery self. I hadn't seen below the blue hospital blankets, below the anger...

"What's the matter, Cas? Can't deal with seeing it first-hand?" she sneered, her voice shaking with barely controlled fury. I shook my head, confused. "I told you what they did to me. More or less. Didn't they give you a full report?"

My brow creased, and I sat back on my heels. "Faith, I... they told me..."

She shook her head and scrambled up from the bed. "I'm sick. Sick and twisted." She turned away from me, grabbing her shirt and pulling it on.

"No, you're not. Scars don't mean you're ugly, they're just part of you. Faith, Peaches, you're—" She whirled around and slapped me so hard I jerked backwards. "Faith, fucking hell—"

"Don't you dare call me that! Don't talk to me like that! I'm... I've had it, Cas. No more. I don't know what the hell is wrong with me. Inside. I'm completely fucked. After all you did..." She paced beside the bed, her fury mounting. She stopped and stared at me, pure hatred etched on her features. "After what you did... I still feel it, that pull I can't resist. How seriously fucked up am I? Angel descended? Ha! I'm a fucking sick and twisted demon."

I stood up and moved towards her, but she recoiled. "Faith, I'm so, so sorry. It was a job, I was undercover, and I needed to keep my cover up. I never meant to put you in danger, but you're right, if I hadn't... if I'd just taken you on a few dates like I was supposed to..." I walked slowly towards her, like she was some wild creature I was afraid to startle with sudden movement. "But I couldn't. You must feel it too, Faith. This thing, whatever it is, between us."

She watched me warily. "Cas..."

I reached out slowly and took her hand. Fuck! The force of her knee slamming square between my legs had me dropping to the floor. My eyes watered, pain filled my lower belly, and I gasped for breath.

She grabbed my hair and wrenched my head back. Her green eyes flickered with a cold fire. "You fucking scum. The only thing that should be between us is a fucking set of bars. I'm assuming it was friends in Concordia who stopped you from going to prison for what you did to me, and when I find out who, I'll make them fucking pay."

My own anger began to burn inside as I remembered what she'd done to me years ago, and I staggered to my feet. "Yes, it was. You put me in a really bad position, and Concordia too. Why, Faith? Why did you tell the police it was me?" I grabbed her shoulders and stared into her eyes. The betrayal, now laid bare, was as harsh as it had been back then. "I went to Hell and back to take care of those fuckers who attacked you, and when I returned, the police were waiting for me." She tried to shake herself free, but I held on, my fingers digging into her skin. They'd leave marks, but I didn't give a shit. I was done taking the fucking blame.

Her eyes burned into mine. "What the fuck did you expect, you psycho? That I was going to let you get away with having me beaten? Did you think that would put me in my place? Well, let me tell you, motherfucker, I'm not the submissive type, and I don't cower to anyone, no matter what you do to me."

"I didn't—"

She pulled away. "You didn't?" Her tone was mocking. She ran her hand down one arm. "You didn't tell them to come after me? Or you didn't tell them to punch me until I fell down? You didn't tell them to stamp on my arm until it broke?"

"No! Faith—"

She opened her jeans to show me the thick scars. "Or maybe you didn't tell them to stab me again and again?" She slid her jeans down, revealing the multitude of shallow scars that marred her legs. "Or maybe you didn't exactly tell them to slice me over and over again while I cried and begged them to stop?"

I felt sick. My words froze in my throat as my eyes fixed onto the scars I'd found when she'd been in my arms only a few minutes ago. She stepped forward and pressed her body to mine. Confused, I slid my arms around her, thinking she wanted to be held. My head was spinning as her hands slipped behind my neck, and she pulled my head down so she could whisper into my ear.

"What didn't you tell them to do, Cas? Cause they told me their orders were from you. They told me I'd seen too much, and you'd commanded them to give me a good warning of what happens to girls who've seen too much, who've out-stayed their welcome. They told me over and over again while they punched me, while they stabbed me, while they sliced into my skin. They even took pictures to show you."

I jerked back in horror, staring at her in disbelief, the pieces finally coming together. "Faith, no—"

"Did you like the pictures? Did you have a good laugh while you flicked through them? The little girl who thought she loved you? Did you plan it all along, or just take the oppor-tunity? When you were taking my virginity, Cas, so gently, so tenderly and loving, did you know then that you'd order your thugs to hold me down and take turns raping me?" She screamed the last sentence, and I broke.

Something inside me shattered, and I couldn't focus any-more. I stepped back from her, my gaze dropping from the look of sheer fury and hatred on the face of the woman I loved beyond measure. The blood in my veins felt like ice, and I thought I was going to throw up. "I—"

"Get out, Cas." Her voice was low and controlled and full of hate.

"Faith," I whispered.

She turned her back on me. "I said, get out."

I turned and stumbled towards the door, not even stopping to do up my shirt. I fled downstairs as though the Hosts of heaven were after me and charged out into the rain. I wanted to scream and cry and hit something and really, *really* hurt something. With a scream of defiance into the torrential downpour, my wings burst from my shoulder blades and I took off into the dark sky, throwing all of my rage and torment into each downwards movement of my wings as I hurtled through the night, leaving my ravaged heart behind.

Chapter Twenty

FAITH

"This is the refectory?" I asked, staring up at the imposing stone edifice from where the taxi had dropped us off in the piazza. "It looks more like a church." Even with the grey skies and heavy clouds, the cream stone stood out against the dark sky like some kind of renaissance painting.

"This is the Santo Spirito Church, the refectory is part of it." Euriel stood next to me, looking up at the stone facade. Even with rain dripping from his nose and his silver hair plastered to his head, he still looked like some kind of stunning marble sculpture. Our afternoon yesterday had been spent wandering around the cathedral. He had certainly known a lot about it, and it was the most I'd heard him talk since I'd met him. It had been nice to see him looking more animated as well. Normally, he just sat in the corner and sulked or sent death glares at whomever he was hating that day. Obviously, the sullen mood had returned as soon as we had met up with the others, but the freshly made pizza and the gorgeous wine had more than made up for it.

Alex stood on the other side of me, his phone open to the museum website. "He's right. The refectory is known as the Cenacola, and is the only surviving gothic-style wing of the ancient Augustine convent built around 1350 and features a large fresco on the eastern wall by the well-known gothic painter Andrea Orcagna."

I looked at him. "Is he important?"

Alex nodded. "He might be. He's the one who painted the fresco that is on your mother's card."

"Oh. Well, I guess he is then. How do we get to the refectory—the Cenacola?"

Alex gestured towards the door of the church where Cas stood chatting with someone in what looked like a security uniform. Cas nodded, thanked the official, and then headed back over to us. My stomach churned as his eyes met mine.

He'd walked straight out of the door last night and had only returned when the rest of us were eating breakfast. He'd been dripping wet and shivering, and he'd smelled strongly of alcohol. I hadn't thought he could feel the cold, but it seemed he could. He'd not said anything, just headed up to his room for a quick shower and met us on the way out. I'd avoided being anywhere near him, and now, close up, I could see how haggard and drawn he looked. His eyes were desolate, almost empty, and there were dark circles under them. If I didn't hate him so much, I'd be worried about him, but all his appearance did was make me angrier. What the hell did he have the right to be broken up about? I was the one he'd fucked over. Or maybe he was just upset his normal magnetism wasn't working on me anymore. I rolled my shoulders, shifting my skin against the fabric of my t-shirt, and relaxed my face into a neutral expression before looking the other way as he came up to us with his information.

"The fresco is in the refectory, but it's not in great condition. Apparently, it was damaged when the church was abandoned for a while in the nineteenth century. Obviously, the fresco is the main reason we're here, but it could just be that Rose was trying to get us to the church itself, so I think we should spread out inside and see what we can pick up."

Sam and Amadi nodded in agreement, and Alex hummed his acknowledgement, still distracted by the website on his phone.

Walking into the church, I paused and looked around at the cream plaster walls and the towering grey columns and archways.

"Beautiful," I breathed. I wasn't religious myself, but I still had a great deal of respect and admiration for the splendour of the buildings religion had been responsible for.

Euriel came to stand next to me, his eyes drifting over the columns and the shine of the organ pipes. "It was designed by a man called Brunelleschi. He devised it with the notion that the church should be a stage for the priest, as well as considering how the physical building would interact with nature such as light, shadows, and space. He wasn't just an architect, he had an idea about how the word of God should be taught and wanted to build the perfect platform for it."

I smiled at him, but Cas glared. "Funny, I don't see the pens for the mindless sheep anywhere about," he muttered.

I reached out and smacked his arm. It didn't hurt him, but I wanted to head off the argument before it began. "We don't have time for your petty arguments, Cas. Behave."

He stared at me, grunted, and moved away without arguing. "The refectory is this way," he called quietly over his shoulder. I sighed and followed him. To my surprise, Euriel did too.

Reaching the refectory, the three of us stood in front of the fresco on my mother's card. It was huge, covering the entirety of the eastern wall, but most of the bottom half was sadly missing.

"Do you know what would have been at the bottom?" I asked Euriel. He shook his head.

"It was supposed to be the Last Supper," Alex said quietly, coming to stand on my other side. I noticed he deliberately stayed far away from Euriel. He glanced down at his phone screen. "It was commissioned by Florentine patrons between 1360 and 1365 to a great gothic master, Andrea Orcagna, and it's thought his brother as well."

Euriel stepped forward, tipping his head up to take in every detail of the crucifixion scene. "Beautiful. Just stunning. Look at the details in the armour, the head coverings. All medieval Florentine costumes. Putting his people at the crucifixion so they could witness it for themselves."

"Who's that guy?" I asked, pointing at a man to the right of the cross, gesturing with his arm. He seemed to stand out more than anyone else.

Euriel frowned. "I think it is supposed to be Longinus."

"Longinus?"

He looked down at me. "The soldier who pierced Christ's side with his lance to make sure he was truly dead. It is the last of the five wounds Christ received during the crucifixion."

"Why would they remember him?"

"He was supposed to have said that Christ was truly the Son of God. And of course, the Lance of Longinus became a highly sought-after religious relic."

"We should have a look around, see if there is anything Rose might have wanted us to notice," Cas spoke up. I had almost forgotten he was there without his constant snide digs at Euriel.

We split up and began to search the refectory, but none of us had any idea what we were looking for. I felt the frustration and desperation growing inside me as it became clear there was nothing to find.

At last, Alex sighed. "There's nothing here. Let's go back to the church and see if Amadi and Sam have turned anything up."

"Can I..." They turned towards me. "Can I just stay here for a few moments? On my own, I mean. I need a couple of minutes."

Cas studied my face then nodded. "Sure. Don't wander off though. Come back through to the main church, we'll wait for you there."

I nodded, and they left.

I turned back to the fresco and sat down on the nearest pew, dropping my face into my hands. I hadn't wanted to show it in front of Cas, but I was becoming convinced this whole trip was a waste of time. I was so certain there would be something here.

"Miss Matthews?" the soft, Italian voice called, and I sat up, brushing the stray tears away.

"Yes?" I answered before realising no one here knew who I was. A stern-looking, middle-aged woman stood in front of me.

"I am Giada Bianchi. May I ask your first name, please?"

I sat up straighter, suddenly feeling nervous. "It's Faith. Who are you?"

She smiled and sat down next to me on the bench. "Giada. I work here at the church. I am sorry for the interruption, but I was asked to deliver something to a young woman by the name of Faith Matthews." She handed me a thick brown envelope with my name on the front. I grabbed it tightly. It was my mother's handwriting.

"How did you... When did you get this?"

"About a month ago, I think. A dark-haired woman approached me and inquired if I worked for the church. When I said I did, she asked me if she could leave something for her daughter who might be visiting in the next few weeks. She described you quite accurately and gave me your name."

I stared down at the package in my hands, trying not to let the tears spill over. "Did she say anything else?"

"No, I'm sorry. Just to make sure you were on your own when I gave it to you."

I nodded and swallowed hard. "Thank you." I smiled at her. "I really appreciate the effort."

She smiled back. "Not that I wouldn't have done it anyway, but your mother insisted on paying me for the service. A donation for the church. I'm glad I was able to pass it on. She seemed like a nice woman." She got up to leave.

"Did she say where she was going after she left the church?"

Giada thought for a moment. "She said she had to get back to the hotel, she seemed like she was in a hurry. I'm sorry, that's all I remember."

"It's fine, thank you so much." I waited until she left the room and then opened the envelope. Inside was a dark blue leather notebook, about half used. I began to flick through it, finding pages and pages of my mother's handwriting, sketches, printouts, and photocopies of paintings and drawings. Choosing a random page, I started to read.

"...*pilgrim Antoninus of Piacenza described in AD570 seeing the crown of thorns with which our Lord was crowned and the lance with which He was struck in the side... Basilica of Mount Zion, Jerusalem. In 615AD Jerusalem was captured by the Persian forces of King Kosgrav II...*" I frowned. It was just another of her research notebooks. I had thought it looked familiar. I flipped through again, scanning over the entries, drawings, and photographs. Yep, just another notebook about relics and artefacts.

I closed it and stood up, tucking the notebook into the back of my jeans under my jacket. Maybe Alex could find something in there that might give us a clue about what was going on. I glanced back up at the fresco, and a wave of worry and sadness washed over me. "Where are you, Rose?" I murmured aloud. "I don't know what you want me to do, to find. What am I missing?" I rubbed my eyes and ran my fingers through my hair in frustration. I hated feeling so helpless.

"Miss Matthews?"

"Yes?" I turned again, thinking Giada had remembered something and come back to tell me, but it wasn't Giada. The woman was tall, with closely cropped blonde hair and... white eyes? Fuck. I turned, but she reached out and grabbed my arm.

A shock wave of pain ran through my body, and I opened my mouth to scream, but the man with her slapped his hand over my mouth and grabbed my wrist, twisting it up behind me so I couldn't pull away without breaking my arm.

"Quiet!" he muttered into my ear. "Or she does it again, and this time it will hurt."

I nodded and forced myself to relax. As I did, so did his grip. I slipped my wrist out of his grasp then snapped my head back as hard as I could. The impact left me slightly disoriented, but my reward was the satisfying crunching sound of his nose breaking. I slammed my elbow into his stomach, and I felt him double over, gasping for breath. The woman narrowed her eyes and came straight for me, but there was no way I was letting this bitch touch me again. I spun around, away from the gasping muscle behind me, with a kick aimed straight at her head. She saw it coming and ducked, but I followed through with my second foot, which caught her in the middle. She recoiled in pain, but her reflexes were like lightning, and her hands fastened tightly onto my ankle. Before I knew it, she had flipped me over, and my back hit the stone floor with a force that left me breathless and stunned. Grabbing my arms, she crossed and knelt on them, pinning them to my chest. Her cold, slender hand fastened over my mouth, and the pain began again. This time, though, she had taken the dampeners off, and agony lanced through me. The world faded away, and all I could feel was the pain until that, too, suddenly eased. My sight didn't return though, and I stood alone in darkness with an increasing sense of panic. Had I blacked out? It was very possible with the torture she was putting me through, but surely I wouldn't be able to think coherently? A familiar feeling crept over me, like I was being watched. There was a presence here in the darkness with me. Unable to resist the need to know, I turned slowly, taking in the darkness until I met a pair of glimmering, cold silver eyes. A rustle of feathers surrounded me, and I felt their razor-sharp edges brush against me, slicing through the skin of my back like a thousand tiny knives. The eyes glided closer, and a raspy, disused voice drifted over the space between us.

"Pain... pain for alwaysssss..."

Terror flowed through me, and I closed my eyes and screamed and screamed.

Someone shook me hard, and my head rebounded off the floor with a crack. My eyes flew open, and I looked up into the white gaze of the blonde woman. She dragged me to my feet, her hand fastened around my wrist.

"What the fuck was that?" The man was staggering to his feet, looking at me with a weird expression. His navy suit was slightly rumpled, and he had a grey sheen to his face that cheered me somewhat.

The woman shrugged. "Damned if I know. I thought I'd lost her for a moment there, and that's never happened to me before." She pulled me around to face her. "That's my little gift, you see. I can inflict pain without doing injury, which comes in handy because you can't die when I punish you. That means you can never escape what I'm doing to you. Just something to keep in mind." She grinned, revealing particularly sharp teeth.

I smiled back sweetly then spat in her face. She pulled a long white cloth out of her pocket and wiped her face with it, keeping her eyes on me. I kept smiling. Her eyes narrowed again, and I braced myself for the pain, but instead of using her ability, she slapped me hard. The man grabbed me again and forced me towards the small door in the side of the room. I tried to glance back at the main door to see if any of the guys were coming back to check on me, but I saw nothing. Fuck.

The small door led to a narrow corridor, and then out into a cramped side street behind the church. A dark-coloured van was parked at one end, and something told me that was my ride. We moved towards it, and I relaxed a little—not enough to make him think I was trying something again though. With that evil bitch and her shock treatment, I wasn't getting out of here anytime soon. The muscle in the suit was holding onto my right arm like a vice, but my left arm was hanging loose at my side next to the blonde. As we moved closer to the van, I slowly slid my hand up behind me and tugged the journal out of my jeans, holding it in place until we reached the van. A tall, skinny man with a shaved head and a tattoo of flying birds on his face jumped out of the driver's seat and slid open the back door.

"Get in, and no messing around." Suit pushed me towards the van roughly, and I took the opportunity to trip and fall onto the step. As I struggled to right myself, I slid the journal under the van past the wheel where they wouldn't catch sight of it.

"Sorry," I muttered, and crawled into the van.

White Eyes got in with me, and I was spun around and pushed onto the van floor. She pinned my wrists behind me, and I felt the tight nip of cable ties slide against my skin. She didn't leave any slack either, pulling them so tight, they pinched badly. I bit my lip and said nothing, not wanting to give her the satisfaction. Suit climbed in with her, and the white cloth passed over my eyes. I panicked as I realised he was going to gag me with it.

"No, please, I'll be quiet, I promise—" My words were cut off as he stuffed a wad of fabric into my mouth and pulled the white one tight between my lips. Dread overwhelmed me, and I struggled, but the cable ties held firm, and the woman sat on the backs of my legs, attaching more ties to my ankles.

When I was secure, the man dragged me up and threw me into a corner so I was half sitting up. "Sit still and stay fucking quiet. Any shit from you, and you'll regret it."

I nodded, my head ringing. I felt sick and dizzy from banging my head on the floor earlier, and for a moment, I thought I might pass out. The idea of falling unconscious while gagged brought on a new flood of panic, and I forced myself to breathe slowly and calm myself down. The van had started up and pulled away while I was struggling, and I realised I had no way of telling where we were going. A vibration in my jacket pocket started me, and I jumped. Suit Muscle cast a suspicious glance my way, but when he saw I wasn't trying to cause trouble, he looked back at White Eyes. They were muttering together in a language I didn't recognise, and I was just grateful he hadn't heard the phone. The rumble of the van must be covering the noise. It vibrated again and again, and I realised it must be the guys wondering where I was. Even though I couldn't answer, it gave me some comfort to know they were looking for me, and I found myself waiting for the buzz as the van bumped along mystery roads. As time dragged on, the space between the vibrations grew longer until they stopped altogether. I leaned my head against the metal panel and closed my eyes, praying they hadn't given up on me.

Chapter Twenty-One

FAITH

I came awake when the van door slid aside with a crash. Whether I had fallen asleep or just blacked out, I wasn't sure, but we had obviously travelled some distance. We were in the countryside. In the growing twilight, I could make out rows of grape vines stretching off into the distance and the dark outlines of cypress trees standing like formidable guards around the building we had arrived at. The cable ties had cut off the circulation to my feet, and pins and needles flooded my legs from sitting on them for too long. I could barely stand, and they seemed to have no intention of removing the ties. Instead, Suit and Bird Boy slipped a hand under my arms and dragged me towards the door that White Eyes was unlocking.

The building itself looked like a derelict farmhouse, and with a sinking feeling, I realised I couldn't see another building or lights anywhere. The door came open, and I was hauled through it and down the corridor beyond into a large kitchen. They'd obviously been here a while. Dirty cups and dishes were piled in the sink, and a rather large rat was gnawing on an old chicken carcass. White Eyes stepped forward and, with a movement faster than I could see, reached out and grabbed the rat. I watched in disgust as she stared at it, smiling coldly. I didn't know rats could scream, but the sound it was making was fairly close. Her eyes flicked up to Suit, and he stepped forward, licking his lips. Sliding his hand behind her head, he pulled her mouth to his, crushing her back against the wall. She moaned loudly and rubbed herself against him. My eyes dropped to the rat in her hand, who had stopped squealing as she squeezed it tighter and tighter. Blood started to stream from its eyes and mouth, and I looked away, fighting the urge to vomit, which with the gag would surely end in me choking to death. Bird Boy cleared his throat, and I heard the two pull apart. I opened my eyes to find White Eyes right in front of me. She smiled and raised her hand slowly. It was covered in rat blood. Gently, as though she was touching a lover, she ran her fingertips down my face, streaking it with red, then she slipped her fingers into her mouth. I swallowed but met her stare.

She grinned. "We're going to have so much fun with this one."

Suit came up behind her and put his arms around her, staring at me over her shoulder. "And I fully intend to reap the benefits."

Bird Boy grunted and began to drag me towards another door at the end of the kitchen. It opened to reveal a flight of stairs descending into the darkness. Another cellar. What the fuck was it with people having cellars? There was only one large room below the building, and it was fairly bare. The sight of a plumbed toilet, a filthy sink, and three dirty mattresses around the edges of the room gave me a sick feeling that they had used this building for this purpose before—whatever this purpose was. At the top of the stairs, Bird Boy paused and took out a switchblade. I held my breath until he bent down to cut open the cable ties around my ankles.

"Down," he grumbled, and gave me a shove. It wasn't much of a shove, except that I was still feeling fairly numb. My knees were weakened, and his push threw me off balance. I rolled down the stairs, unable to break my fall because of my bound wrists. I lay on the concrete floor, breathing hard and wondering if any of the limbs that hurt like hell were actually broken. Bird Boy gave a huff of frustration and clomped down the stairs.

A groan of pain escaped me as he rolled me onto my stomach and cut the ties around my wrists. I gasped as the blood started to flow properly again, but he seized one wrist and dragged me over to a mattress. I dug my heels into the ground and started yanking back. He was stronger than he looked though, and he pulled me onto the mattress, kneeling on my back and pressing my face into the grimy fabric. I held my breath, praying to whatever god would listen that he was simply going to tie me up. I heard the clink of metal behind me and felt him tugging my boots off. Forgetting that I was gagged just for a moment, I turned, trying to tell him if he damaged my boots I would not be fucking impressed. Metal cuffs clicked around my ankles, and then I felt his hands on my body.

Horror filled me, and I began to struggle, trying to kick him, hit him, but his legs pinned me down and his hands still roamed over me. He rolled me over beneath him and grabbed my wrists, transferring them to one hand as he continued. I realised he was only searching me, and I stopped fighting. It only took him a few seconds before he located my phone, which he pocketed. I wasn't carrying anything else. Sam had put my wallet in his pocket after he'd spotted it sticking out of my jacket in case we were cased by pickpockets, and other than my phone, I didn't need much with me. Satisfied I wasn't carrying a weapon, or another phone, he stood up, and without a backwards glance, climbed the stairs to the kitchen and slammed the door shut, leaving me in darkness.

Shifting my legs onto the mattress, I ignored the aches and pains from my treatment and curled up, pulling my leather jacket tight around me. It didn't give much warmth, and it was chilly down here. Refusing to let myself think in case I plunged into useless hysterics, I concentrated on the footsteps I could hear above me until they finally faded into silence.

"Are you hurt badly?" a soft voice asked from the far corner.

I sat bolt upright. "Who are you?"

"My name's Amara. Are you okay? You fell down those stairs pretty hard."

I stretched slowly, wondering the same thing myself. "I think so. It doesn't seem like anything's broken, but I think I'm going to feel it tomorrow."

Amara gave a short, sharp laugh. "Trust me, tomorrow you'll be wishing all you had was a broken bone."

I drew my knees up to my chest and wrapped my arms around them, trying to stop my heart from hammering. "Why? What happens tomorrow?"

"Well, if you're here for the same reason as me, I imagine Fisher will be here in the morning, and then they'll start questioning you."

"Questioning me about what? I don't know anything. I have no idea who these people are!" My voice grew embarrassingly high-pitched, and I forced myself to breathe.

"Quiet! You really don't want them to hear you."

I looked over to where the voice was coming from. As the moon rose outside, the small window let in increasingly more light, and I was starting to see grey outlines in the shadows. Amara was lying curled up on another mattress, though I only spotted her because she shifted positions.

"Why are you here?"

I saw a small movement, which might have been a shrug. "I'm not entirely sure where here is. I know I'm not in England anymore, because when they took me, I felt us taking off and landing. I figure we must be somewhere in Europe because the flight wasn't that long, but I'm not sure where."

"We're in Italy. Well, I think we are. I was taken in Florence, but we drove for several hours, so I guess we could be anywhere now. I definitely didn't get on a plane though. How long have you been here?"

She sighed. "A little over five weeks. I've been keeping count, watching the sun rise and set. They keep questioning me about this ancient relic, but I don't know anything. It was my colleague's project, but they insist she must have told me about it. I mean, she told me bits, but nothing I've told them seems to be helpful."

I freeze, my skin growing cold. "Amara, what do you do?"

"I work in an archaeology department for a university." She laughed, but there was no humour in it. "I mean, I'm not exactly concealing classified information terrorists would want."

I swallowed. "Who... who was your colleague, Amara?"

"What?"

"The colleague you mentioned. What was her name?"

"Oh, her. Matthews, Dr Rose Matthews. Ring any bells?"

I nodded, even though she couldn't see me. Wetness dripped down my face, mixing with rat blood. "Yes. It does. She's my mother."

"Oh." Amara went quiet and wouldn't speak anymore. The darkness seemed to grow around us again. I pressed my face into the mattress and cried as quietly as I could.

The next morning dawned, cold and damp. I cringed at the thought of moving from the tiny pocket of warmth I'd created where my body was in contact with the mattress, but judging by the quiet snores in the corner, I could tell Amara was still asleep, and desiring to preserve my dignity as much as possible, I wanted to use the loo before she woke up. The chains stretched just far enough for me to relieve myself and splash some water on my face. I scrubbed at my face, trying to remove any remaining rat blood, and then ran my fingers through my hair.

My back itched again. It never seemed to stop now, and I rubbed myself against the rough wall, trying to relieve it. I slid down slowly, stretching my legs out in front of me as I sat on the mattress. After crying for what felt like hours, I'd given myself a stern, silent talking to. I'd seen the resources the guys had first-hand, and I was certain they would come for me. I just had to hold out until they did. I'd worked out that they couldn't possibly have my mother, otherwise they wouldn't need to question me, and I had convinced myself that she was hiding out somewhere away from these evil fuckers. I wasn't going to disclose anything that might give her away.

When Amara woke, she wasn't in the mood for talking. She relieved herself with no apparent embarrassment and then laid herself back down on her mattress, staring up at the ceiling and refusing to speak. I studied her from my own mattress. Her limp, shoulder-length brown hair was dirty and matted with what could have been blood, though I saw no external injuries. Her face was sunken and gaunt, her eyes like golf balls in deep sockets. She was dressed in suit trousers and a light-coloured shirt that hung open to reveal the vest underneath. Her low black heels were placed neatly together at the end of the mattress, and at the sight of them, I turned my head to see my own boots in a similar position.

Seeing them made me feel a little better after viewing Amara's state in the light. I was starting to get very nervous about what was coming. Okay, terrified. I was fucking terrified. But there was no way I was going to let them know that. Plus, I was a witch, wasn't I? I mean, I'd never been taught how to use magic for practical purposes. It was more like studying the theory for a driving test before you were allowed to get behind the wheel. But I had to be able to do something, surely. I was still pondering this when the door above creaked open and footsteps sounded down the stairs.

Suit and Bird Boy came down the staircase. To my surprise, Suit offered me a bottle of water. I looked closely at it, but the seal didn't seem to be broken, so I turned the lid and drank deeply. I watched as Bird Boy grabbed a chair from the side of the room and dragged it slowly into the middle of the space.

"Take a seat." Suit gestured towards the chair.

I stretched out on the mattress, my back up against the wall. "I'm good here, thanks. I was never one for upright chairs, always being told off for slouching when I was a kid."

Suit cocked his head, then he lunged at me suddenly, making me jump, and his fingers twisted into my hair. I gritted my teeth hard as he dragged me to the chair and slammed me down into it. Bird Boy was waiting with more cable ties, which he used to attach my wrists to the back legs of the chair. Crouching down, he did the same for my ankles, binding them to the front legs. I aimed a kick at him, but he caught my foot easily and twisted it sharply, causing me to cry out. I glared at him, imagining kicking his ass once I got free. Suit stepped back and turned to leave.

"Now what?" I asked.

He turned his head. "Now, you wait." The two of them went back up the stairs, closing the door behind them. I heard the key turn but noticed they didn't pull the key out of the door. I filed that bit of information away in my mind for later.

"Amara?"

"Mmmm."

"Amara!"

"What?" She didn't move.

"This Fisher, what does he do exactly?"

"Oh, he doesn't do anything. He just asks the questions. It's the others you need to worry about."

"Why? What are they going to do?" I don't know why I asked. I was assuming I wasn't going to come out of this particular situation unscathed, but I wanted to be prepared for what was coming.

"They hurt you."

Great. Fan-fucking-tastic. The door opened again, and this time Suit and Bird Boy brought up the rear. White Eyes came down first, dressed in a white trouser suit and looking very out of place in this dump. Behind her was a man I didn't recognise, and who, I guessed, was the infamous Fisher. He didn't appear very threatening. In fact, he looked more like an accountant with his tweed suit and red spotted bow tie. He even carried a leather briefcase. When Suit and Bird Boy reached the floor, they went to a corner of the room and dragged a table and chair forward, which looked a lot more comfortable than the one I was currently strapped to.

Fighting the sick fear rising inside me, I lifted my chin. "Mr Fisher, I presume?" That was good. All I needed was a fluffy white cat in my lap.

He nodded in my direction and set his briefcase down on the table. "Miss Matthews."

"I'd shake your hand, but I'm afraid I'm rather indisposed at the moment." I nodded at my restraints with an apologetic smile.

A flicker of surprise crossed his face, although he didn't respond. He sat down, opened the briefcase, and took out a lined pad of paper and a posh-looking pen.

"Am I to understand you are in charge of this motley crew?" I continued.

He raised his eyebrows. "They are here at my bidding, yes."

"Good, good. In which case, I'm afraid, I have several complaints to make about their treatment of me. Firstly, the van. I mean, I'm all for the 'oldie is a goodie' scenario, but really. Mercedes makes vans too, and they're a lot more comfortable inside. I would advise upgrading before your next arranged kidnapping." I smiled politely.

He frowned, obviously confused. "Miss Matthews. I am here to question you about your mother, Rose Matthews, and her recent work on the Arma Christi."

I smiled and nodded. "Yes, yes, of course, and we'll get to that, but I haven't quite finished. My second complaint is the lack of refreshments. Granted, after a few days in Florence, I could stand to lose a couple of pounds. Too much pizza and ice cream, if you know what I mean. But still, the absence of some nibbles and a glass of something to drink was rather irritating, to say the least." Trying to strike the balance between delaying him as long as possible and annoying the hell out of him was tricky, but I swear he almost smiled. Clearly, I was amusing him. Well, that was something. He glanced over at White Eyes, and at the look, she walked over to me.

I stared straight ahead at Fisher. "Thirdly, I'm afraid you need to sack your cleaners. The facilities are simply—" I screamed as White Eyes brought her hand down on my shoulder and pain flowed through me. When she finally released me after a nod from Fisher. I was trembling and breathing hard. Fuck. Come on, where the fuck were the guys? Taking a deeper, slightly shaky breath, I smiled up at White Eyes. "Thank you, that really woke me up. I was feeling a little drowsy there for a moment."

She glared at me and lifted her hand again, but dropped it at the sound of Fisher's voice. "Miss Matthews, did your mother discuss the Arma Christi with you?"

I shook my head. "No, not that I recall. Now, as I was saying—" White Eyes brought her hand down again, and again I screamed as the pain filled every cell of my body.

Fisher leant forward on his elbows. "Miss Matthews, as much as I am enjoying your little wisecracks, I'm afraid I have a train to catch this evening, and I require you to divulge your information before then."

"I guess you'll be missing your train then. I hope you can get a refund." I cringed as White Eyes moved, but nothing happened, and I realised she had stepped behind me, out of sight.

Fisher sighed. "Then we shall have to work together to persuade you." He nodded to Suit and Bird Boy who walked forward. Suit stepped behind me and placed a hand on each of my shoulders, holding me still. Bird Boy reached into his jacket and pulled out a rather sharp-looking knife.

All pretence forgotten, I recoiled at the sight of it, and Fisher smiled. "Miss Matthews, would you like to tell me now?"

"I told you, my mother didn't discuss her work with me." Bird Boy knelt down in front of me and began to use his knife to cut up one leg of my jeans. When he reached the knee, he took a piece in each hand and tore until it reached the top of my thigh.

Fisher watched with a calm, detached expression. "Mr Blake here is a very useful chap to have around. He's part demon, you see. Only part, and yet we think an ancestor must have been fairly high up in Hell's hierarchy, because he's very handy with controlling the elements." Bird Boy leaned back, and with a twist of his wrist, a small fireball appeared in his hand.

I looked back at Fisher. "Look, I'm telling you, I have no idea what an Arma Christi is. I'm sorry, but I really, really don't."

Fisher nodded seriously. "I'm sorry too, Miss Matthews."

Bird Boy blew on his hand, and a lash of flame darted out, licking my ankle. The heat was seriously intense, and I screamed as he moved slowly up my leg, burning my flesh as he went. When he reached the top of my leg, he sat back on his heels, and with a small *pfff*, the fireball went out. I hung my head for a minute, breathing hard. Tears dripped onto the charred skin, and I winced. The itch across my back had intensified, and I felt like my skin was burning there too.

Fisher's voice broke the silence. "Miss Matthews, if you, as you so insist, do not know anything about the Arma Christi, then I will ask another question. Where is the Spear of Destiny?"

I gave a forced laugh. "Oh, for fuck's... I don't know what the fuck you are talking about!" I jerked back hard in my chair as Bird Boy moved, but instead of changing to my other leg, he got to his feet and stepped over to stand next to Suit. Suit brought his hands to my face and tilted my head back against his chest.

I looked up at him, breathing heavily. There was no pity or hint of mercy in his eyes. They were just... flat. I took a deep breath. "Sorry to disappoint you, but I was never very good at deepthroating. Sensitive gag reflex and all that." Suit just smiled and moved his hands so one was on the back of my head with his fingers twisted in my hair, and the other was around my lower jaw. I felt the panic rising up inside and started to struggle, but I was pinned still. Bird Boy held his hand above my face, and I flinched, waiting to feel searing heat on my face, but instead his hand began to drip. Surprise struck me first, and then the horrifying realisation of what was about to happen slammed into me. Seconds after it did, so did the water.

Chapter Twenty-Two

Cas

CAS

I scrubbed my hands over my face, hoping it would make me feel slightly more awake. Last night, there had been no question of getting any sleep. I could barely sit still, let alone lie down and close my eyes. Everything Faith had told me was hurtling through my mind over and over again. I replayed that night so many times, becoming angry, heartbroken, irate, and tormented. She was right. It had all been my fault. I was the reason she was attacked and hurt so badly. I'd seen her in the hospital, but she'd been full of bravado and fire when I'd visited, I just hadn't realised how far they'd gone. The thought of their hands on her made me see red, and I could feel my heart racing and fire flooding my veins again. I took a deep breath.

Alex looked up from his phone. "You okay, Cassiel?"

"Fine," I muttered.

"You don't seem like your normal, cheery self today."

I looked at him, raising my eyebrows. I'd only known Alex for a few decades, and he was not usually one for cracking jokes. Faith was obviously having an effect on him too. He smiled shyly.

"What makes you think there's something wrong?" I inquired. "I could have just slept badly."

He nodded. "Well, yes, that's true. Only..." He trailed off and glanced back down at his phone.

I sighed. "Only what?"

"Um, well, I saw you leave last night. I was down in the reception doing some work. You seemed... well, upset. And..."

I rolled my eyes. "And?"

He shrugged. "I was there working all night, and you didn't come home before dawn. Plus, there's the minor detail of major storms over the Sahara last night. Witnesses report seeing lightning and fire streak across the sky many times. Meteorologists are at a loss as to what caused it." He held his phone up to show me the news story. "I'm guessing seriously frustrated and pissed off fallen angels aren't on their list of possible causes, but they're definitely on mine."

I shifted my eyes from the phone screen and met his, and I grinned guiltily. "Anyone see me?"

He shook his head. "Not in any report I've read yet. I think you were lucky though."

I took a breath. "Good. Look, Alex—"

He shook his head. "I haven't mentioned it to the others, and I won't. Just, if you need someone to talk to, I'm here. Or if you need to let off steam, take Amadi and beat each other up. Let's try to avoid the exposure of divine beings to humans just because a girl told you to get lost."

I opened my mouth to retort, then thought better of it, and glanced over at the door to the fresco. "She's been a while. Maybe someone should check on her." Alex nodded. He walked over to Amadi and murmured something to him before they both disappeared through the door.

I wandered over to Sam, who was making a slow circuit of the church. He seemed antsy. "You okay?"

"Yeah, it's just... it's been a few days. I could do with getting somewhere with some open spaces."

"Not a problem. There's clearly nothing here, nothing obvious anyway. Maybe tomorrow you and Faith could hire a car and go to the beach. I think it's only about an hour away."

The mere mention had Sam's eyes lighting up. "Oh yeah, that would be cool. We could go early and pick up some stuff from the bakers and do a whole picnic thing..." His voice trailed off, and I turned to see what he was looking at. Alex and Amadi had come back through the door and were heading straight for us, identical expressions of worry on their faces. *Faith.*

"What's up?" I asked as they got to us.

"It's Faith. She's not there." Amadi's voice was rough, and I frowned.

"What do you mean, she's not there?"

"I mean, she's not there! She's not in the refectory. We searched the place, she's gone." His voice rose slightly, and I put a hand on his shoulder to try to calm him.

"Well, she didn't come back in here, I'd have smelled her." Sam looked at me, concern etched across his features.

"There's a door out into the alleyway behind the church, but she wasn't there either. We came to let you know before we went wandering out into the city. Maybe Sam could catch her scent?" Alex was calmer than his partner, but I could still see the doubt in his eyes.

I nodded. "Let's go. Alex, could you find Euriel? I think he wandered off to the other gallery." The rest of us headed through the refectory and out into the alley. Pausing, I let Sam step forward.

He sniffed at the air, then bent down towards the ground briefly before straightening up. "She definitely came this way, but there are other scents, too, that I don't recognise. I think someone was with her. Maybe more than one, but I can't really tell."

"Are you sure someone was with her? Could it have been someone else who came through here recently?"

He shrugged. "It could be, I suppose, but, I don't know, something tells me she wasn't alone."

"Okay, which way?" He gestured down the alleyway towards the road at the other end, and I jogged towards it. She hadn't been gone that long, so she couldn't be too far ahead. Stepping out onto the road, I glanced up and down to see if I could catch any sight of her, but there was nothing. Just a few Florentines going about their everyday life.

I sighed with frustration and waited for the others to catch up. "I can't see her. Any idea which way she went, Sam? If we go quickly, we might catch up with her."

Sam sniffed the air again, trotting off down the road one way, then doubling back and trying the other direction. He shook his head. "Sorry, Cas. There's nothing. Her trail ends here."

I ran my hands over my face and made a loud noise of frustration that had a few passers-by giving me slightly worried looks before crossing over to the other side of the street. "Now what? We go back to the hotel—wait, has anyone tried calling her?"

Amadi rolled his eyes. "Only every few minutes since we realised she was gone. Both Alex and I have been trying. It rings out to the answerphone."

"Cassiel, I may have something." I glanced over to Euriel, who had drifted behind us, clearly less worried about the disappearance of a lowly human than the rest of us. He was bending over at the side of the street, and as he straightened, I saw he held a notebook. Flicking through it briefly, he handed it over. "It appears to be a journal concerning some religious artefacts. Possibly belonging to her mother?"

I thumbed through it, but my head was spinning, and I practically threw it at Alex. "You look, I can't make heads or tails out of this stuff."

Alex nodded. "I'll take a look. Why don't you go and speak to the church security? Let them know you think a friend of ours might have been taken against her will."

I scoffed. "Why do you think humans could be of any help right now? Surely if she's been taken, it'll be by someone with supernatural abilities."

Alex shrugged. "That's a safe assumption, however, the humans have something we don't."

"And what's that?"

He turned and pointed to the corner of the building. "Security cameras." Smartarse.

"Ah, *gracias, gracias.*" I waved at the security guard as I left the office. It had taken more than a little persuasion to stop him from going to the *polizia*, but I had assured him we were a private security firm and it would be extremely detrimental to the wellbeing of our client, and he seemed convinced. The video had been fairly damning, and I had struggled not to put my fist through the stone wall at the sight of Faith being dragged into the van, her hands bound. She had looked furious rather than afraid, which had brought a brief smile to my lips. Obviously, the van's registration had been covered, and the cameras had lost them heading towards the centre of the city, so it had been of little help other than giving me a brief look at her kidnappers.

I walked back to the hotel, staring at the pictures I had taken of the footage on my phone. The guy wasn't really known to me, but I had a funny feeling I knew the woman from somewhere, I just couldn't place her. Her face was blurred, but I thought I remembered someone from a while ago who tended to wear all white and had white hair. I growled at myself, cursing my lack of memory when I needed it. Maybe if we hadn't had that fight last night, she wouldn't have gone off alone. I should have left one of the guys in there with her, no matter what she wanted. She would have been pissed at me, but at least she would have been safe. The shadows were growing long as I finally arrived at the hotel. Just as I reached out to push open the front door, it swung open and Euriel stepped through. He said nothing, just moved down the steps to the street.

"Where are you going?"

He stopped and didn't look back. "I'm off to find dinner."

I shook my head in disbelief. "Faith has been kidnapped, and all you can think of is your stomach? Fucking hell, Euriel!"

He spun around. "Don't use that language with me, Cassiel, and don't forget, it's Lord Euriel. As in your superior. In case you had forgotten, I am here on a different assignment than you, and a simple human will not derail me from that task. Nor am I about to put myself in danger for her."

I stalked down the steps. "Are you for real? She's been taken, I saw it myself on the fucking camera. And you are just going to pretend nothing's happened?"

He turned away, shrugging. "Humans go missing all the time. She's just another lost soul. No one important." I reached and grabbed him by the shoulder, pulling him around before driving my fist into his face. He jerked backwards, but I gave him his due, he didn't go down.

"I'll overlook that minor mistake, but just this once, Cassiel. I suggest you get a grip on your emotions. One such as you should not be forming emotional attachments to a human. It weakens you."

I really saw red then, and my fist smashed into his jaw. I swung again, but he blocked me, and I got a well-placed jab to the stomach that had me gasping. I didn't pause though and swung out again, hearing a very satisfactory crack as his nose broke. He yelled and jumped back.

"Control yourself, Cassiel. I suggest if you care so much about the girl, you would be better off directing your anger towards her assailants rather than at me. But keep in mind, I shall not be letting this go, whatever your pitiful emotional state." He turned and began to walk away.

Gasping, I leaned on the railing by the steps of the hotel. "You're a fucking coward, Euriel. You don't care about anyone other than yourself. And you're too afraid to. If you won't risk your life for a human, then what are you fucking good for?" The last comment was shouted loudly as he disappeared around the corner. For the second time that day, a couple of people crossed to the other side of the street. Right now, I couldn't give a shit. I turned and went back into the hotel, making my way two steps at a time to Alex and Amadi's room.

Amadi looked up as I burst in without knocking. "Good job we weren't in a compromising position, Cas. I'd have had to give you a good ass kicking if I caught you lusting over my pretty boy's fine behind." I glared at him, and he grinned, but the smile didn't quite reach his eyes. He turned back to Alex, who was sitting on the bed with his back against the headboard, tapping away on his laptop. Glancing over to the open French doors, I saw Sam on the balcony, leaning on the railing.

"Where's Euriel?" Amadi asked.

"Went off to get something to eat. I don't think he's going to be much help." I took a breath, trying to control my anger, which seemed to be constantly bubbling under the surface at the moment. "Sam!" I called through the door, and he came back into the room, perching on the edge of the small sofa. I looked around at them, not wanting to confirm what they probably already knew.

"I looked at the security tapes, and yes, they show Faith being put into a van at the end of the alleyway. No license plate and no clear view of the attackers, though one was a woman with very light hair, dressed in white."

Amadi's head snapped up. "All white? Was her hair short?"

I nodded. "You know her? I thought she looked familiar, but I can't place her."

Amadi tipped his head back and stared at the ceiling. "I ran across her in Dis. In Gehenna." He looked straight at me. "Cas, this is bad. She was an enforcer there. If she's one of the people who took Faith..."

Sam straightened. "An enforcer? So basically a torturer?"

Amadi nodded. His skin had turned greyish. I knew he had horrific memories from that time and didn't want to imagine what this woman could do to Faith.

I pushed the thought away and leaned against the edge of the desk. "Alex, anything?"

Alex looked up, and his face started to turn an interesting shade of red. "Well, um, actually yes. So, back at home, I may have... kind of... possibly... put a tracker on her phone..."

"What?"

Everyone turned and stared at him, and the blush deepened. "Well, I just thought... and Hargreaves suggested... just as a precaution, you understand..."

I walked over to the bed and turned his screen around to see a map. "So you can track her?"

He shook his head. "Could. And did. The tracker only works if the phone is turned on. I traced as long as I could until it disappeared."

"Someone found her phone," Sam surmised, also walking over to look. "They obviously turned it off. Where was the last location?"

"Here." Alex pointed to the middle of a long stretch of road then zoomed out, showing an area several hours' drive from the city.

"Fuck!" I ran my hand over my face, wishing I'd managed to get more sleep the night before. "Okay, we'll need a car. We should all go. If that white bitch is as bad as Amadi thinks, we'll need all of us to get her out."

"Already on it," Amadi inserted. "I spoke to the concierge an hour ago. There's a car hire place about four blocks from here, and he's organised a pickup for us first thing in the morning. We can leave early." I wanted to punch the wall at his words. The morning was still several hours off. He seemed to sense what I was thinking, as he stood up and put his hand on my arm. "We'll find her, Cas. She's strong, she'll be okay. She knows we wouldn't abandon her."

I nodded. "Yes, I... okay. I'm going to have a shower and get changed. Try to clear my head. I should probably fill Hargreaves in too."

Amadi shook his head. "It's the middle of the night. He'll be asleep and can't help anyway. We'll fill him in tomorrow once we've got Faith back. Right now, you need to rest. You look dead on your feet, and you won't be much help if you can barely keep your eyes open. Alex is going to keep trying to find out more about who's taken her."

I sighed. He was right, I needed to be at full strength tomorrow. Pacing the floor would not help her right now. I turned towards the door, and for the second time, nearly collided with Euriel coming through it. To my astonishment, he was carrying four pizza boxes and a carrier bag, which he dumped on the table.

"Any news?" he asked quietly. I stayed silent while Sam quickly filled him in. He nodded, careful not to look in my direction. "So we leave early. Fine. I thought you all might need something to get your strength up." He turned and left, pushing past me without comment, and I looked back at the others who were still sitting there in shock. After a moment, Sam walked over and opened the bag.

He looked up at me with such a stunned expression, it might have been comical in a more relaxed situation. "It's beer. Euriel bought us pizza and beer. I didn't think the world was ending for another few millennia."

"Hmm... what I want to know is who broke his nose?" I looked over at Amadi and shrugged, trying to appear innocent. The break had almost healed, but Amadi had seen the thin white scar that remained for now. Amadi narrowed his eyes at me, then turned his attention to the pizza box Sam chucked his way.

I glanced back out into the empty hallway, then shut the door and sat down to eat, trying desperately not to think of what Faith was doing and praying she was okay.

Just a few more hours, Peaches, and we'll come and get you. Just hold on.

CHAPTER TWENTY-THREE

FAITH

I lost it. I'm not ashamed of that at all. Drowning has always been my greatest fear, and once he began to pour water over my mouth and nose, all coherent thought flew out of my head except to survive. I pulled hard at my ties and felt the solid plastic cut through my skin, but the pain wasn't even a distraction. The chair shook under me as I attempted to throw my head from side to side, but Suit held me fast and the water just kept coming. It filled my mouth and nose, and every time I tried to draw a breath, I choked and coughed. It felt like it went on forever, but it probably only lasted a few seconds. Bird Boy pulled back, and Suit let go of my head. I sat upright, coughing up water and shaking violently. My heart was racing, and when I opened my eyes, I could see the cable ties had drawn blood where I had pulled at them. Fisher got up from behind the table and walked over to stand in front of me.

Bending down, he used his pen to push a lock of hair out of my face and then looked into my eyes. "Now, Miss Matthews, this can all stop. All I need to know is what your mother told you about the location of the Spear of Destiny." I coughed again and spat into his face with what energy I had left. He backed up and pulled out a thick cotton handkerchief to wipe his face. After he had, he passed the handkerchief to Suit. "Continue."

"No, please... please!" I wasn't beyond begging now.

Fisher went and sat back down. "Miss Matthews, you can end this at any point."

"But I don't—"

Suit grabbed my hair again, wrenching my head back, but this time he draped the handkerchief over my face so I couldn't see. I struggled again, ignoring the sharp pain of the ties. There was no warning. The water cascaded onto my face and the fabric made it worse. I tried to hold my breath, but that just meant the cloth stuck to my face with the water, and I felt like I was being smothered. I opened my mouth to try to inhale, but my mouth and throat were instantly filled with water, and I began to splutter again.

"The location, Miss Matthews."

The water kept pouring, and I couldn't have told him even if I knew what he was talking about. All I could think about was trying to get as much oxygen as possible. I was drowning. Desperation overtook me, and I fought as hard as I could. No way was this fucker taking me down. I was not going to die in this fucking shithole with these wankers. A sensation rose from the ground, through my feet, and throughout my body. My shoulder blades burned, and I thought I heard bones crack. My fingertips sparked and tingled as though I had received a static shock, and a jolt went through me. I heard shouts, and the grip on my hair released. The water stopped instantly, though the wet cloth stuck to my skin, and I could feel my air supply dwindling. I couldn't spit the water out with the cloth on. With a sudden thought, I threw my body weight to one side. The chair toppled, and I hit the floor hard. The cloth detached slightly, allowing me to take a ragged breath of air.

Two polished shoes appeared in front of my face, and I heard White Eye's voice. "How the fuck did she do that? She's supposed to be mundane. We weren't told she could channel electricity. What the fuck, Fisher?"

"Mundane, my ass," I muttered. Hands grabbed the chair, and I was yanked up again. Bird Boy stood in front of me, and the expression in his flat black eyes was terrifying. I felt sick to my stomach, and I couldn't stop violently shaking. I felt certain he was going to kill me. My heart was still hammering from the water torture, and I could feel adrenaline racing through every cell. The thunder of my heartbeat seemed to spread throughout my body, and it felt as though the ground itself began to rumble. In horror, I glanced down at the crack widening across the concrete floor as it started to shake under our feet. Dust began to fall from the ceiling.

"Everybody out!" Fisher shouted, grabbing his briefcase and starting up the stairs. He paused briefly. "Bring the girl."

"I'm not fucking touching her again. Bitch shocked me good." Suit followed Fisher up the staircase. "Let her get fucking crushed."

Bird Boy reached out and slashed the cable ties on my ankles with his knife, then he took a key from his pocket and unlocked the manacles. White Eyes stood behind me and released my wrists, grabbing hold of one and tugging me up off the chair. The ground was really shaking now. Plaster and loose bricks began to fall down around us as the two of them dragged me towards the stairs. I could barely walk, and the burn down my leg was really starting to hurt. I cried out in pain.

"Come on, this whole place is going to go," White Eyes yelled at me as I fought against them.

I grabbed hold of the stair rail then turned. "What about Amara?"

White Eyes looked up at Fisher.

He shrugged. "Leave her, we don't need her anymore."

My mouth fell open in shock, but they paid no heed and dragged me up the stairs. "No, wait—" I stopped as pain lanced through me.

White Eyes glared angrily at me, and my body trembled. "I am not getting buried under here. Now move, or I'll show you pain like you've never felt before!" We stumbled up the stairs and out into the hallway. The shaking was getting worse, and parts of the ceiling had already come down up here. We skirted around a large piece on the floor and staggered outside through the open door—right into absolute chaos.

Still unsteady with the pain that danced through my veins, I leaned heavily against the wall as I took in the scene before us. Blocking the driveway was a large dark-coloured car, and from behind it, a flurry of gunfire sounded. Suit had pistols in both hands and was firing back, covering Fisher who was making his way towards a second car parked near the building. Bird Boy was conjuring fireballs and sending them flying into the car in front, leaving deep charred dents in the bodywork. Something blurred across the courtyard, and Bird Boy flew back, slamming into the wall of the house. At the same time, a massive wolf leaped over the car and headed straight for Fisher. I gasped as Cas and Amadi ran around the car and headed for Suit as he paused to reload. He raised his guns and aimed straight for them.

"Look out!" I screamed. My voice was still ragged, and it hurt to yell. White Eyes shocked me again, and I fell to my knees, crying out in pain. She hauled me to my feet and down the steps, following Fisher. A shout came from Suit, but I couldn't turn and watch because the wolf was now bearing down on us fast. He leaped at White Eyes, but she sidestepped him and put her hand out, brushing his fur. Sam howled with pain, crashing to the ground where he lay shaking and whimpering. I tried to pull forward, but she held me back. I twisted around and attempted to fight her off, but she shocked me again and again until I screamed. Suddenly, she staggered under a blow, and I looked up to see Cas towering over us. He was in full fallen angel form, and his black wings stretched out around us. His eyes burned with hellfire as they landed on me, and then he slowly turned to White Eyes.

"Release her now!" His voice was deep and terrible, and even I trembled a little at the full force of his power. White Eyes stared defiantly up at him, and I felt pain raging through me again. I crumbled to the ground, and she twisted my wrist viciously. Cas wrapped his hand around her neck and lifted her clear off the ground, squeezing tightly. I tried to pry her fingers from my wrist, but the pain was constant, both from her and from my upper back, which was burning inside, and I hadn't the strength. Suddenly, the pain coming from her stopped completely. I gasped and looked up at Cas, realising where she was concentrating her energy. Beads of sweat appeared on his brow as he tried to ignore it, but I knew what she was capable of. His muscles tensed, and he shook like a rag doll, but she wouldn't release him. I couldn't bear it.

"Let him go!" I begged. "Please, I'll go with you, just let him go!" White Eyes dropped her gaze to me and laughed.

Cas fell to his knees and tears ran down his face. "I'm sorry," he pleaded with me. "Faith, for everything..."

"No!" I cried out. "Let him go, you let him go now!" I hated him, God knew how much I hated him, but it became clear in that instant how much I loved that bloody man, and I wasn't going to let her take him from me. If anyone got to cause him excruciating pain, it was me.

"I'll let him go when he's dead," she sneered, as his grip loosened around her throat and she plummeted to the ground. She staggered to her feet and placed her hand on his head. He roared and grabbed her wrist, but he no longer had the strength to tear her free. I sobbed and reached forward, trying to rip her hand away from him, but I could barely kneel, and she pulled back on my injured arm. I screamed. Cas dropped to his hands and knees. Any attempt at fighting her off was gone. My desperation began to turn from terror to fury. I looked at her, her white eyes gleaming, her mouth drawn up in a cruel sneer, and I wanted to *hurt* her.

Her eyes widened in surprise, and she swung her eyes from him to me. "What—"

I stared back at her with a chilling hatred I never knew I could feel. I could sense my abhorrence travelling through my body to where our skin touched. Her face went even paler, and she cried out. Cold realisation dawned that I was hurting her the way she had hurt me and Cas. She released my wrist, but I grabbed hold of her hair with my hand, concentrating on pushing the cold feeling into her body. I wanted her to feel all the pain she was inflicting on him. I wanted her to shrivel up with the agony, to curl up on the ground in torment for hurting him this way.

She let go of Cas and brought her hands up to grab mine. I refused to release my hold. With what little strength I had, I held on. Icy cold hatred poured out of me. It was like releasing the floodgates on everyone who had ever hurt me. Images danced through my mind of the men who had come after me and injured me. Who had held me down and raped me. Who had taken away any power I had. Except they hadn't. I had my power back now, and no vindictive little bitch was going to hurt me or someone I loved ever again.

I gave myself up to the feeling of raw power that surged through my veins. It moved from ice to fire, and my skin burned and stretched, my bones seeming to shift of their own accord. I felt the skin on my back tear open, and I dimly recognised the pain and the feel of blood streaming over my skin, but it didn't matter. I didn't care about anything except wanting this demon to hurt. I gazed down at her and watched with detached interest as her face grew gaunt and her eyes sank into the sockets. Her skin seemed to wither, and she cried out, but I ignored her as her body withered and dried in my hand. Blood flowed from her eyes, mouth, and ears then slowed to a trickle. Her white eyes darkened to grey and then black, and she fell silent.

I knelt there for a moment, my hand still tangled in her white wiry hair, staring down at her blank eyes, feeling blank myself.

"Faith. Faith, she's gone. It's over. You can let her go now, we're safe."

I felt Cas's arms wrap around me, his fingers disentangling mine from the corpse, because that was what she was now. I stared down at her in shock as her remains fell to the ground. "Faith, please. Faith, look at me. Look at me!" I blinked and swung around to face Cas. He was now back in his human form, and his dark eyes sparkled with unshed tears.

"Hey, there you are, Peaches." He managed a weak smile, but I couldn't do anything other than look at him. I couldn't think. I couldn't talk. He sighed. "Come on."

Standing, he scooped his arms beneath me and cradled me against his chest. He carried me to the car and stood me gently next to it. "Faith? Sweetheart, you need to retract your wings." Cas's voice was gentle, but I couldn't comprehend what he was saying in my dazed state. I stared at him blankly. Sighing, he placed his hands on my shoulders and turned me. I looked down at the car window and my slightly distorted reflection.

I looked like hell. My hair was wet and plastered to my head. My skin was pale, and I appeared exhausted. My eyes seemed to be bright though, and I wondered briefly if it was just the sky reflecting on them, but the real difference was the large, black feathered wings that stretched out from my sore, aching shoulder blades. I hunched my shoulders and they moved, curling around me. Keeping my eyes on the reflection, I ran one hand down the soft black feathers. They were soft and fluffy, like a duckling's.

Already at breaking point, my mind couldn't process the image properly, and I simply gazed up at Cas. "I have wings."

He nodded slowly. "It would appear so. You need to retract them so we can get you in the car. Pull them back in."

I looked back at the reflection and moved my shoulders. Nothing happened. *Pull them back in. I need them in to get into the car. They won't fit.* My mind stumbled over the concept, but my body reacted as though I had always had these incredible appendages. With the thought in my mind, they retracted, folding close to my body before fading from sight.

Cas wrapped his arm around me and guided me into the back seat before climbing in next to me. He lifted me onto his lap, and I didn't say anything, just cuddled in close and concentrated on the warmth of his body as it heated my cold one. My skin felt like it was buzzing all over. I was faintly aware of Sam and Euriel climbing in next to us.

I reached up and touched Euriel's face. "When did you break your nose?"

He gave me a small smile. "Don't worry about it, it'll heal."

Amadi glanced back from the passenger seat. "Alright, Faith? You gave us one hell of a scare."

I felt Cas shake his head, and his arms tightened around me. "Leave it until later, mate. I think she's in shock. You'll not get much out of her now."

Amadi smiled at me sadly. I turned away from him and closed my eyes. Alex started the car and pulled away, and within minutes, the rumble of the engine and the beat of Cas's heart had lulled me into welcomed darkness.

***

I came awake in the dark with a jolt, and my hands reached out wildly, scrabbling at my face to pull the cloth away from my mouth. It took me a few moments to realise I had been dreaming. A rustle of movement in the dark made me sit bolt upright, my heart hammering madly in my chest.

"Faith? It's Cas. You're okay, you just had a nightmare. You're in the hotel with us, and you're safe. Go back to sleep." He sat on the bed next to me, and I felt the mattress creak under his weight.

"Cas?"

I felt a featherlight touch on my hair, stroking gently. "It's just me, Peaches. Lie down and sleep. You need rest."

He stood up, and I reached out to him. "Don't leave me." I sounded like a little girl who was scared of the dark, but I couldn't bear to be alone again. He sighed, and I heard the sound of his belt being unbuckled. Moments later, the buckle clunked on the floor, and his weight descended on the bed next to me. He moved close, and for a moment I thought he was going to take me into his arms, but he didn't. I was glad, I didn't think I could handle any sense of containment or restraint, as caring as the gesture might have been.

Instead, he reached out and brushed my hair away from my face. "Sleep, Faith. I'm here, and I'm not leaving." I closed my eyes and fell back down into the blackness that awaited my exhausted mind. As I drifted off, I thought I heard him murmur, "I am never leaving you again."

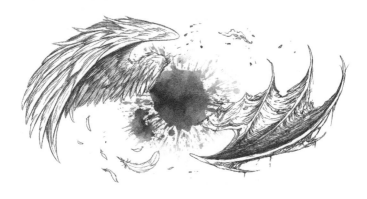

CHAPTER TWENTY-FOUR

FAITH

I was in the cathedral again. I recognised it with a dull sort of acceptance. I sat with my back against one of the huge columns, my knees pulled up to my chest. It was full daylight, so no setting sun this time, just a cold winter light that filtered through the high windows. Even the colours of the stained glass seemed muted. The chill seeped through my body, and I shivered but made no move to get up off of the stone. I just sat and stared into space, waiting to wake up. The silence was almost deafening, so I jumped when a small noise sounded behind me. Then another. And another. Until it was constant. The drip, drip, drip of water soon became faster, and I watched the tiny rivulets trickle down the columns and the walls, pooling on the dusty floor. Another rivulet ran down the column above me and fell onto my hair. I screamed and jumped up, expecting to see Bird Boy as I turned, but he wasn't there. Just running water. I backed away as the silvery pools grew wider, and I could feel myself shaking violently.

Suddenly, I collided with something hard, and I turned to see Cas standing behind me. He opened his arms, and I stepped into them, burying my face into his chest as the water rose around us.

He stroked my hair, and I pulled back and looked at him. "Cas! Cas, we have to get out of here!"

He stared down at me with a blank expression, almost zombie-like. I felt a sick sense of fear creep over me, and I tried to pull away, but his arms tightened around me like bands of metal. I raised my hands and pushed against his chest.

"Cas! Let me go, we have to get out!"

The water was around our ankles now, but he still wouldn't release me. I struggled, and he stumbled slightly. The two of us went down, crashing into the water. I gasped and spluttered as my mouth and nose filled, and panic charged through me like electricity. I fought to get up, then I felt his hands clamp down on my shoulders, holding me to the ground. He murmured something, but my ears were underwater, so it was muffled. I pushed up against him and felt his hardness pressed between my legs.

"Cas, please!" I begged him, and he laughed. He sat back, holding my throat with one hand while he reached into his jacket and took out a knife. Leaning down, he brushed his lips against mine, and then I felt the sharp shock of pain as the knife sank into me, again and again, three times, deep into my belly. I gasped with the agony, and water flooded into my mouth. The level had risen further, and he held me down, watching as I struggled and fought under him. When it covered my eyes, my vision went red, and I realised the water was stained with my blood. I could feel the knife slashing at my legs, and the man on top of me changed from Cas to one of my assailants then back to Cas again.

I stared at him, feeling the pain in my chest as my lungs begged for air. Sliding my hand down my body, I felt the cuff of his jacket, the skin of his hand, and then the cold steel of the knife. I wrapped my hand around the blade and dragged it from his grip, ignoring the agony, and it sliced through my fingers, down to the bone. He released my throat and sat back, observing me. I used my elbows to push myself off the floor and drove the knife deep into his chest before pausing to take a breath. He began to laugh, and I lost it.

Screaming at him, I drove the blade into him over and over. I felt his hot blood splatter across my face, saw it soak my hands and my clothes, but I couldn't stop. His face was dripping with it, and the surrounding water was crimson, but I couldn't stop until I needed to breathe again. He reached out and grabbed my shoulders and stared into my eyes. I froze as the cold silver orbs gazed deep into me, his mouth twisting into some kind of depraved grin. Black wings enveloped us, the soft brush of feathers hardening to silver steel blades, and I screamed as a thousand knives began to slice through my skin...

"Faith! Faith!"

I snapped awake as I was shaken roughly, and I scrambled back against the headboard. "Don't touch me!" I wheezed, my heart hammering in my chest. I pushed my matted hair back from my face and felt the wetness on them. Looking down at my hands, I could still see the blood covering them. There was blood everywhere. I could feel the sodden wetness of my clothes and the bedsheets, and feel the stickiness as it dried on my face and in my hair. Cas was sitting on the edge of the bed, and his face was dark as blood streamed from his eyes and nose. I could see the knife buried deep inside his chest where I'd stabbed him, and as I raised my eyes back to his face, his eyes glittered silver in the faint light that flowed in through the window from the streetlight outside. I closed my eyes and screamed.

Cas grabbed my arms and pulled me against his chest, just like in my dream, and I could hear him murmuring softly to me. "Faith, you're fine. You're safe. We're in a hotel. The guys are next door, everyone is safe."

"No, no, let go of me!" I shrieked at him, hammering at his chest with my fists. He wrapped his arms around me, holding me tight so I couldn't get away, and we fell over, tumbling onto the mattress. He held me close, hooking his leg over mine so

I couldn't kick him, and rolled on top of me to pin me down. The sound of his voice paused, and I felt his lips against my hair, my temple, my eyelids. He kissed me gently, over and over, and I realised his lips were soft and warm and dry against my skin. I opened my eyes and looked at him. There was no blood, only his tanned skin, shadowy in the darkened room. He was murmuring softly into my ear.

"What?" I whispered in disbelief. He didn't stop brushing his mouth along my jawline.

"I said, you don't need to worry. You're safe with me, you always have been. My beautiful peaches. Why didn't you tell me? Why didn't you let me in, let me help? Things could have been so different. I would have shown you what I did, broken the rules for you. Always, my darling." I took a shaky breath. He pulled away gently, looking deep into my eyes and brushing my hair out of my face. No blood. I shifted under him and he moved back, letting me sit up.

"I... I'm sorry, I was dreaming again. I'm fine now. You don't need to stay." My hands twisted in the sheets, which were simply white now as the last vestiges of my nightmare passed. He sat up but moved so he was in front of me.

"Don't apologise. And don't send me away."

I looked up at him. "I don't need your help. I'm fine." There was no hate or anger in my voice, I simply didn't have the energy.

"Don't shut me out, Faith. You always shut me out. Even when we were dating, I couldn't get into that heart of yours."

I stared at him in disbelief. "It's a bloody good job I did, otherwise you really would have fucked me up with what you pulled. What, you think this whole supernatural, perilous danger situation means I'm going to let you try again?"

"Look, I was going to wait until... well, until you felt better, and maybe when it wasn't the middle of the night, but will you let me tell you what happened? Please, Faith."

I didn't want him to. I felt exhausted and drained, and I needed time to process what had transpired the day before.

Pain shot down my leg as the sheets moved over my skin, and I desperately tried to ignore the fact I probably had third-degree burns. But I didn't have the energy to argue, so I simply nodded and reclined back on the pillow. At the very least, it would stop me from falling asleep and back into my own personal horror film.

He took a deep breath and shifted so he was lying next to me. "Okay, so... six years ago, I was working undercover for Hargreaves in this gang that was forming in the city. They're an offshoot of a larger machination that spans several countries that deals mainly with sex trafficking."

I frowned. "Why did you have something to do with sex trafficking? Surely that's more for human police to deal with."

He shrugged. "Not when the people running it are incubi." At my blank expression, he continued, "An incubus is a type of demon that needs lust or sexual energy to live. There are quite a few earthside, since they can live very comfortably here. Some live off one-night stands, others can have long-term relationships, even marriages if they find a human partner with a voracious sexual appetite."

I blushed, suddenly becoming uncomfortably aware that I was wearing panties and a camisole, and he was topless and rather close to me. Either he didn't notice, or he ignored me.

"Anyway, this particular gang does not merely indulge in consensual fun. They traffic humans in order to satisfy the darker desires of their demonic clientele, running illegal brothels and living off the endless lust emitted by their clients. When Hargreaves became aware that this group had spread up here, he tasked me with infiltrating the gang to discover and... neutralize the ringleaders."

I nodded, sickened. "So that was what you were doing in all those clubs and bars we went to. The products you were talking about? Human beings?"

He sighed. "Yes, and it sounds cold, and I hated it, but I couldn't do anything. I needed to earn their trust enough to get to the leaders, or I'd get found out and wouldn't be able to help anyone. Plus, we hoped that if I could get in with the ringleaders, I'd be able to discover the identities of those higher up the food chain, running the international scheme, and we could do some real damage."

I swallowed. "I get it. So what was I? Another product you preferred to keep to yourself?"

His eyes shot up to mine. "No," he whispered. "Never. You were..." He stopped and took another deep breath. "It sounds awful, and I'm not going to come off looking good, but... you were a cover."

"I was a fucking cover? That's all?" I felt like I'd been slapped. I mean, I knew from what had happened after that I didn't mean that much to him, but knowing he'd never been interested in me at all just drove the knife deeper.

"I had spent nearly a year trying to get in with those guys, and there was no way on earth I was going to do it by becoming a client. I required a reason why I wasn't trying to partake of their 'offerings,' so I needed a girlfriend, someone I could tell them was already filling my every desire. When I saw you... well, it wasn't hard to pretend that I was obsessed with you, because I was." I snorted at this, and he reached over and took my hand. "Faith, I know you were young back then, I know you hadn't had much experience with men and relationships, and I know your self-esteem wasn't the highest, but believe me when I tell you that I fell head over heels for you."

I pulled my hand away. "Even if I believed you, that makes what you did that night even more of a betrayal. "

"Faith, the night everything went wrong, you weren't supposed to be there. I had deliberately made sure you were not around that night so I could keep you out of it."

I nodded. "I know. I was convinced you were cheating on me with that woman. That's why I came over."

Cas frowned. "What woman?"

I twisted the sheets in front of me, not wanting to look at him. "The posh-looking blonde with the short hair and the legs that went up to heaven. The one we ran into at that bar one time, and you were both trying to pretend you barely knew each other," I muttered.

"Rosemary? She was my handler. My go-between with the Concordia." He laughed. "You thought I was having an affair with *her?* Hell's gates, Faith, would you really have put me together with someone like her? Twinsets and pearls?"

I smacked him on the arm, and I wasn't gentle. "Like you said, I was young and naïve, and my self-esteem was pretty low. Of course, it plummeted after that night. I get you were on a case, Cas, and I get that you were undercover. But that doesn't explain or excuse why you did what you did to me. I didn't even understand what I heard. I thought you were drug dealers. And even if I had, why couldn't you have just told me everything like you did this time? You'd already broken the rules by fucking me."

He ran his hand over his face and sighed. "No, it doesn't excuse what happened to you."

I shot him a cold smile. "So you finally admit it then?" He took my hand and held it fast, even when I tried to pull away.

"Yes, I admit I saw you in the shadows when I was talking to those incubi, but no, I didn't follow you when you ran out of there. I had just tried to get a young teenage girl out of one of their houses and I'd been caught. They thought I was an agent, and I was trying to persuade them it had been for my own sexual needs." He shuddered, then stopped and suddenly looked at me, his eyes bright. "You're right, fucking hell, you were right. It was my fault you were attacked. *Fuck!* I saw you in the shadows, and I was trying to get them to think I liked young girls. I gestured towards you and said you were only pretending to be eighteen, that you were really fifteen, but I'd scored you a fake ID. I said that you... you followed me around everywhere like a puppy. My own little pet."

I sat up and slapped him across the face.

"You fucking bastard." He didn't respond, he just stared at me, so I hit him again. And again. He caught my hand the fourth time and held it, not tightly, but firmly enough to stop me from snatching it back.

"I am *so* sorry, Faith. The incubi seemed to take my word for it. They insisted on coming inside for a couple of drinks. One of them stepped out to make a phone call, but they were at my apartment for hours. As soon as they left, I went inside and called Rosemary to tell her what had happened and to say I would need to get out soon, then I came over to yours."

I stared at him, feeling like I might be sick. I wanted to hear it from his own lips. But I didn't. I didn't want to hear exactly how he'd betrayed me. I pulled my hand back and rolled over, pulling the covers around me. I suddenly felt very naked and vulnerable, and I really didn't want to look at him. I felt him sit up, but he didn't move any nearer.

"When I got there, they were waiting for me. Not the incubi I'd been talking to, but the ones who worked for them. The ones they send out to find girls. I felt sick with fear, but so damn thankful I'd got there quickly. They laughed at me, Faith. They laughed at me and told me I shouldn't have done what I did. Then they showed me the pictures on their phones. Pictures of you, what they did... some of what they did. I had no idea if you were even still alive. I pushed past them and ran up the stairs. When I opened your door and saw you—" His words choked off, and I turned as he moved to sit on the edge of the bed, facing away from me, his head in his hands. I felt like I'd been hit with pain from White Eyes again, except this time the pain was emotional. It still flowed through my body, burning me with its power.

He hadn't betrayed me. It wasn't him.

I sat there for a few moments, trying to absorb it. To be honest, I felt lost. When I was around Cas, the hate I'd had for him was what drove me. Now it had... not gone, exactly, since he'd still put me in that situation, but it had faded dramatically, and I wasn't really sure what to do or how to act. I rolled back over and placed my hand on his back.

"Cas? Cas. Look at me." Slowly, he raised his head and turned to look, and the sight of the tears streaming down his face hit me like a punch to the stomach. "If you didn't give the order, why did you leave me there alone? Why did you take so long to come and see me in the hospital? You could have explained it all to me."

He barked out a laugh, dashing away the tears with the back of his hand. "I called an ambulance and waited outside until they arrived. Once I saw them loading you into the back, I went after them." He looked straight at me, and I shivered when I saw the pure hatred in his eyes.

"What did you do?" I whispered.

He averted his gaze. "I found them," he said simply. I quivered at the venom in his voice. He looked back at me and laid one of his hands on mine. "It got all mixed up after that. When I went home a couple of days later, I found the police waiting for me. I was arrested and detained for a couple of days while they investigated me. Took some pretty quick work on Hargreaves' part to deal with that mess, and the whole time I sat in the cell, my mind just kept running through why you'd go to the police and why you would tell them it was me who attacked you. I became convinced you'd heard everything, and it broke my heart that you'd immediately believed something that bad about me, even though you'd told me you loved me. You never even gave me the chance to try to explain."

The blood drained from my face and I pulled back. "They told me you'd sent them. I'd seen them before, drinking with you at the club. I—"

"You believed them," he stated quietly, giving me a sad smile. It felt like a knife to the heart.

"Cas, I..."

He sighed as my words trailed off. "When I finally came to the hospital, I thought I might be able to forgive you. And then I saw you all wired up, with bruises and cuts on your face. And I was still angry with you, so fucking angry, but I could see then that I had put you in that danger. Whatever happened afterwards, the attack was still my fault, and you'd always be in danger if you were with me. You were still human. Still fragile. And you always would be. I knew I had to walk away." He shifted slightly, leaning on one arm to look at me, and brought his free hand up to capture a lock of my hair.

"So you did."

He nodded. "I did. And I blamed you for it." He chuckled. "A fallen angel, millennia old. I've lived in Heaven and been through Hell. Literally. And I spent five years blaming you and hating you because I couldn't bring myself to accept the real truth."

"What was that?" I asked quietly.

He closed his eyes. "That I loved you beyond anyone or anything I've ever loved. Something changed in me the day I met you, and it's never been the same since." The tears that had been threatening to appear spilled over, and I bowed my head so he didn't see them. He sighed. "I know you have feelings for Sam, and, well, maybe even Amadi and Alex too. Hell, I don't even know if you can forgive me, or if you even feel anything for me anymore." I looked up and caught his gaze, and before I could overthink it, I slid my hand around his neck and pulled his mouth down onto mine.

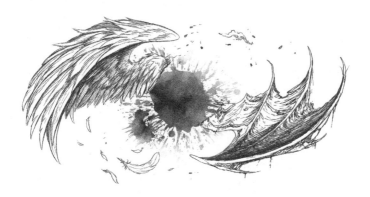

Chapter Twenty-Five

FAITH

It wasn't a romantic kiss. The type you see in films where a couple finally comes together, where he reaches up and touches her face softly before lowering his lips gently to hers. This wasn't one of those. I'd meant it to be, meant it to tell him how sorry I was, how I hated myself for hating him all these years. I meant it to say that I loved him too. But it wasn't that kind of kiss. With the two of us, how could it be? The moment my lips touched his, it was like the gates of my soul had been opened and everything I'd buried deep inside came flooding out into that one small touch. I wanted him to see it all, feel it all, to know and understand why I had hated him so much. That it had been because I loved him beyond anything I could have imagined. That every day apart from him had felt like torture, and what had made it worse was that I thought I had meant nothing to him. Now to find out he had felt the same, I just couldn't control it anymore. I wrapped my arms around his neck and pulled him close, my mouth hungry for his taste. He took it all, holding me gently against him and meeting my frenzy, but not adding to it, letting me release what I needed.

He was my rock in a storm of emotion. My strength. My fallen angel.

Our teeth clashed, and he slipped, crushing me into the mattress as his chest pressed into mine. I couldn't breathe, but I didn't care. I could happily die this way with his lips on mine and his hands in my hair. He seemed to sense my lack of oxygen though, because he pulled back. My body still ached, and my leg burned and tingled against the sheets, but I didn't care. I looked at him, too full of what I was feeling to say anything. He didn't say anything either. His breath was ragged too, and I managed a quick gasp of air before he leaned down and took my mouth again, claiming what was his, what had always been his—my heart and soul. Moments later, to my dismay, he broke away again, breathing hard. His eyes glittered darkly in the shadowed room, and I reached up to run my fingertips over his face. He brushed my hair behind my ear then leaned in and began to kiss me gently, one for each tear that had fallen down my face. When he finally pressed his lips to mine again, I could taste the salt on them. He closed his eyes, leaning into my touch, and my heart ached with how much I loved him.

"Cas," I whispered. He opened his eyes and looked down at me. "Hold me. Please, just... hold me and never let me go again." His expression hardened, and he slid his hands under my neck and back, raising me off the pillows to crush me against him.

"Never," he muttered hoarsely, his breath hot against my ear. I felt his lips trail along my jaw and down the delicate column of my throat and sighed with pleasure as I felt his teeth graze my skin. It sent a shudder through me, and I moaned quietly. I heard him chuckle as he kissed along my collarbone, sliding the strap of my top down so he could bare my breast and take my nipple into his mouth. Lowering me softly onto the bed again, he cupped my other breast, rubbing his thumb over my skin gently at first, then firmer as I began to squirm beneath him.

"Cas, I want to feel you, please!"

He raised himself up on his arms and tugged the sheet out from between us. I reached down and grabbed the hem of his shirt, yanking at it impatiently until he laughed and sat back on his heels to pull it over his head. I stared at him in the moonlight, hungrily taking in every detail of each sculpted rise and dip all the way down to where his hips sank into his jeans. Leaning forwards, I ran my hands slowly and firmly up his stomach and chest, fanning out over his shoulders. I had always loved his shoulders. Seeing that broad expanse in a tight T-shirt, under his biker jacket, or especially now with just smooth skin caused my belly to flip. I pulled him down on top of me, shifting so his body lay between my thighs. I cried out, and he pulled back instantly.

"Faith, what's wrong?" He glanced down and seemed to freeze. I was breathing heavily, and not just from wanting him so badly.

"I'm sorry... it's just... it hurt a bit."

He gently ran his fingers over my leg, and I whimpered.

"Faith—"

I turned my head away. "It's fine, I'm sorry." I bit down on my lip, trying to ignore the burning sensation across my skin. "I had forgotten. How stupid am I?"

He reached down and cupped my face, bringing my eyes back to his. I didn't want to look at him. I felt sick and ashamed of... well, my body. How could he want someone as scarred and deformed as me?

"You aren't stupid, Faith. We gave you some pretty serious pain killers. They're probably just starting to wear off. But you're healing *really* fast."

I nodded, fighting against the tears that were threatening to spill over. *Stupid girl, you're lucky to be alive. Stop getting so fucking morose over a few scars.* Cas leaned down to kiss me again, but I turned my head away.

He looked at me for a moment before shifting to my side and lying next to me, his face inches from my own. "Talk to me, Peaches. What's spinning around in the pretty, screwed up head of yours?"

I swallowed hard and flickered my eyes up to his briefly before closing them so I didn't have to see him watching me. "I just, I forgot that I'm probably... well, permanently scarred. You don't want to see or feel that when you touch me. I don't want to see it or feel it. I can understand if you change your mind about wanting to be with me."

There was a moment of silence where I honestly thought he was trying to find a way to let me down gently, and then suddenly, I felt a puff of air in my face. I opened my eyes to see him grinning at me.

"Did you just... blow on my face?" I asked him incredulously.

"Yep. You about done with the dramatics?"

I slapped his arm. "I wasn't being dramatic, I was trying to do the right thing."

He rolled his eyes. "There are enough martyrs in Heaven, Faith. Come here." He opened his arms, and I moved into them, one arm slipping under my neck to cuddle me in tight. "If that's what you still think of me, then I'm rather concerned. I'm not leaving you ever again, and even if you were permanently scarred, which you are *not*, I would still never leave your side. And neither would the others."

I tipped my head up to look at him, and he kissed the tip of my nose. "The others?"

He sighed. "I'm not going to pretend I wouldn't love to have you all to myself, Faith. But I've seen the way you are with Sam, and you've made it pretty obvious you have feelings for Amadi and Alex too. I don't want to get in the way of that."

"Cas, I—"

He laid his finger gently against my lips. "I'm just saying there are other... You know, in Sheol, it's quite common to have several partners."

I stared at him. "It is?"

He nodded. "Faith, I'm just thankful to have you back in my arms again after all this time. If that means sharing you with the other guys, then I'm good with that."

I paused for a moment as all kinds of thoughts whirled through my head. Eventually, I settled on something safer. "You don't think I'm permanently scarred?"

He shook his head. "The great thing about having a bunch of supernaturals at your beck and call means we have fairly incredible healing abilities between us. We'll get you sorted. And you seem to have some kind of rapid healing of your own. The cuts and scrapes you had are already gone, and the burn is nearly healed, though it might be sore for a few more days. But you need rest for that. So maybe we should let you get to sleep."

I paused, considering his suggestion. "Will you stay with me?"

He pressed a kiss to my hair and reached down to pull the covers gently over my legs. "Of course I will."

I snuggled close and closed my eyes, listening to his breathing. Trying to keep my breathing as even as his, I slowly dragged my fingertips down until I could brush them gently over his nipple. I smiled as I felt it harden beneath my touch.

"Faith," he growled.

"Mmm?" I trailed my fingers down his chest, scraping my nails lightly against his skin.

"Faith!" he hissed, taking a quick breath. "I thought we were sleeping now."

"I can't sleep. My head is all over the place."

"Is it really? Well, maybe I can give you something to focus on." He slid his arm out from under my head and propped himself up on his elbow, looking down at me with a smile.

"You're not going to teach me to meditate, are you?" I asked warily.

He grinned. "Not exactly." He leaned down and kissed me, his lips moving tenderly over mine.

He took his time exploring my mouth with his tongue and gently nibbling my lower lip. Anytime I tried to rush him, he slowed, and I felt him grinning as I made a sound of frustration. Eventually, I surrendered to his touch and sank into it. He kissed me as though I tasted like the best whisky he'd ever had and he wanted to savour every taste he could, and the thought made heat pool in my belly. Pressing tiny kisses on my lips, he brushed his lips along my jaw, stopping to breathe softly into my ear. The heat made me shudder with pleasure. I turned my head and cupped his face with my hand. I could feel the stubble on his face under my fingers and smell that delicious whisky and smoke scent I loved so much.

I pressed my face into the crook of his neck, inhaling deeply. He was my drug, and I was his addict, there was no more denying it. He emitted a sigh that might have been a moan, and sucked at my skin, flicking his tongue over the sensitive flesh. By the time he reached my collarbone, I was fairly sure I'd be displaying several marks in the morning, but at that moment I didn't care. I turned towards him, trying to press my body against his, but he put his hand on my shoulder and firmly pushed me back down.

"Shush, be still. I don't want to hurt you."

I sighed and relaxed, gasping suddenly as I felt his mouth on my nipple again, pulling it deep into his mouth. He bit down gently, and I moaned, sliding my hands into his hair. Moving to the other, he cupped first one and then the second, stroking the skin and rubbing his thumb over and around my free nipple as he caressed the other with his tongue. Letting go, he glided the tip of his tongue all the way down my breastbone to my belly. He slid his thumbs over my hips and hooked them through my panties, then slowly dragged them down my legs, lifting one side so the fabric didn't brush against the burnt tissue. As he pulled them free and dropped them onto the floor, I raised myself up on my elbows to look at him. Hell, I could stare at this sinful delight for eternity, but he had other plans. Bending down, he trailed kisses up the inside of my uninjured leg, careful not to touch the other, until he reached the apex of my thighs.

I felt his hot breath dance over my skin, and I ran my hands over his head, pulling him closer. His tongue flicked up my slit once, then a second time, before slipping inside my folds.

"Cas!" I cried out, grabbing his shoulders. He didn't reply, but his tongue slowly explored my core, teasing me.

"Cas, please..." He lips fastened softly around my clit, and I felt him slip a finger inside me as I cried out again. I arched my back, moaning loudly as his tongue began flicking back and forth over my clit, getting faster. He slid a second finger into me, and I grabbed his shoulders, sinking my nails into his skin. I felt a vibration as he growled in pleasure, and it sent shivers over my skin. I could feel my entire body heating at his touch, like he'd lit some kind of fire inside me. Not one that tortured and hurt like my leg, but a warm, heavy flame that flickered along every nerve ending. His fingers slid in and out of me, and the flames began to consume me as I felt my climax rise.

"Come on, Peaches," he murmured against my wetness. "Come for me, let me see you explode." He sucked hard on my clit and slid a third finger inside, curling them to press against my wall. I came apart, one hand on his head and the other gripping tightly at the bedsheets as I screamed his name. He didn't pause though, even to let the waves subside.

I moaned as I felt the head of his cock press against me. He rubbed it up and down my wetness until I arched my back, pushing up to meet him. With one thrust, he buried himself deep inside me. He stilled for a moment, as though reminding himself to take it slowly, and I slid my arms around him, pulling him close as I dragged my nails down his back. He released a ragged sigh.

"Fucking hell, Faith. This feels like coming home."

I grinned. "Heaven or Hell?"

He groaned as I tightened my muscles around him, slowly squeezing and releasing him. "I don't fucking know anymore."

"Well, wherever you go, take me with you," I murmured, closing my eyes as he started to move inside me.

"Always," he whispered in my ear before driving into me hard. I cried out again and again, unable to keep quiet as he slammed into me, all thoughts of being careful forgotten as years of pent-up rage and loss and love overwhelmed us both. My hips rose to meet his thrusts, and my nails scored his back.

"Cas! Oh fuck, Cas..." I wrapped my legs around his waist, pulling him deeper, and with the change of angle, something must have tipped him over the edge, because he roared as his release took him, gripping me hard and pulling me tight against him. The friction between us and his reaction shot a bolt of pleasure to my pussy. I screamed his name as I completely fell to pieces, soaring on wave after wave of sensation until I lay completely sated and breathing hard.

Cas moved up the bed, lifting the sheets and blanket to cover us both. He pulled me into his arms and tucked his body against my back. I smiled when I felt him still slightly hard against me, and when I pushed against him, he laughed.

"Don't even think about it, Peaches. You've had yours. Come back to me when you're recovered."

I grinned and closed my eyes. Taking a deep breath, I breathed in his scent and drifted off to sleep, safe in his arms. He was right, it did feel like coming home.

CHAPTER TWENTY-SIX

FAITH

Cas wasn't in the bed when I woke up. Sunlight was streaming through the window, and the pane had been opened slightly to let a fresh breeze drift through the room. I loved the touch of it on my face and took a deep breath before struggling to sit up.

Sam was sitting in the easy chair by the desk, but I caught his attention when I began to move. "Faith, take it easy. You've been through hell." He got up and came over as I lowered myself down in a slightly more upright position. I looked around the room, not recognising it.

"Where are we? This isn't our hotel."

Sam shook his head. "No, we thought it would be safer to move hotels, in case they came looking for us again. We're on the other side of the city."

He perched on the bed next to me. His face was paler than usual, and there were dark circles under his eyes. "Are you okay? You look awful."

He chuckled. "I'm on top of the world, baby girl. Just glad we found you when we did."

"I saw you get shocked. I know what it feels like." I reached up to touch his face, and he took my hand in his, stroking his thumb gently across my knuckles.

"Yeah, that wasn't fun. But I'm fine."

"Did you find... At the farmhouse, there was a woman in the basement with me. She said she worked with my mother. They'd taken her too, to answer questions..." My voice trailed off as I remembered the shaking walls and crumbling ceiling. "Oh my... Sam, did the farmhouse collapse, or did I just imagine that part? I'm not sure what's real anymore."

He squeezed my hand, and I looked up into his baby blue eyes. "Faith, there was no one else in the building. The two men got away. We didn't go after them, I'm sorry. We all needed to see that you were okay."

I sat up again, gripping his hand. "No, no, not outside. *Inside* the farmhouse. Down in the basement. She was down there. They left her, and I didn't tell you she was there."

He gently pushed me back against the headboard. "It's fine, Faith. Alex checked, there was no one else in the building. He can... well, let's just say he would be able to tell. Whoever it was got out before the building collapsed, I promise you."

I stared at him. "You're sure?" He nodded. She must have got out. I let out a breath, then asked, "What about Cas? He was here last night, but he's gone..."

Sam smiled at me. "Cas is fine, better than fine. He just needs rest—as do I—and not to worry about you, so you need to get as much rest as you can too. He's out with the others getting some dinner. I volunteered to stay with you on the proviso they brought pizza and ice cream back for us."

I smiled, my first real one in what felt like forever. "Pizza and ice cream?" He nodded, and I grinned. "Beer?"

He laughed. "I don't think you're quite ready for beer yet." I frowned, and he stopped smiling.

"You okay?"

"I don't know, am I? I shouldn't be okay, I should be in a hospital." I lifted my arms from the covers and glanced down at my shoulder then up at Sam.

"Cas and Euriel healed you when we got back. Don't you remember?"

I shook my head slowly. Sliding my hand below the blankets, I inched my fingers towards my leg, cringing as I expected to touch bandages or horrifically scarred flesh. My eyes widened as I felt a smooth expanse of skin, and I wrenched the covers up to see for myself. There wasn't so much as a blemish. I dropped the covers and twisted around to try and look at my back. Nothing but pale skin.

I stared at Sam. "How...?"

He dropped his gaze uncomfortably. "I think it's best if we leave it until the others get back. They'll be better at explaining it than me."

"Tell me."

"Really, Faith, I don't understand the details."

I took his hand again. "Sam, please, why do I look like nothing happened to me?"

He sighed, and his blue eyes met mine. "Fine, but you're not going to like it. When you grabbed hold of the demon—"

"The woman with the white eyes?"

"Yes. When you grabbed her, something happened."

"Yes, I... Oh. Oh my God! Sam, what did I do?" I stared at him in horror as the memory came back.

He twined his fingers with mine. "You killed her."

"I... she was hurting Cas, she had hurt me."

He grabbed my face and pulled it up to meet his earnest gaze. "Faith, please don't think you're in trouble. You were acting in self-defence and defending Cas as well. You had every right to do what you did."

"But I'm not even sure what I did."

The door opened, and I looked up nervously. Cas and Amadi came into the room carrying pizza boxes. When they saw I was up, they dumped them on the table and came over to the bed.

"How are you doing, Peaches?" Cas sat down on the other side of me, opposite Sam, and took my hand in his.

Amadi perched on the end of the bed. "You gave us a hell of a scare, Faith. Just glad we got you back." The door opened again, and Alex came into the room with a box from the ice cream parlour I had visited with Euriel only a couple of days before. It felt like a lifetime ago since we had wandered the streets of Florence talking about art.

"Where's Euriel?" Cas asked Alex, raising his eyebrows.

Alex pulled the chair up near Sam and sat down. "I asked him to arrange our journey home, seeing as Faith was feeling better."

Cas nodded and seemed to relax a little.

Sam cleared his throat, and Cas looked over at him. "I was telling her about what happened to the demon." Cas arched an eyebrow, and Sam added, "She asked! I told her you could explain better. Or maybe Amadi?"

Cas leaned sideways against the padded headboard and squeezed my hand gently. "Before I tell you what I know, I need you to understand that that woman was evil. She earned her living inflicting pain and torture, and she would have killed both of us without a second thought."

I nodded. "Okay, but, what did I do to her? Sam said I killed her, but I just held on to her and..."

Cas sighed. "Yes, you killed her, but you used a magical ability we had no idea you had."

"Magic? Okay, that makes sense."

"The ability you used, it's a magical skill known as ravage. It basically causes things to wither, age, and dry up from the inside out. How did you feel just after doing it? Physically, not emotionally, I mean."

I thought for a moment. "I felt, I don't know... numb, and like I was buzzing all over. And my back was burning." I shuddered, remembering the feeling, and Sam slipped his arm around my shoulders.

Cas nodded. "Ravage allows you to drain life from something. You actually absorbed the life force you drained. It filled the cells in your body, that was the buzzing you felt. I don't think you'll remember, but you kept trying to scratch at your leg the whole drive back in the car. The one they... burned." A shadow crossed his face, and he swallowed before continuing, "The life force you absorbed from the demon's body had nowhere to go except into your cells. It does what life always does, it repairs and rejuvenates those cells."

"With a horrific cost." I looked down at the outline of my legs under the covers, feeling slightly sick. "But if I took all of her life force, why do I still feel exhausted, like I ran a marathon or something?"

Cas leaned in and brushed his lips against my hair. "You subconsciously transferred some of her life force into me. It worked faster on me. I wasn't nearly as damaged as you were."

I laughed shakily. "Great. So here I was, excited about being a witch and having powers, and the one I get is the stuff of nightmares."

Cas glanced over at Amadi who leaned forward on his elbows. There was a strange look in his eyes.

"What?" I looked from him, to Cas, to Sam. "What aren't you telling me?"

"Faith, witches don't have the ability to use ravage. It's a full-on demonic power." I stared at him, and he licked his lips nervously. "The angels have an ability we call regenerate. It does the opposite of ravage. It takes their life force and restores something to what it was before. However, the angels have an external source of power that they can draw on so they don't use their own."

I shook my head, confused. "What are you saying, Amadi? That I'm a demon? Or an angel? Can angels use ravage?"

He shook his head. "Only fallen angels. When they were condemned to Hell, God cursed them. Part of that curse was that although they retained the powers they were created with, they became warped. The power to regenerate became a power to destroy. If you can command ravage, then you are not merely a human witch, you have pure angel blood in your veins. Well, fallen angel anyway."

"But... you're saying I must be a fallen angel. How can that be? I remember growing up as a kid."

Amadi looked back at Cas, who hugged me gently. "Faith, when you let your power take control, something else happened to you as well. Do you remember?"

I looked at him, his dark eyes gentle but worried. I thought back, cringing at the memory. "Just the buzzing and the pain, memories of... and I thought I was..."

"What?"

I shook my head. "I don't know. I felt like my bones were breaking, like my body was being torn open. I thought it was part of my nightmare again. I saw things like that sometimes when she caused me to feel pain."

Cas ran his hand slowly up and down my arm in a comforting gesture. "That wasn't your nightmare, Faith. That was real. Only your bones weren't breaking, they were reforming."

I stared at him in horror. "What?"

He paused, his lips parted, and I could see him searching for what to say.

"You grew wings, baby girl," Sam chimed in softly.

I whipped my head around to look at him, but he wasn't joking. He was deadly serious.

"Wings? Real, actual wings? But where..."

Cas rubbed his hand over the top of my back. "They're out of mortal sight right now. You should be able to call them back with practice, and it won't hurt after a time."

I gaped at him. Oh fuck, I remembered. My mind flashed back to my reflection in the car window, the feel of down against my fingers. How the fuck did I forget I suddenly grew wings? My gaze drifted to Cas's mouth as his tongue darted out and swept over his lips. Oh, yeah... that was probably how.

"Wings," I said again, knowing I sounded stupid, but unable to really grasp the concept.

"Black ones. Like Cas," Amadi added. "Add them in with the power to ravage, and there's only one real explanation."

Cas sighed. "He's saying you are the child of a fallen angel. One of your parents fought in the War of Heaven and was cast down to Hell."

"Like the watchers who slept with human women?"

Cas nodded. "If we're right, and that's what you are, it means one of the original fallen angels returned earthside and created you. You're the first nephilim to walk the earth since the great flood."

I stared at him in horror, feeling cold terror creep over me.

"Cas, Hargreaves, and Deliah told me what Heaven did to the nephilim..."

He wrapped his arms around me, pulling me tight against his chest. A moment of panic surged through me, but the memory of what I had experienced paled now in comparison to the danger before me. I circled my arms around him, holding on as tight as I could.

"I am not going to let anything happen to you, Faith, I promise you," he murmured into my hair.

"We," Amadi corrected, and I looked over at him as he crawled up the bed and took one of my hands.

"Yes, we," Sam added. "*We're* not going to let anything happen to you, baby girl."

Alex leaned forward and touched my face. "You've got some pretty strong protectors here, sweet one. Whatever comes, we'll face it together."

I met each of their gazes and gave them a weak smile. Alex was right. Whatever danger was coming, I had them. And I knew they'd fight for me. All of them.

I looked into Cas's eyes and nodded. "We still have to find Rose."

He smiled. "I know, we will. If anything, she might be able to give us a clue as to who your parents were."

And what I am, I added silently.

"There's just one thing I need to know," Sam said suddenly, staring hard at Cas and me.

I shifted uncomfortably, wondering if he'd overheard us the night before. "What's that?"

"Why does Cas call you Peaches?" My face flamed red, and Cas burst out laughing.

I smacked him on the arm. "Don't you dare!"

Chuckling, he moved out of reach and turned to Sam. "Well, it's fairly simple. When Faith and I started going out, I first met her in a bar. I walked up behind her and thought she had the most perfect ass I'd ever seen. Like a lovely, juicy round—"

"Peach!" Sam finished, and the guys erupted into laughter.

I sulked, secretly trying not to grin at the sight of my tough, supernatural men giggling like little girls. My men. I quite liked the sound of that, and Cas's suggestion danced briefly through my head. I smiled to myself, snuggling under the covers and leaning my head against Sam's arm. My men. My guardians. My lovers?

Afterword

For news on upcoming releases, please visit my website;

www.elizabethblackthorne.com

If you are on social media, please feel free and very welcome to stalk me everywhere! I love to chat about the paranormal and hot men in general, so do reach out. Click on the link for all my social media:

https://linkt.ree/Elizabeth_Blackthorne

About Author

In the northeast of England with her husband, four minions, a crazy sprocker spaniel and seven cats. An avid reader since she was a kid, she decided at the age of seven that she wanted to be a writer. Since then, she has been an archaeologist, barrister, photographer and a cake decorator, but story telling will always be her true passion.

Sitting down at her computer any chance she can get means she can type out a few lines in between kids, pets and never ending housework (just kidding, she tries not to do much housework – it's bad for the soul!)